YOU ME & TWENTY SEVEN

BETH LOURE

mily

The clock dings twice. Danggg. Dangg. The deep, low hum vibrates in my stomach. It's twenty past the hour.

Exactly ten minutes have passed since our last exchange. Well, Tom said *mmm* when I asked him if he liked my rabbit slippers. It can't be considered even a whole syllable. That settles it—our conversation has deteriorated to the level of noise. I sip loudly from my rosé while squinting at him. No reaction.

I sulk. Quietly. I hate how good I've become at sulking quietly over the last few months. That's another thing I hold against him.

Tom's sitting in his favorite spot on the maroon couch, stooped over his phone, laptop on the coffee table in front of him, adjacent to the martini I placed there half an hour ago. He gives occasional attention to the drink but keeps most of his concentration on the screens. Unlike most evenings, tonight he's even turned on the big TV.

"Come on," I said when I saw him fiddling with the remote control. "You're not even going to *pretend* we're hanging?"

"Just a short while, Emily," he said. And then, piercing at me with his lucid blue eyes, he said, "I didn't forget." That was comforting for about five minutes or so. Then I began questioning his priorities. Maybe it would have been better if he had forgotten instead of choosing to do this instead.

It flickers now, the TV. Showing graphs and scrolling numbers in green on black. It's like I've been kidnapped into the Matrix.

"Mmm," Tom repeats absentmindedly when I share that specific thought. I bet he didn't hear me. I bet I could say whatever and get the same reaction. So, I say casually, as if talking about some mundane household chore, "I talked to your father today. He says hi."

"Not funny, Emily." Tom doesn't take his eyes off the screens. Mine are getting all teared up. That was a nasty thing for me to say. I blame Tom for making me be mean to him. Another foul added to the list I manage in my head.

Tom's going to turn fifty in exactly one month. Other men his age get a lover, preferably in her twenties. Or buy a leather jacket and ride heavy motorcycles. Maybe I should be grateful that Tom's midlife crisis has him sitting on the couch, playing with his digital coins.

Only I'm not. I miss him. And I'm offended and mad at him for ditching me for this weird new hobby. I don't care how much money he makes, I just want my husband back. Hunched over his electronics, he reminds me of an Emperor penguin protecting a precious egg.

I chuckle a little, uncontrollably. Will the noise would penetrate Tom's bubble? It doesn't.

I'm sitting cross-legged on the burgundy wing chair and admiring my new rabbit slippers. They look so sweet and the fabric so soft against my finger, like a real rabbit. Trying to get my mind off him, I think about the furry fabric I used to sew my new rabbit slippers. I wonder what else I could sew from it while slowly sipping my rosé. Maybe a clutch purse? It would be a hilarious twist for a chic evening accessory.

Tom keeps hammering away, tapping, the clicks barely audible over the grandfather clock. It's ticking, ticking, ticking. Ticking me out of my mind out.

I'm about to scream when Tom looks up and smiles. His smile still takes my breath away. Reaching for his martini, he says, "Well, I've just made a grand."

"That's great, honey. Maybe we should use it to indulge ourselves. I read an article today about a couple of empty-nesters who took a year off to hike the Appalachian Trail."

After another moment of unresponsiveness, Tom finally says, "I've changed my mind, Em. I'm kind of hungry. Let's go out for dinner." His gaze is captured by the phone again.

"I thought it might be something we'd enjoy. Remember that one time we went camping with the kids? We always said we should do it more." My legs are getting stiff. I pull them out from underneath my body and shake them vigorously. "We don't have to take a whole year. I mean, we don't have to hike *all* those thousands of miles of the trail. We could start modestly. Just a week or so one summer and see if we like it. Wouldn't that be a thrilling experience? Tom?" I lean forward, as if getting closer to him would get me the reply I long for.

"I'm thinking... Hmmm... French. What do you say, Em? Should we go to Ma Maison? We liked their soufflé, didn't we? It was so puffy and tall." Now he looks directly at me.

I look the other way and get up. "There's no way you could get a table." My throat is dry. I sip my wine and let the sweetness spread in my mouth. Looking at him, I want to say I have some leftovers I could heat up, but there's no use. He's already calling the restaurant. I take another sip and wait patiently for the inevitable.

Tom scoffs as he hangs up. "She literally laughed in my face. So rude."

"What did you expect? It's Valentine's. You should have booked a table weeks ago." The grandfather clock dings again. It's ticking away my youth. With every second that passes by, I'm closer to my own demise.

The clock was a wedding gift from Tom's parents. I hated it from the first tick, but who can say no to an heirloom? It's been in Tom's family for three generations, and I'm the first one to put it in exile in the garage where it can tick and ding and chime with all the other stuff we don't want around the house but are too nostalgic to get rid of, like Tommy's baby clothes, or Marni's Mother's Day crafts.

A few months ago, Tom brought the clock back into the house and placed it on the mantel, stacking all the family photos by the edge and saying it reminded him of his child-hood. How could I deny the wish of a grieving son? I've been telling myself it's only temporary, while literally counting the seconds until Tom became his old self again and I could banish the demonic creature back to its old hiding place.

I take a deep breath. "We could go dancing. You would have a chance to wear your tux." I gasp as the visual of Tom in a tux hits me. "You *do* look handsome in a tux." In fact, he looks good without any clothes on whatsoever. I down the rest of my rosé. It's my third glass this evening, but no one's counting.

"Em, concentrate. Please. We're talking dinner here, not renewing our vows. What about the Olive Garden?"

"Huh. I counter that offer with a pizza and a spaghetti

western, right here on the couch. Unless..." I start to waltz around.

"You're in your pajamas, for heaven's sake!"

"It's a unicorn jumpsuit!" I protect the dignity of my outfit, which I've designed and made by myself from scratch.

He shakes his head.

"I could wear that black gown from Marni's wedding if we go ballroom dancing." I smile.

"Fine," Tom says, and I halt in place.

"Really?"

"Of course not!" He knits his eyebrows at my gullibility.

I pace glumly to the panoramic window. It's snowing. Again. Already the snow is piling up on the front lawn.

"Sorry," Tom says. "That was uncalled for." His voice is soft, but the damage is already done.

Turning back toward him, I'm astonished by how gray he looks. He seems to have aged overnight. With this new look, he's more attractive than ever.

"Will you get dressed to go to an Outback Steakhouse?" Tom asks.

"I would rather get *undressed*," I shoot back. His eyes are the color of washed denim, clear as ever. "We could make out in front of the fireplace like a couple of newlyweds."

Tom isn't hooked. "Dammit, Em, I'm hungry. I'm absolutely famished!"

"Well, so am I." My voice is deep. I cross the short distance between us and sit close to him. He draws back when I put my hand on his thigh. It's just a tiny, unconscious flinch, but we both know it happened. Now it's the elephant in the room. I move to the edge of the couch, wiping up teary sniffles on the sleeve of my jumpsuit. I put my hood on. Damn. The damn clock is driving me crazy.

I'm about to get up and leave when Tom scoots closer. He flicks the horn on my head then whispers in my ear, "how about we go out to dinner, *then* come home and make love?" His tone is appeasing.

I take a deep breath as I turn to face him. "How about we have sex right now, then I'll heat up some leftovers?"

"We should go out, Em, it's our anniversary."

"Fine," I say, some ticks after. I'm exhausted. "Let's go to Beirut." That's our default go-to eatery. We're kind of regulars over there.

"Beirut?" Tom twitches his face. "That's hardly a celebration."

"What's to celebrate?" I grab his martini and pour it down my throat. I hate gin.

He's trying to come up with a clever response before his phone pings and he retreats to his screens.

Sighing, I return to my post by the window. "In this weather, I would rather get a takeout. Maybe we could watch a movie on Netflix. Or maybe I could just die." I say the last bit in a low voice.

He puts down the phone. Picking up the remote, he turns off the graphs and switches to Netflix. "A comedy?"

"Nah. I'm not in the mood for goofy."

"A political documentary, then."

"Na-ah. That's a hard pass. Let's just go to Beirut and get it over with." I'm too tired to argue.

"I'm going to change," he announces as he gets up. I have no intention of doing the same.

Tom returns wearing a heavy, hand-knitted Icelandic sweater his mother knitted for him ages ago.

"Gee, where did you find that?"

"It was way back in the closet."

"I know. I hid it there. It's hideous."

He shrugs. "It's scratchy as hell too" Tom says. He keeps tugging the sweater away from his body. It looks so funny, I can't help but laugh.

"Huh," Tom says. "That's the reaction I was rooting for when I put it on." He smiles at me and everything seems lighter.

"Fine." I cross my hands. "We'll watch one of your stupid sci-fis. But you'd better not fall asleep halfway through."

"Let's eat first." Tom says. He changes back to his casual jacket. I put a fleece cardigan over my jumpsuit.

"I just wanted to do something different, is all," Tom says when we're by the door.

"I've been wanting to do something different for months," I mutter as I pull on my Uggs.

"I'm bored with Beirut."

"I'm bored with everything!"

We face each other as if we're in a staring competition.

"Oh, I almost forgot." Tom is the first to blink. He reaches into his pocket. "Happy Valentine's Day and Anniversary." He pecks me on the cheek and hands me a small golden box. I don't know whether it's the dry touch of his lips on my cheek or the fact he bought me a gift that gets me overly excited.

"Tom! We agreed!" I do my best to sound angry.

"It's just a little something."

There's a metal thimble inside the box. It looks vintage. I heave loudly.

"Don't get all emotional, Em. I saw the little thing when I picked up the dry cleaning and thought you'd like it. So, there. I got it for you just so you'd know I still think of you. That I still care. Despite—" He tries unsuccessfully to hide his emotional state. After almost three decades of marriage, you notice every little nuance in your partner.

"Thank you, honey. It's beautiful." I wipe my eyes. "I'll be right back." I have a present for him too. I rush upstairs to my sewing studio and search frantically for a little box or something to wrap my gift—a handmade key fob with the gray Litecoin logo embroidered on the fabric. Finally, I slide it into one of the pink floral bags I've had custom made. It's not masculine, but it'll do.

Tom checks the handmade item carefully, giving it the proper attention required to appreciate my work.

"That looks great, Ems. Really. Truly professional."

I beam at him. "It's a new embroidery design. I uploaded it to my Etsy store earlier this week. I've already had three sales."

"Then, dinner's on you."

I scoff. "That's barely seven dollars, Tom. *Before* tax."

He shrugs humbly. "No worries, then. I just made another fifty while you were gone, so..."

I grind my teeth. It would have been so much better if he'd just put down his phone. I don't care about the money he's making. It doesn't make me happy.

Tom grabs my hands. "Twenty-seven years, Em," he whispers. "Can you believe we made it this far?" His eyes sparkle.

No, I can't. Especially because the last few months have been a daily struggle. As we step out into the snowy night, I promise myself to make it stop. To do everything in my power to bring the old Tom back. And if I can't, if he continues to take me for granted, then his next birthday gift is going to be a divorce.

Beirut is a small family business. Leila is in charge of the pots and pans, while Nasim takes care of the guests. They look the same age as Tom and me, but that's where the resemblance ends. Leila is an exceptional cook, something I've never been interested in being. And Nasim is a sweet gentleman with the manners of long-gone chivalry. They seem very happy together, content in their quiet way of living. It's beautiful yet heartbreaking to watch.

When we enter, Nasim is stood by the opening between the kitchen and the sitting area, his left elbow resting on the railing as he leans against the wall. His face is illuminated from the strong kitchen lights, while his body is in darkness. Leila stands on the other side of the wall, inside the kitchen.

She's says something I can't hear. Even if I could, I probably wouldn't understand because Leila doesn't speak English. Her lips move and Nasim listens carefully, his head tilted. He nods, and the slow smile that spreads across his face matches the one already on his wife's.

A stab of pain knots my stomach. Tom and I used to communicate so fluently and effortlessly. We used to be best friends. Every night after we'd tucked in the kids, we'd sit in the living room, sometimes for hours. We shared our experiences and random thoughts. We laughed. We kissed. We made love.

Oh, how I miss that intimacy. Money was always a struggle, but we were happy. And now that we're rich, I'm miserable. These days, I see only glimpses of what we used to be, like that moment earlier, when Tom surprised me with an unexpected gesture. Then, his sweetness sweeps me off my feet and leaves me baffled, wondering whether his current detachment is just a phase I should wait for to run its course, or if it's our blunt new reality. Twenty-seven years is not something you break up lightly. I shiver as I remember the promise I just made to myself. One month. I'll give it one more month.

Nasim welcomes us with his big smile. It's so wide and genuine I have to smile back, although there's not even one happy organ in my body.

"Emily. Tom. So good to see you again!" He takes our coats. I wrap the old, oversized cardigan around my torso. This is the first time I'm wearing the jumpsuit outside the house, and I'm too aware of my looks.

"How are you doing, Nasim?" Tom asks. "How's business?"

Nasim kisses the tips of his fingers and points them upwards. "Inshallah," he says. I already know that means all is good. "I took your advice, Tom, and invested in that dog money."

"Dogecoin," Tom corrects. "Did you make a profit?"

Nasim nods. "Enough to upgrade the stove in the kitchen. Leila's been complaining about it for a while, and now she's happy." Nasim glances at the kitchen. Leila can't see us because the sitting area is so dim while the kitchen is so bright. "And I am telling you, my friend, a happy wife is the most important thing in life."

There's so much love in Nasim's voice. I can't stand it.

He gives me a quick glance. Does he notice my misery?

Tom looks at me. I squint back. I'm definitely *not* a happy wife.

"Speaking of Leila, she was hoping you would come today." Nasim quickly changes the subject and prepares the ground for his catchphrase. "She has cooked all your favorite dishes." He laughs. It's a deep, throaty laugh, although it comes straight from the heart. We can't help but join the laughter even though there's nothing funny about it. Nasim says the same thing every time.

There are no menus at Beirut. You eat what Leila decides to cook that day, and there's no telling what that will be because it depends on her mood and the ingredients she finds in the market. It doesn't matter, though, because she's such an ingenious chef. Everything she makes tastes absolutely divine.

While we wait for our firsts, Tom is back on his phone and I'm on the verge of turning from an unhappy wife to a furiously crazy one. I tap my fingertips on the table. I inhale deeply, trying to restrain my rage.

Tom doesn't lift his head.

There's nothing much to explore in Beirut. It's one of those small joints, only eight tables and a total of twenty chairs. I've counted. There aren't two chairs alike. I don't know if it's supposed to create a certain Middle Eastern atmosphere, or if it's simply because each chair was purchased at a different yard sale. They all look kind of used, ragged.

Besides us, there's only one other patron in the restaurant. He's one of the regulars too. I can see only his partial profile, but I recognize him by the bald patch on top of his skull. I know he's wearing glasses and has a beer belly. His jaw moves as he bends over the table, eating.

Soft Arabic music pours out of a large TV screen hanging on one of the walls. It looks like a foreign version of X-Factor—different judges but a similar set. The singer is a young woman wearing too much makeup around her eyes and I can't wrap my head around the music. It sounds like a cat in heat.

Tom moves his head with the beat, shooting it back and forth like a chicken. He's doing it subconsciously while still tapping his phone.

I choke back a giggle. Then a brilliant idea overtakes me. "Hey, Tom." I touch his forearm to grab his attention. "I know what we should do! We should learn Arabic." I touch my cheeks, certain they're flushed.

It takes him a few seconds to complete whatever he's doing on the phone. As he lifts his face to look at me, the affirmative no is already formulating on it. He opens his mouth to say the word, but something shifts. His eyes darken as footsteps come closer.

It's Nasim with our firsts, eight small appetizer plates each containing a different salad sample. He uses exaggerated gestures to describe the hummus, tabbouleh, fattoush, baba ganoush, and all the rest.

"This is also very good." He points to yet another plate. "That's eggplant." He forms the shape of the vegetable with his hands. "It's grilled on an open fire, so it gets this smoky texture. Here," he brings the plate close to my face, "you can still smell the smoke, can't you?" I sniff. The smell is so good, I almost drool.

"Hey, Nasim," I say, "do you happen to know an Arabic teacher who could teach us the language?"

"Emily!" Tom snaps. I don't get why he's so jumpy.

Nasim smiles. "Well, Emily, I can't just pull a name out of my sleeve, but I can certainly make some inquiries for you if you wish."

"Thank you," I say sweetly at the same time as Tom says, "that won't be necessary."

Nasim looks at Tom. He doesn't understand what's going on. That makes two of us.

"We don't want to impose," Tom says and gives me a fiery look. I'm a berated child. I swallow the tears of my offended pride.

"That's alright, my friend," Nasim says. "You share investment tips with me, and now it's my turn to give you something in return. Please, enjoy your food." And with those words, he leaves us.

"What's wrong with you?" Tom scolds me the minute Nasim's gone. "That's racist!"

"Really? I thought he was flattered we're interested in his culture."

"You assume he knows Arabic teachers only because he speaks Arabic!" Tom whispers.

Although his voice is hushed, the accusing tone is obvious. Tom's right about my train of thought, but is it racist? I don't think so.

I turn back to look at Nasim. He's standing next to the other regular customer. They're chatting, and the customer laughs. Are they laughing at us? Nasim notices me watching them, and he nods. I smile. He doesn't seem offended, but who knows? I wish we hadn't come.

"And I don't want to learn Arabic!" Tom concludes the argument with a thunderous whisper.

"I should go over there and apologize."

"No!" Tom shoots back. "It'll only make things worse. Just eat!"

I need a drink. Too bad Beirut doesn't serve alcohol.

Tom dips the tip of his fork in the hummus and licks it clean.

"Hmm." He purrs with pleasure. I don't understand what he likes in this murky chickpea mash but since he gives it the gurgle of approval, I dig in too. It's delish. The taste certainly doesn't fit the neutral color. The salads are great too. They're crispy and bursting with flavor. Parsley, onions, and lemon hit my palate.

We eat quietly, except for the occasional *hum* and *ah*. I still feel bad for earlier, and on top of that, my mouth is burning. Maybe it's the onions. I nibble on the pita bread, but it doesn't help. Icy water numbs the pain for a while, then it gets stronger.

Tom notices my distress. He clicks his tongue and opens his mouth to say something. I shoot him a warning glare. That shuts him off. After being married for so long, we know how to press each other's buttons. I can't take any more pressing. Not tonight.

Our entrées arrive.

"This is mujadara." Nasim points at a dish of lentils and rice. Leila cooks it often, so there's no need for lengthy explanation. "Kibbeh," Nasim says and places the plate on the table. There's no nice way to tell him that this kibbeh looks like a turd. "And this is lahm bajeen. It's minced beef. Very good."

As he folds the tray under his arm, I look up at him. "Nasim, I apologize for earlier. It was thoughtless of me, and I didn't mean to offend you."

His eyes cloud and his gaze shifts to the horizon, like he's trying to recall what that I'm talking about. Oh dear, I've just made things worse.

His face clears. "Oh, you mean about the teacher? No worries, Emily. All is good. All is great!" He looks at Tom when he says that last beat. I look at Tom too. His nostrils flare. Oh well, it'll pass once he takes his first bite.

I swoop the caramelized onion garnish off all the plates. Tom *hates* caramelized onions. I cut the kibbeh into halves, lengthwise. It makes them look less turdy. I put some on my plate and some on Tom's.

"You shouldn't have said that," he says when we make eye contact.

I shrug. "Well, I did. It's done now. Eat."

The soft, whiny music fills the silence between us. The food is not moist but also not dry, it's soft enough to melt on my tongue without turning into a sticky goo that clings to my teeth. It's gourmet cooking at its best. Now I'm glad we came. It won't be long before the masses find out about this gem and Beirut will change forever.

"Try putting some tahini on your kibbeh," Tom says. His lips shine with olive oil when he smiles at me. The food smooths the tension between us.

"Maybe we could take cooking classes together?" I'm back at it. For the past six months, I've been trying to find an activity we would enjoy doing together. "We could *both* use some tips in that area."

Tom swallows before answering. "You've gone full circle

now, Em. That was literally the first thing you offered when you decided to go on this quest."

"Really?" I wipe my lips.

He nods. His mouth is full again.

"I can't remember."

"That's because you're trying too hard."

"Maybe it's because you're not trying at all!" I slam the napkin against the table.

"Em. Please. This is not the time nor the place."

I leave it—for now. But my mind is made up. We're going to tackle this issue *today*. No more delays. No move cover-ups. I've had enough; I'm done. The minute we get back home, I'm going to confront Tom about it. I'm going to share my feelings. I'm going to do whatever I can to get my best friend back.

Tom's phone beeps. Again.

"Come on! We're having our anniversary dinner!"

"Sorry," he says. "I've put a lot of money into this, and I need to complete the transaction." He taps the phone as he speaks. "There. Done. Just made another hundred." He's smug. "This has been a good day."

"Maybe for you," I grumble.

Not a minute passes by, and the damn thing beeps again. He picks it up without even a blink. It's like a reflex. I drop my utensils on purpose. The noise startles Tom. He jumps a little in his seat, but my message doesn't get through. The phone is like armor.

I sigh. "Tom," I say. There's a quiet determination in my tone. Or maybe it's despair.

"Oh, yeah, no, sorry. It's Tommy. He sends his regards."

I mellow in an instant. My baby remembered our anniversary!

"He's going to spend spring break at a friend's house in Miami." Tom updates.

"Woo!" I mimic wiping the sweat off my forehead. Tom Jr. was a shy boy growing up. I'm so happy he's found a friend in college. "Is that a *female* friend?"

"I don't know." Tom's still tapping. The glow of the screen radiates on his face. I'm waiting for more, but he's not sharing.

"Well, did you ask him?"

"What's that?"

"Did you ask him about his friend?" My voice is slightly high pitched.

When he doesn't answer, I grab the phone from his hand.

"Em!" Tom's yelling now. He gets up and tries to take his phone back.

I look at the screen and of course, he's looking at one of the crypto coin market trends and *not* texting with our son.

Teaching art to unwilling, rowdy kids finally pays off. I use evasive maneuvers to keep the phone out of his reach, pulling away and dodging. I had to confiscate so many phones during my class, then deal with the hysterical, distressed teenagers trying to get their gadgets back. It wasn't funny for me to fight with the students, but it *is* funny now—in an evil kind of way. I take pleasure in seeing Tom's efforts to get his precious back.

"Give it back! Emily! Stop that! You're making a scene!"

"You're the one jumping around and *I'm* making a scene?"

There's no reasoning with him. He's possessed.

"Fine," I say. "Give me the car keys, and I'll give it back."

He puts the keys on the table. Now it's a demilitarized neutral zone. I put the phone on the other side. As he leaps forth to grab it, I take the keys.

"Now use your phone to get yourself a cab, because I'm leaving." I grab my coat on the way out. I don't look back.

CHAPTER 2

May 27th, 2016

I don't think Mom is really dead, she's just turned into something else. Like a bumblebee. One buzzed next to my face when I went to visit her—that was the first clue. Because what's a bumblebee have to do with a graveyard? I'd started telling Mom about the horrible day I'd had when this bee just appeared out of nowhere. I tried to wave it off, but it flew away then came right back, circling me before it stopped and hovered in front of my face.

"Mom?" I asked.

She kind of nodded with her whole body, then she started flying away. I followed her. She stopped for a minute on a tulip tree, and I waited for her while she dug out some nectar. It was just like Mom and her sweet tooth—she could never resist a candy. Huh. Emerging out of the flower, Mom was covered in yellow pollen. She didn't seem to mind. It was exactly like when Mom would get dirty cooking.

At first, she flew at a steady rate, then she picked up the pace. So, I asked her to slow down—and she did. Isn't that proof it was really her? I was so happy to see her, telling her how much I've missed her and that I'm so happy she came back as a bee.

She led me to a little grocery store on South Maple. We never shopped there. It always looked so dark and neglected. Mom landed on the ads board hanging inside the window. There were all kinds of ads there—people who had lost their pets, people looking for jobs. A locksmith offering super unlocking services for the folks of the neighborhood. I browsed the ads for a second, and when I looked up, Mom was gone.

"Mom?" I called. She didn't come back. "Mom? Mom!"

The cashier, an Indian guy wearing a large white turban, lifted his eyes from the book he was reading.

"Did you plan to meet your mother here?" he asked politely. "Maybe she's a bit late."

"My mom is a bee," I said. He looked at me like I was a crazy person. I knew that look. "No time to explain. She brought me here, and now she's gone. Have you seen a bumble bee?"

The man left his post behind the counter and came toward me. "Was it a regular bee?"

"Yes. It stopped right here—" I pointed to the board. And then I saw it.

Seventh row, second from the left. Mrs. Tomlin is looking for a housekeeper.

Second row, seventh from the right. Mrs. Tomlin is looking for a housekeeper.

Chills.

That's why Mom led me here.

I went straight to Mrs. Tomlin's. I didn't even bother to call. I was so confident it was meant to be. On the way over, I pictured her as a grumpy old lady with gray frizzy hair, curved witch nose, and a hairy mole on her left chin. Surprisingly, she looked exactly like I'd imagined, which was another good sign, because how do thoughts come into our minds? Someone puts them in there. Only, she wasn't that old. Probably in her early sixties.

The house she lived in looked abandoned, the front lawn a field of grass with piles of leaves lying about. At first, I thought I'd got the wrong address. But the ad, both ads, listed this exact place. I knocked, the sound echoing inside. I had to knock several times before she finally appeared at the door. She opened it but left the inner screen door shut. I grinned. She grunted.

"Jehovah's Witness?" she asked.

"No."

"Any other religion?"

"No. I—" I raised the ads.

"Whatever you're selling, I'm not buying." She began closing the door.

"Wait! Are you still looking for a housekeeper?"

She opened the door again, gave me some scrutiny. "I pay minimum wage for a 24/7 job."

"Okay." I'd thought it was a volunteer position. Getting paid was even better.

She examined me from top to bottom through squinted eyes.

"Do you do drugs?"

"No. Do you?"

She chuckled bitterly. I hadn't meant to be funny. I was genuinely concerned. She looked weird. Her eyes were just slits. I couldn't even get their color.

"Are you a serial killer?"

"No, Ma'am. But seriously, if I were a serial killer, would I have said yes? Maybe you should have asked me if I'm a liar first. I would've told you straight away that I'm not." I kept on talking like I do when I'm nervous until she stopped me by opening the screen door.

"I'll show you your room," she said, and I marveled. It came with a room!

The lease on Mom's apartment was due by the end of the month and with the medical bills eating all our savings, I couldn't afford to live there anymore. Getting a job and a place to stay was something I hadn't even dared to dream of. Thanks, Mom, for looking after me even after your death.

The inside of the house looked as dreadful as the yard. Mrs. Tomlin was either a hoarder or just didn't care enough to take a trip to the dumpster. There were old newspapers lying around, and lots of plastic bags, empty beer cans, and pizza boxes.

We passed through the living room. The TV was on, some nature show on National Geographic. The curtains, full of dust, were drawn shut although it was a beautiful spring day. There were dead flies on the floor.

My room was in the back of the house. It was small and dirty, but the bed seemed comfortable enough.

"Your work here is to deal with anything that requires leaving the house," she said, still grumpy. "I hate leaving the house."

I nodded.

Giving me another inspection, she asked, "And, I don't know— Is it too much to expect an intelligent conversation every now and then? I get bored sometimes."

I shrugged. "What do you consider as an intelligent conversation? I have a graduate degree in Applied Mathematics from Brown. I can talk for hours about polynomials and methods to calculate probabilities. Does that count?"

She just grunted, so I didn't say anything about the power of numbers.

"Do you cook?"

"Yes, Ma'am. I'm an excellent cook. My mother was a chef, so..."

"Hmm." She grunted.

Tears began welling up. "Yeah. She died three weeks ago. It's still fresh."

"Sorry for your loss." Her tone was softer. "A smoke?" She pulled a wrinkled pack of cigarettes out of her pocket and offered it to me.

I sniffed the air. It was moldy, with only a hint of smoke. She wasn't a heavy smoker. What a relief.

"My mom died of lung cancer, so, definitely not." I didn't know why I said that.

She sighed and put it back in her pocket. "What about your father?"

I shook my head. "Never knew him."

"Any siblings?"

I shook my head again. "Sorry," I said and wiped my face.

She pressed her lips together into a thin line. "That's my Charlie." She opened the locket she was wearing around her neck. Inside was a picture of a little boy, smiling. He had smart eyes and a sweet smile. He looked like a miniature version of her. "Stepped onto a land mine in Afghanistan two years ago."

"So sorry for your loss," I said.

"Yeah. Thanks. I wish I could tell you it gets easier. But as you can see," her gesture included the entire house, "it doesn't."

"Was he your only child?"

"Yep. I'm all alone in the world. Just like you."

Did Mom lead me here so I could get a glimpse of the future me?

"So, are you staying?" she asked.

I nodded. "I can start right away. Would you like me to fix you some dinner?"

She shrugged. "There's nothing in the fridge. I usually order in."

Some people say there's nothing in the fridge when they're out of beer. I had to check it out and oh boy, was it empty. The only thing in there was two slices of old pizza.

"I was planning on having that for my dinner," she said.

So, it was back to the grocery store. I decided to cook pasta with fresh tomatoes. The Indian guy helped me pick out some fresh produce, and put everything on Mrs. Tomlin's tab. So that part was easy. There was a stack of notebooks by the cash register—hardcover, black leather. I took one. I needed a new journal for this new adventure.

And now I'm writing this first entry while lying in bed. Mrs. Tomlin has fallen asleep on the recliner by the TV. Earlier she told me she can't sleep in her own bed. Poor thing.

CHAPTER 3

om

Emily fades into the whiteness. One minute she's here, and the next she's an ambiguous figure struggling through the blizzard. It's dark and foggy outside, and I can't tell if it's her coming back, or if it's just my terrorized mind playing tricks on me, making me see arms and legs in a rising wave of snowflakes created by a mischievous gust.

The whole world is shifting on its axle, just like that terrible day last fall. September 12th. I can't move, like the biblical figure who turned into a pillar of salt after experiencing a horrifying vision. I can't produce any sounds, as if I'm a kindergarten toddler and not a middle-aged man.

The sudden shock of the loss is paralyzing. It's one of those moments that stretches on for eternity. It's one of those sports slow-mos where one player is about to kick another in the face, and the realization of the unavoidable, upcoming pain slowly forms in his expression.

The same goes for my face. My mouth is wide open, but I can't make any sound. It's probably been just a few seconds since Emily's dramatic exit when I hear the voice. *Go after her.* I don't know if it's the voice inside my head. It's slow and distorted. *Go after her.* I don't recognize the speaker. Have I just experienced a disassociation of the mind? Do I have a multi-personality disorder? *Go after her, Tom.* Cold sweat covers my back as I finally get a grip. The voice has an ovular 'R'. I know the speaker. I exhale with relief, yet my stomach is still a stiff knot. His name escapes me, like everything else. What just happened?

"Go, Tom. Go after her," he urges me again.

"She's coming back," I mumble when my voice returns. I point outside. The lamp post on the other side of the road is flickering. Is it her? The figure outside keeps moving, shifting. One moment it's Emily coming toward the door, and the next, it's just the falling snow, filling me with despair.

"Go, Tom, she can't be too far away."

"Nasim." The fog in my mind disperses, and I get my memory back. He's right. I should go after her. I hurry toward the exit, just reaching for the doorknob when my Infiniti Q50 comes to life with its unmistakably sweet roar. Two beams of lights shine through the fog, and a glimpse of cherry red catches my eye as she speeds down the road.

"She's gone," I say, and my mother's words echo in my mind. *He's gone,* she cried. *He's gone, Tom.*

My knees get wobbly; I hold on to the knob. The door swings open, letting the cold draft in. I can't get a hold of my body. I'm sliding down, the fibers of the dirty brown rug getting closer to my face when a pair of strong hands catch me. A silver flask is pushed inside my blurry field of vision.

"Drink that," an authoritative voice says. The flask is pressed against my quivering lips. Liquid spills over my shirt, my pants. Cold. My throat clenches as the drink burns its way down.

"Better now?" the voice asks. This isn't Nasim's. He would never give me alcohol.

I nod. But is it really?

Those strong hands help me up. I look outside through the glass door. The storm is weakening now, the fog beginning to disperse. An engine revs close by, but it's not mine. A Toyota. My instincts are coming back. Still not confident about my knees holding me up, I grab the back of the chairs as I feel my way back to the table Emily and I just shared. Her plate is still there, napkin draped over a half-eaten kibbeh, the utensils a mess. She hates it when her fork handle gets sticky. I wipe it clean with the napkin and set it nicely by the plate. She'll be happy when she returns.

A pinch in my heart. She's not coming back.

"You're all right, my friend. You're all right." Nasim comes and taps me on my shoulder hesitantly. I look up at him. His eyes are dark as the night and there are acne scars all over his face. It's so funny, seeing a grown man with those pimply reminders of his youth. I choke back a giggle. Leila stands next to Nasim. She smells like cumin and turmeric, and her apron is stained. She has a worried look on her face.

"Oh, hi, Leila, how are you doing?" My cheerfulness sounds fake. But they don't say anything. Well, not to me. Leila shoots something in Arabic at Nasim, and he replies in his gentle manner. I know they're talking about me, only I don't have a clue what they're saying.

They start fussing over the table, gathering plates, clearing everything away. I should probably go.

I can never come back. Emily has ruined Beirut for us. Now I'm furious. How dare she desert me here like that? The memory of her grabbing my phone and not giving it back makes me even angrier. And now I need to rectify *her* mistakes. Clear up after her.

"I'm so sorry for Emily's behavior, Nasim, Leila. You know her, it's not typical."

Nasim nods. Leila gives me a harsh look. Her mouth is so tightly closed, it looks like a button. She storms off to the kitchen, an echo of Emily's act. I sigh. I'm as good as dead here. Nasim goes after her, plates balanced all over his forearm.

As I reach down to get my wallet out of my pants, I look around the restaurant, observing it one last time. I have good memories from this place, like the time Marni and Marcus announced their engagement, and we toasted with apple juice. Or almost a year ago, when we celebrated Tommy's acceptance to MIT.

And then it hits me again. The certainty of the loss. Everything is spinning when I try to get up.

"Easy, easy now." The man who gave me the drink earlier is by my side again. He's vaguely familiar. He helps me back to my seat as if I'm a million years old, although I can tell by his silver hair and turkey-like neck that he's older than me. He wears frameless glasses and has a beer belly that stretches out his button-down shirt.

"Thank you."

He waves a dismissal.

"I've seen you here before," I recall.

He nods, "As have I. You and your beautiful wife."

I swallow hard. "Twenty-seven," I say, choking.

"Sorry?" the stranger kindly asks.

I raise a finger, signaling that I need a minute. "Emily and me. It's our twenty-seventh anniversary today. We got married on Valentine's Day." My voice is barely a whisper.

"Mabruc—it means congratulations." Nasim has come back from the kitchen to pick up the rest of the dishes. "I am certain you and Emily will overcome your recent hiccup in the most agreeable way."

I grimace. "Thank you."

"You are one of the finest couples I know." Nasim says and puts his hand on my shoulder again, only for a second before disappearing back into the kitchen with the last of the dirty dishes.

The familiar stranger takes Emily's seat. He uncorks the flask and slants it toward me. I shake my head. Bourbon neat was never to my liking. He shrugs and imbibes a vast quantity, examining me over the silvery bottle. The way he looks at me makes me uneasy. It's like his dark blue eyes are probes penetrating my soul, poking into my deepest secrets and fears.

Nasim returns. He pours bitter black coffee into tiny cups and places a dessert plate in front of each of us. It looks like a piece of cake made from thin, orange noodles, green pistachio crunch spread on top. I've eaten it before. I remember it being sweet and creamy.

"Sweet kanafeh is the remedy for a wounded soul," Nasim declares. "Eat, my friend. It will make you feel better."

It does. The mixture of sweet pastry and salty goat cheese is a feast to my palate. I close my eyes and savor each bite, knowing it will probably be my last kanafeh here. I've overextended my welcome.

"You must have done something pretty upsetting for her to flee like that," the man in Emily's seat says.

I sip the coffee. The sizzling hot beverage burns my lips.

"Did you cheat on her?" he asks bluntly.

"What? Of course not!" I shake my head vigorously. I don't know why I need to defend myself, but I still do it. "It's not like that at all."

My phone beeps. An alert. The noise clears my head. I can't be emotional when I trade. It's Trading 101. "Excuse me, I need to take care of this." Ethereum has reached a lower threshold, and I need to put in an order to buy.

"I'm an expert in crypto coins," I explain to the stranger while I set an alarm for the price at which I'm willing to sell the coin. "I hope to reach six-figures by the end of the fiscal year."

Most people are very impressed by this little speech. My current conversational companion isn't. He slides me a business card. *Sex Therapist* it says. There's no name, just the title and a phone number. I turn it over and turn it again. I wonder.

"I can help you," he says simply. "If you'd like."

"I don't have a sex problem." I slide the card back.

He pauses, his eyes piercing me while I look at my phone. "Sex is just another gateway to the psyche," he says softly. "It's a snapshot of your emotional state."

My nostrils flare as I pick up my phone and scroll my open alarms. Who is this charlatan? How dare he exploit my vulnerability so bluntly? I shake my head, "I don't believe in therapists. And even if I did, as I said, I don't have a sex problem."

"Of course, you don't. It's for the wife," he says quickly and winks.

"How dare you! It's not your place to make such...accusations!"

He has the best poker face I've ever seen, like nothing touches him.

"We're done here." I get up. "Nasim! would you please give me the check?"

Nasim rushes to the table. "Oh no, Tom, today's dinner is on the house." He bows apologetically.

"Absolutely not!" I take out my wallet.

"A woman doesn't get so frustrated at her partner just

because he spends too much time on his phone. There's always something deeper," The sex therapist says.

I stop mid-movement. "We've had a rough year, if you must know. Our daughter got married last June. Our son left for college. And then my father died." My voice breaks.

He raises an eyebrow. "I'm sorry for your loss."

"Thank you." I browse through the notes in my wallet.

"It's not easy being just the two of you in that big empty house," he says softly as someone who knows exactly what he's talking about.

I put a Benjamin Franklin on the table. I could just leave. It would be so easy. Consider the change as a tip. As a damage fee. But I stay.

"She keeps coming up with these stupid ideas. Activities we should do together." Like her enthusiasm for Arabic earlier. I turn to explain to Nasim, only he's gone. Evaporated into thin air.

The therapist looks at me encouragingly, waiting for me to state the obvious. I sit down. "Do you think she's depressed?"

He nods. "I might be wrong, of course. I wouldn't diagnose someone based on an insulated incident in a restaurant. But if you were to ask me to make a calculated guess, I would suggest you're dealing with the Empty Nest Syndrome. It's nothing to be ashamed of. Many parents feel sadness and grief when their kids leave home. It's not a clinical condition though, and can be treated quite easily with great results."

I look at his card.

"Sometimes sex isn't the problem, but it *is* the solution." He taps twice on the side of his nose.

I don't get what he means by that, but I take the card and put it in my pocket.

"I must warn you, though. My methods are highly

unorthodox. Incredibly successful," he smiles, "but still, quite innovative. Not what you'd expect at all."

"What do you mean?" I take another bite of my desert and a tiny sip from the bitter coffee to balance the sweetness.

"Well..." He pauses for a second, thinking. Soft Arabic music breaks the silence. It comes from a commercial playing on the TV. I recognize the brand, Palmolive dish soap, but the text and message are so different than what I'm used to."Tom." It's Nasim again, and I'm immediately overcome with shame.

"Nasim. I can't apologize enough."

"Please." He rolls his eyes as he picks up the hundred-dollar note, "don't insult me, my friend." Reluctantly, I take the money back. I don't want to cause another scene.

Nasim puts a business card on the table in front of me. What's with the business cards today? It's for Beirut. I look up at him, puzzled. The therapist looks perplexed as well. He sits quietly with his hands crossed over his heavy chest.

"Earlier, Emily asked about an Arabic teacher. I would like to humbly offer myself," he says plainly. He smiles. It's not his usual wide, welcoming smile—this one is somewhat apologetic. Timid. "You see, I was a teacher in the old country. And I would be honored to teach Emily. And you, of course," he adds quickly, as if Emily and I are not a couple anymore.

"Oh." It's unexpected, and I don't know what to say.

"I was very touched when Emily asked to learn my language. I sincerely hope I didn't scare her off with my casual reply." He wrings his hands and lowers his gaze. It takes me a second to get the subtext. He thinks Emily left because of *him*.

"Oh, no, Nasim." I touch his forearm. "Please, don't blame yourself for her leaving. It was my fault." Probably. God knows what ticked her off.

He exhales loudly. "That's such a relief. Leila was all over me for being too shy to offer myself for the job in the first place." He turns his head toward the opening between the kitchen and the restaurant. Leila is peeking out at us. He puts a thumb up. A slow smile spreads on her face.

Watching the two of them communicate, something opens inside me. I realize I wronged Emily by assuming she'd offended Nasim. I realize this is my way back in. A peace offering.

The taxi pulls up to the curb. I can't get out quickly enough. While hurrying to the house, I smell the fresh clean scent of the snow. The front lawn is white, and there's salt on the path leading from the street. My heart warms to my Emily. She's so thoughtful, making sure I won't stumble on the ice.

The house seems dark, only the outside light on. And the front door is locked.

I knock. I ring the bell. "Emily," I call out, not too loud. I don't want to alarm the neighbors. There's a spare key under a fake rock by the garage. My Infiniti is parked inside.

Emily!" I cry as I rush upstairs to her sewing room. It's a mess, and she's not there. She's not in the bedroom either. Nor in the kitchen.

There's a note on the counter by the coffee maker. *Gone to visit Katie for a few.*

It's signed with her fancy *E*. No '*Love, Emily*'. No Xs for kisses or Os for hugs scribbled by her signature like usual when she leaves me casual notes.

She's never done this before. She's *threatened* to go to Katie's on numerous occasions. It was kind of our thing. But she never actually *acted* on it. It was like an empty mantra she chanted every time we had a big fight. I'm taking the kids and going away to Katie's for a few days, she would say with her quivery voice and teary eyes. It was a signal we'd exhausted the fight, reached the end of the line. Her saying she was going to her sister's was a cease and desist moment where we could choose to forgive and forget or throw more wood onto the fire and end life as we knew it. We never did the latter. We never took that leap.

Going away to Katie was our emergency code during heated arguments and it was our private joke during happy times. I can't believe she actually went to Katie's. And why now?

The last time she threatened to leave was a few years back, when Tommy wanted to cash out his college fund and use the money for programming summer school. Emily sided with him, which was reckless. Although in retrospect, it wasn't so stupid.

Why now? The dispute over Tommy's whims kept us agitated for weeks until my father came through and loaned us the money for summer camp. Tonight, all we'd had was a stupid, childish argument in Beirut. No big deal. What did she want me to do? Put down the phone while I'm bringing in money to pay for the meal? It was stupid, *nothing.*

The house feels empty without her bubbly energy. Even when I turn on the lights, it doesn't seem as bright. My phone beeps. *Emily!* My heart sings. But it's just one of my alarms. I toss the phone aside. I'm not in the mood for trading, which is weird, because it's my go-to activity whenever I'm down.

I'm spent, physically drained. It's only half-past eight, but there's nothing left for me to do. I climb upstairs slowly, sighing with every step like my father did in his final years.

I tuck myself in Tommy's bed – my bed now since Tommy's at college, and lie with my eyes open. I look at the charts on the wall and wait for them to work their charm. Usually, the numbers relax me into an easy sleep.

There's a beep from somewhere in the house. My phone, informing me the battery is about to die. I should get up and plug it into a charger. But I don't. It's fine to take the rest of the night off. I've earned enough for today. *That* makes me grin.

For a second.

Then, fear of missing out on a good deal overwhelms me. I ignore it. The irony makes me chuckle. Isn't this exactly what Emily wanted? For me to take the night off. Well, she finally got her wish and she's not even here to enjoy it. I should call her and apologize for ruining our anniversary. I sigh. The house is a big black hole without its sun to balance the gravity. Maybe she didn't go. *Maybe* this is just a new level in the "going to Katie" strategy. She's probably sitting in her car somewhere, waiting for my call. As I ponder it more, I'm certain that's the case.

Then, like every night since my father died, my mind drifts to Monday, September 12th.

The day started with an early morning phone call. It was barely seven, and it was my mother, despite how many times I'd told her not to call before seven-thirty. I pressed *ignore*. She called again a minute later. Getting angry, I dismissed her one more time. When she called for the third time, an hour later, I was in the shower. She left a voice message. It was nothing but silence. I was about to delete it when I heard her say, "Tom?"

She sounded confused, lost. My heart was pounding hard when I called her back. She didn't answer. And then, there were classes and meetings and more classes. She slipped my mind. It was lunchtime when I finally got a hold of her, and by then, it was already too late.

Such a stupid death, falling off a ladder while cleaning the gutters.

"But I told him I'd come to do that!"

"He had to go up there. A storm is coming tonight." Mom was crying.

I'm still so angry at him. But I'm also filled with guilt. I should have been there on Saturday like I'd promised. My laziness killed him.

Stupid. Stupid. Stupid. Why didn't I pick up the phone when she called? He had two full hours after the fall before his organs collapsed. I could have been there with him. I could have said goodbye. I keep spiraling about all the things I should have done differently. I miss him so terribly.

And now Emily has left.

A heavy boulder falls out of nowhere and crushes my chest. Choking, I struggle for air. Odd cracking sounds come out when I breathe.

I'm having a heart attack. I'm going to die here, all alone in Tommy's bed.

Slowly, I crawl out. The pain is excruciating. A burst of cold sweat covers my skin. I'm shaking, my teeth chattering uncontrollably. The pain is so strong I can't straighten up, so I crawl on all fours toward the staircase. I wish I hadn't canceled the landline, hadn't left my phone downstairs.

Sitting at the top of the stairs, I scoot myself down on my bottom. One step at a time, pushing through the pain. My whole upper body is bent forward; the pain is more manageable that way. I make little noises like weightlifters do.

I'm focused on survival. On the next step. Each one gets me closer to my dying phone, which continues to beg for juice. Hopefully, I'll get there before it drains completely.

I pray to a god I don't believe in. *Oh god, please don't let me die tonight.* Then I try to contact Emily telepathically, which I also don't believe in. I concentrate all my being into the message. *I'm sorry. Please come home. I need you.*

There's a rattle by the front door. Someone is trying to break in. But I don't care. At this point, I'd give away all my belongings for a ride to St. Helen's. With a soft touch, the door is opened. A cold breeze shakes me to the core, and I cry out. "Help!" I try to say. "Help me!"

And there's Emily. Holding a duffel bag and a dripping umbrella. I can't believe it worked. I love her so much.

"Tom!" She rushes over and immediately, I feel better. I try to mumble something, but my mouth is dry, and my tongue is too heavy. She presses her lips to my forehead to check my temperature. I've seen her do it a bazillion times when the kids were little. Sometimes they were healed by that simple touch. The pressing on my chest has loosened up a bit. I'm saved.

CHAPTER 4

May 28th, 2016

$\mathscr{I}$'m updating what's gone on with me since Mom directed me to Mrs. Tomlin's house yesterday.

Well, after coming back from Sunjay's grocery store, I charged into the kitchen with mops, scrubs, and detergents. Most of the time, Mrs. Tomlin minded her own business. When she did drop by to check on me, I already had the fridge, stove, and counters sparkling clean and was making my way through the dusty cabinets, tackling cobwebs and dead insects.

"What's going on here?" Her sharp voice startled me, and I banged my head on the cabinet top. "I didn't ask you to do the cleaning around here, and I'm certainly not paying you for that."

"Okay." I shrugged. We stood there for a few seconds staring at each other. I waited for her to dismiss me. She didn't. "It's a matter of hygiene, you see. I can't cook in a dirty kitchen. And I plan on cooking all your meals here."

She continued to stare at me silently.

"Well, unless you want me to leave?"

She looked around the almost-sparkling-clean space. Then she grunted something incoherent and went back to whatever she'd been doing before.

I stayed.

Dinner was fabulous. We ate quietly by the breakfast counter. I tried to think of an intelligent conversation topic but couldn't come up with anything. I was too tired from all the cleaning and kept hiding my yawns.

Mrs. Tomlin didn't seem to mind. She took a second helping. Then a third. "Thanks," she said when we were done. She pushed her plate away.

I grinned. It was good seeing someone enjoy my cooking. Mom was so weak toward the end, she could barely digest the watery soup I'd prepared.

"Let me do the dishes," she said when I began picking them up. I sat by the counter and watched her clean. She was so meticulous about it, she'd obviously been tidy and organized before.

Today, I decided to tackle the garden. I found a rusted lawnmower in the shed and mowed the grass in the front yard and raked all the leaves into a huge pile. She watched me through the window. At one point, when I leaned against the rake and wiped the sweat off my forehead, she stepped outside with a glass of water. It was a nice gesture.

I was nearly done when I heard a man's cheerful voice saying, "Hello there!" It startled me. It was a middle-aged gentleman walking a dog. He introduced himself as Elijah.

"I live right across the street, young lady." He pointed to a well-groomed cottage.

I giggled. The last time I'd been called a young lady was in my twenties.

His garden was a marvel, with wisterias hanging over the front porch and a row of English roses instead of the usual white picket fence. "Are you the new gardener?" he questioned.

"Oh no, I'm Mrs. Tomlin's new live-in housekeeper. Gardening is my initiative. I've never gardened before."

"Yes, I can see that," he said. The little dog sniffed my boots, then tinkled on a pile of leaves.

"Well, if you need any help, feel free to stop by. And please give my regards to Audrey. Mrs. Tomlin, that is."

I did. She made a dismissive gesture and said he was a nosy veteran who should mind his own business and stop criticizing his neighbors. Whatever that meant. She's so weird. Is it her grief?

I liked the physical work. My muscles burn as I write this. I'm so tired that I didn't go to visit Mom today. It's the first time since she died. Is that progress? Does she like it? I keep looking for bees.

om

Emily's doing two, maybe three things at once. I don't know how she does it. She's calling 911 while wrapping me up in the afghan from the living room and putting an extra pair of socks on my feet. She's efficient, like a bumblebee, not missing a thing. I'm safe and secure in her hands.

I can relax now. Well, as far as the pain allows. I even sleep for a few seconds before the EMT arrives. Then I'm probed, examined, turned, and tossed around. I'm an object. Stripped of my free will. I'm not a human being anymore, just a sick lump. The EMT has taken control of my body. They're talking about me as if I'm not present, no longer a man. Humiliation is more painful than the actual pain. I close my eyes, bite my lips. I try to dissociate myself from the situation.

It seems like I've been lying on the stretcher for an eternity before Emily grabs my hand. Hers is nice and warm and comforting. I open my eyes to see her soft gaze. She nods at me and tries to brave a smile as the team lifts me into the ambulance.

Emily sits in the jump seat by my side. Leaning forward, she's still holding my hand, caressing the back with her thumb. It's nice, but it would have been a million times nicer if I didn't need to pee so desperately. The bumps along the way don't help. I bite my lips in an effort to hold it in, closing my eyes every time we hit one. Wetting myself isn't an option. I've disgraced myself enough as it is.

"Are you in pain?" Emily asks. There's so much worry in her voice.

I shake my head. With my eyes closed, I signal about the pressing matter. Pointing toward it with my hand.

"Oh, you need to pee, honey?" she whispers in my ear. I nod. She's trying to balance herself while rummaging through the bag of essentials she packed earlier. With a smile, she pulls out a zippered pouch. It's homemade, one of those she sews. My toothbrush and toothpaste and contact lens gear are inside. She wraps all the toiletries in a fresh Kleenex and throws them back into the bag. Holding the small pouch with one hand, she unzips my pants with the other.

"What are you doing?" My voice suddenly comes back, hoarse and sharp.

"Shhh," Emily says. She pulls my penis out.

"Everything alright back there?" the EMT guy asks. I don't see him, but I get a sense he's watching us. What the hell is she doing?

I try to reach down, but she holds me firmly. To my embarrassment, I'm getting half erect. "Emily! Stop!" I demand through gritted teeth.

"Are you kidding me? This is the most action I've had in

months." I can't dispute that. She puts the pouch over my penis and zips the opening half-closed.

"Go!" she orders.

"But it'll ruin it!"

"So? I'll just make another one. It's a quick sew. Oh, and it's waterproof, so no worries about leaks either. Thank you very much." She says the last part as if in my voice.

I can't just let go. I close my eyes and focus, then the sound of trickling water fills the small space in the back of the ambulance, and everything flows. It's such a relief.

Emily zips up the urine pouch and places it carefully on the floor. "Remind me to get rid of it when we reach St. Helen's," she says with a smile. "Or the next passenger is going to have a special treat."

"What was that trickling sound?"

"Oh, it's just an app. Marni taught me about it. I use it when I need to go in public restrooms."

I look at her with wonder.

"Because of my shy bladder," she adds coyly, avoiding eye contact. That surprises me. Twenty-seven years. I thought I knew everything about her. I wonder what else she hides.

"Glad it could help you too." She fixes me back in my pants and pecks me on the cheek. It would have been less humiliating to be castrated. I'm spiraling into self-pity. What a wuss I've become. A helpless old dude who needs his wife to hold his penis while he pees. Great. Overcome with shame, I close my eyes again. It's the only way I can feel some privacy.

"Well, Tom, didn't we just have a moment?" Emily's amused voice penetrates my bubble. "Or did I read it wrong?"

I flinch. It's so embarrassing. "I'm dying here. Are you sure you want this to be our last exchange?" I'm looking at her directly. planning my last words. "Tell the kids I love them. Tell my mother..." My voice dies. My poor Mom. Losing her husband and her only child within six months. There's a sparkle in Emily's eyes. I wonder about it. "Em?"

"First of all, you're not going to die. Not tonight, anyway. Unless this no-good driver drives us into a ditch. And second of all, yes, if these are our last moments together, I would very much like to know you still find me attractive."

I hate it when she says second of all, and she knows it. I let it slide because there are more pressing matters. "What do you mean?"

"I mean, I felt your reaction when I touched your knob." She raises her brows.

She's enjoying this. I grit my teeth. She's so annoying. "What do you mean about me not going to die?" My voice cracks. I can barely say the word.

"Tom," Emily says softly. She leans over and caresses my cheek. "You're having a panic attack."

We hit another bump in the road, and the ambulance flies into the air for a second until gravity pulls us down. Emily's head hits the ceiling.

"Ouch," she says. Her lips are pressed together as she rubs the bruise. She gives the driver an angry look. In vain. He doesn't see her. His attention is on the road. She clearly wants to tell him off, but she remains quiet.

"Yo, driver, do you mind driving more carefully? You're killing my wife!" Yelling at him makes me feel a little better.

"Sorry man, trying to avoid the ice." He takes a stiff curve and Emily balances herself, so she won't slide off the seat.

"If anyone is going to die here tonight, it's going to be me," she's jokes.

I can't stand it. "You don't need to sugarcoat it for me, Emily. I know I'm having a massive heart attack. I have pressure in my chest that radiates to my left arm. I'm covered in cold sweat."

The urine pouch slides around the floor as the drivers hits another curve. He seems to be taking them more roughly after my request. Emily stops the pouch with her foot before it crashes into the wall of the ambulance.

"Tom, honey." She takes my hand. "Your EKG is fine. All the other parameters indicate that your heart is beating perfectly."

I'm confused. "So why are taking me to the hospital?"

Emily shrugs. "Procedure, I guess. The siren isn't on, hon." She hangs on to the side as the driver zigzags all over the lanes. "I'm sorry, Tom. For earlier. I shouldn't have left."

"But you came back." My fingers feel for hers. "I called you in my thoughts, and you came back to me."

We stare at each other. The road with all its turmoil disappears, and it's just me and her. She's as beautiful as the day we met. I love her so much. "I'm so sorry, Em, for being so distant and self-absorbed lately. You don't deserve it."

She touches her chest. "Oh, Tom. You should be on your deathbed more often."

"Shut up." I turn my head the other way, but I can't keep it there for long. The driver takes care of that. "No, Seriously, Em. I want to make it up to you. Just tell me what you want, and I'll do it."

She looks at me with half a smile.

I begin to regret what I've just said.

She raises her eyebrows mischievously.

Oh, no. I know what she's going to ask, and I can't do it. "I mean, I'll do one of those activities you keep suggesting."

She chuckles as she leans closer. "All I want is for you to take that clock back to the garage."

Our eyes are locked. "*Anything* but that." I'm teasing.

The vehicle comes to an abrupt stop.

~

A ray of sunshine wakes me up, blinding me through my closed eyelids. I open them just a slit and take in the unfamiliar surroundings. It takes me a second to remember where I am. My hand is a little sore. It's the IV.

Everything else feels fine. I inhale deeply. The air is so sweet. There's a hint of chemical cleaning products, but it doesn't reduce my joy of being alive. There's no pain. The huge rock that compressed my chest has been lifted. I look around with wonder and gratitude, and I make a mental note to cherish this feeling. To remember it.

Emily is bundled in her coat on a chair by my side. Her hair is a mess, and her freckles are very dominant in the early morning sun. Outside the window, the storm has cleared, the snow on the ledge melting, dripping. February 15th is going to be a beautiful day.

A nurse walks in. "Good morning, how are we feeling today?" She pushes a thermometer into my mouth, takes my pulse, and checks my blood pressure.

"Top of the morning to you," I say as soon as the thermometer is out of my mouth.

"I see somebody woke up in a good mood." She writes the data on a sheet.

"Is everything okay?" I straighten up and inhale deeply.

She nods. "Looks like it."

Emily stretches in her seat. She's all arms and legs. She yawns and quickly puts a hand over her mouth. "Sorry, my breath is terrible."

"I don't care." I pull myself up and lean closer for a kiss.

"I'll leave you two love birds to it," the nurse says, clicking her tongue. "Doctor Montague will be here soon with your discharge papers." She draws the curtains closed behind her, and we're alone in our bubble. It's private enough, although there's another person less than five feet away. We can clearly hear his coughs.

"So…" Emily says, "I found this in your pocket." She holds up the sex therapist's business card. "Care to explain?"

I lean back on the pillow. Last night's events seem so remote, like it happened in a different life, to a different person. The heated argument Emily and I had at the restaurant seems so petty and childish. I can't even remember why I got so mad.

"He was dining yesterday at Beirut. We chatted a bit after you left."

"Oh." She turns the card over in her hands. Back and forth. Back and forth. I remember doing the same thing less than twelve hours ago.

"So, about those activities you're so keen on us doing—" I reach out to grab her hand.

She wiggles in her seat to avoid my touch. Her smile is crooked.

"What's wrong, Em?"

"Maybe you need to get better first." She doesn't meet my eyes.

"What do you mean get better? You said it was a panic attack. Is there something I don't know?"

The man behind the curtain coughs loudly.

"Shhh." She signals with her hand, and I lower my voice. "What aren't you telling me?"

"Nothing."

We sit quietly for a bit. The noises from the corridor enter our bubble. Someone wheels a cart. A nurse says loudly, "20cc, Gina. Crate three." There are beeps and clicks, yawns and sighs. The fluorescent light flickers.

"What I mean…" She turns silent again. I wait. But it drives me crazy. My heart starts speeding. It's like each second of silence makes my health degrade in years.

"I think you should figure out why you had this panic

attack in the first place," she finally blurts out. Quickly. She's fidgeting with the therapist's card again.

I lie back. There's a hole inside me, like when we leave the house for a few days. As we unlock the car, I'd get a nagging feeling that I'd forgotten something important. I used to go back and do one more sweep around the house. Make sure everything was shut. When Emily realized I had this knack, she'd casually ask me to recheck if she didn't leave the oven on whenever we were about to leave the house. She never ridiculed me about it. Never made me feel less of a man.

But now, as I lie on the hospital bed, I'm full of shame about all my little quirks. The therapist's voice echoes in my head. "It's a classic Empty Nest Syndrome." He tapped his nose right before he left, and now I get it. It hits me like a punch in the face. It's not Emily who's depressed. It's me.

Then something miraculous happens. Twenty-seven years and one day of marriage, yet, it's the first time Emily and I both speak at the same moment.

"I think you should get an appointment," she says, while I say, "I think I should get an appointment."

We laugh. But it doesn't clear the air, especially when the man on the other side of the curtain chooses this moment to fart.

"Really?" Emily asks. She knows how I feel about therapists and such. She stands and opens the window. Just a slit, but it's enough for a gust of fresh air to clear the sulfuric stench.

"Really," I reassure her. And I truly believe it.

CHAPTER 6

June 27th, 2016

It's been a month since I moved in with Audrey. The days have been going by so fast. I work hard and fall into a deep sleep every night. But I want to document my time here. I need to remember this. It's the sixth of my twenty-seven life adventures. I didn't document the first two, but I still have my journals from the trip to Japan, and of course, my time with Michelle, right before Mom got sick. I told Sunjay about the power of twenty-seven, how it guides me through life. He nodded while he listened. "That makes sense," he said. And that was it.

Sunjay and I are friends now. He comes sometimes for dinner and intelligent conversation, as Audrey calls it. Most evenings, we talk theology. Audrey never tires of hearing about the Sikhs. She even got an English translation of The Guru Granth Sahib, the Sikh scriptures, and sometimes, they read it together. Other times, Audrey opens it randomly and reads a few paragraphs. She finds answers and comfort in the ancient text, like any other religious person. She got mad at me when I mentioned it, although it's true.

One would expect Audrey and me would fall into a mother-offspring kind of relationship. After all, she lost her only child, and I buried my beloved Mom. But our relationship is nothing of the sort. Firstly, Audrey is nothing like Mom, who was always nurturing. Even when the tumor had eaten so much of her brain that she couldn't speak anymore, she still looked at me softly, making sure I'd eaten, drank, and had enough rest.

Audrey is not the nurturing type. She doesn't really care about other people. She chose to live estranged from her family. I learned just the other day that she has a sister who lives less than two hours' drive away, yet they never meet. By choice. She tolerates my presence because she pays me, thus, she owns me in some way. I guess she sees us as an employer-employee sort of thing, which is technically true. For me, it's a calling. Mom brought me here for a reason, and I trust Mom to let me know when to move on. I suspect she brought me here for the hard labor I'm doing. It's healing.

Also, I'm nothing like Charlie, her son. Audrey says he was a lazy, filthy boy who didn't mind sleeping in his own shit—her words. They had a lot of fights around the subject of personal hygiene, so she says. When she couldn't make him do his own laundry, she tried to settle on making him pick up his dirties and put them in the basket. That didn't work either.

"He said it was just a waste of time," Audrey said. "Why bother cleaning up when everything gets dirty again?"

I contemplated that for a few seconds. "Well, I guess he has a point," I said finally.

"Thus, this." She gestured toward the dirty living room.

"On the other hand, though, I actually *like* cleaning. Because it helps me clear up my mind, you know? Get focused. Think straight. I can't think straight with all this clutter, so if you don't mind, I'd like to clean it up. At no charge," I added quickly because I knew it was a touchy subject. Audrey lived on a small allowance. "I'd be doing it mostly for me."

She looked at me funny before retreating to her La-Z-Boy. But the next day, she joined me in my cleaning efforts. We took down the dusty, heavy curtains from the living room, washed them, then hung them back up. While they were in the washer, we organized some of the stuff she'd hoarded since Charlie's death. She didn't want to join me on a trip to Goodwill, but she helped me load the bags in my car, saying this is was as far as she'd gotten from the house in years. And she *did* pay me extra, for which I was very thankful, saying it would help me with my debts. I do have my lottery money savings, but I prefer keeping that for rainy days.

I haven't been to Mom's grave in days. The pain of her loss hasn't faded one bit. It comes with me wherever I go, like I've grown another limb. A ghost limb, which no one can see and feel but me. I wish it were a good limb, a third hand or something. Or maybe like a pinata, filled with good memories of Mom and the wise things she used to say. But it's just this hollow, empty absence of her, and it drives me crazy. How can she not be here? I know she's here in some other shape or form, but when I go to sleep every night, I want my Mom. Not a bee. Not a wind. I want to feel the softness of her body when she hugs me and the smell of her lilac shampoo. Oh, Mom. I miss you so much.

Audrey and I made it a custom to garden together for two hours each morning. After breakfast, we put on our sun hats and our gardening clothes. Mine is an old school uniform of

Charlie's. Audrey suggested it. Apparently, he never set foot in there. Audrey used to be an avid gardener when he was alive, keeping a neat vegetable patch and having luck with her roses.

It doesn't take much work to reinvigorate the neglected yard. The flower beds need just a few touches of compost before the chrysanthemums and cornflowers bloom, filling the garden with color. I wait for the bees to come. And they do, but none of them is Mom. They just mind their own business, paying no attention to me. Mom was never like that.

But I think Mom likes the garden. Each day there are exactly twenty-seven flowers in bloom. I know that's a sign. When one flower dries out, another one replaces it. If it was a one-time thing, it would be coincidental, but it keeps happening, and there's a reason for that.

I've never told Audrey about my beliefs regarding the number twenty-seven. Maybe that's why she gets angry every time she sees me counting the flowers.

"What on earth are you doing?" she questions. And I never answer, because what's the point? She won't get it. She reads her holy Sikh book but has no respect for the holiness not written in books.

Today she picked some flowers while I worked on the vegetable patch on the other side of the house. I think she did this just to agitate me. When I came back to count them, there were only four. She stood a little further away and watched me.

"Where did the flowers go?" I asked.

"Oh, I picked some and put them in a vase in your room." There was an ugly smugness on her face.

"Why would you do that?" I yelled.

"You're so obsessed with these flowers! I wanted to do something nice for you."

We both knew she didn't pick the flowers out of the kindness of her heart.

Mom never got angry when I counted stuff. When I got excited about finding new patterns of twenty-sevens, she just smiled and said, "that's nice honey." I think I can hear her whisper in my ears when I'm counting the flowers in the garden.

om

The discharge papers clearly state I had a panic attack. I was kept overnight as a precaution, and I'm being released with all my vitals as good as they can get. Basically, my physical health is perfect for a man my age. They did, however, recommend I get some sort of counseling to find the root of the panic attack. I flip the paper when I'm done; I want to re-read it. Emily stops me mid-way. She's been reading behind my shoulder.

"Would you please stop hovering like that?" I snap at her, and she takes two steps back.

"Sorry. I just wanted to know what the doctor wrote about your condition."

"My condition." I grunt. "is that I'm batshit crazy."

"Don't say that!"

"Why not? You think so too. Isn't that why you wanted to go to Katie's"

"Oh, Tom," Emily says with a sigh.

She wheels me to the elevator, my duffel bag on my knees. I stand when we reach the automatic sliding doors, then we're outside. My legs are weak, barely holding me upright. I need to lean on Emily. She leads me to a bench by the curb. There's no taxi in sight.

The combination of sun and snow hurts my eyes. "Did you bring my sunglasses?" I bark at her.

"Sorry. I didn't think of that."

"Now where is that effing cab?"

She stands by the curb, looking at the road. "It's probably stuck in the morning traffic, Tom, no need to get upset."

I groan as I look for my phone, only to realize she left it at home, too.

"Wait here for a sec." She rushes back inside and comes back two minutes later, smiling widely.

"There." She hands me a bag. "Got you some shades."

"Why did you do that? Do you think we're made of money? I lost out on a huge deal yesterday when you grabbed my phone."

"Forgive me, your royal grumpiness, for trying to help. Give them to me, I'll take them back." She stretches out her hand.

I tear off the tag and put the glasses on. They fit perfectly. I like them, but I don't let her see that.

The taxi arrives. We get in quietly, sitting as far as we can from each other. Emily puts the overnight bag between us as a buffer. Looking at it, I'm reminded of the embarrassing scenario from the ambulance ride last night when she had to help me pee in a bag. If only I could just disappear. *Poof.* I'm such a loser. I try to shrink myself down, take up as little space as I can. And I fail at that too. What must she think of me?

"I'm fine," I say when Emily hurries from her side of the

car to help me out. She retreats and goes back to pay the driver. I have no wallet and no control.

Under the warmish morning sun, the snow on the front lawn is in the process of turning into slush. I walk carefully, placing one foot in front of the other clumsily, like an old man who forgot his walker. The last thing I need right now is to slip on the ice.

Emily rushes to the door. Of course. She can skip like a gazelle over the snow puddles. Why does she need to rub it in my face?

"How about some breakfast? I'm famished." She's smiling like I'm a little boy who needs nursing. I know she means well, but it's annoying, humiliating.

"Nah. Thanks, but I'll pass. I'm going to wash off the hospital stench. All those germs."

When I'm back downstairs, wearing my work outfit, there's a nice spread on the dining room table. Toast, eggs, even bacon. The real kind, not the turkey substitute. My stomach roars and I almost drool. Emily is buzzing around, fixing utensils and the good plates. But there's no cause for a celebration.

"Hey there," she says when she sees me. She's wearing an apron. That's another first.

"You like?" she asks when she notices me checking her out. "It's one of my designs. I had art students in mind when I made it. Look, it has a tool belt and so many pockets to store stuff, but I guess it's good for cooking too." She shrugs, and her hair falls softly over her shoulders.

Her nonchalant coolness Makes me mad. She acts as if nothing has happened, but I can't ignore the elephant in the room. I grab a piece of toast. With my mouth full I say, "thanks, but I can't stay."

"What do you mean?" She crinkles her face.

"I have *school*, Emily. Kids are waiting." Toast crumbs fly out of my mouth as I speak.

"Oh, *that*." She's moving again. Pouring orange juice into crystal glasses as if I didn't just say I needed to go. "I've taken care of it, Tom. You just sit down and relax."

"You've done *what*?"

She jumps a little. "Geez, Tom." She puts her hand over her heart, "I've called Brenda, told her you're sick." She sits down.

"You had no right!"

"Hello, Tom? I think *thank you* is in order here. Come on, sit down." She taps on the chair's cushion and giggles.

"What have you done?" I yell so loudly my throat hurts. "You're going to get me sacked!" I bang the table and all the dishes clatter. I'm breathing at two hundred miles an hour.

Emily's lower lip quivers. "I think you're overreacting, Tom. They wouldn't sack you for missing a *day*. You're the math whisperer, for heaven's sake."

"More like the math *Nazi*," I blurt. My tongue is heavy in my mouth.

"What?"

I've said too much.

"What do you mean, Tom? What's the math Nazi?"

"Enough with the constant nagging, Emily. That's why I didn't tell you. Yap. Yap. Yap. Jesus. All the time. You're like a tick, sucking me dry." I grab the skin at my neck, demonstrating, "Enough! No more planning of grandiose activities. Let me live my life in peace!"

My heart is pounding crazy fast when I finally stop yelling. I'm certain that now *it's* really happening. The heart attack. I knew those doctors were wrong in their diagnosis.

Emily is looking at me. She's pale. Her mouth is open as if she's about to say something, but if she's does, I don't hear it. My ears pound and I collapse to the floor like a bag of rags.

The sharp pain hits me again, much stronger this time. I can't move. I can't even moan.

"Tom?" Emily is by my side.

I deeply regret everything I've just said. Those can't be my last words. She grabs my hand. "I'm sorry," I whisper. "I love you."

"Love you too." She says it automatically, not like she really means it. She holds me close, rocking me like I'm her baby until the EMT arrives. It's two men this time. One of them is built like The Rock, shaved head and masculine body. Emily looks at him like he's some kind of superhero when he spreads the gear out on the floor next to me. It's too damn frustrating being treated by a model of youth and health, especially when there's nothing wrong with me. All my vitals are fine.

"Blood pressure is a little bit high, but nothing to be concerned about," The Rock tells Emily. He doesn't even bother to talk to the agonized, groaning lump lying on the floor.

"EKG is perfect," he updates her when it's done. She's on her feet, rubbing her hands on her apron. Like she's rubbing me off her. She's full of gratitude. "Would you two like a cup of tea? Maybe some breakfast?" She points at the set table.

"But I'm in excruciating pain!" My voice is hoarse from all the yelling before, and my throat aches.

"I'm sorry, sir." The Rock says. "Seems like you're experiencing a panic attack."

I grit my teeth. Not that bullshit again.

"As they told you earlier today, you don't need a surgeon. But I do recommend scheduling some therapy as soon as possible, sir." The Rock writes something down on a sheet of paper and lets Emily sign it.

"I'm going to administer a one-off pretty strong medication, sir." He gives me a shot. The stuff spreads in my veins, cold and calming. I immediately feel better.

"Why don't you go lie down for a while?" Emily suggests after The Rock and his sidekick leave. I can't stand her compassionate kindness, especially after all those nasty things I said earlier. "Would you like me to set up an appointment with the therapist you met last night at Beirut?"

I shrug. "He said you're probably suffering from Empty Nest Syndrome."

"What?" Emily is confused.

"He said you're depressed." I take real pleasure in saying it, taking her off balance just a little bit. But then a huge wave of shame hits me. It's like a tsunami, threatening to drown me and everything I am.

"Tom." Emily sets the ground for a serious talk. I already know what she's going to say. It's the math Nazi thing that I was so foolish to blurt out. Me and my big mouth. The clock chimes three times. I can still make it to the second period if I hurry. I probably shouldn't. The pain killers make me somewhat dizzy. I grab my keys and head out.

"Tom!" Emily yells after me. "Tom!"

I turn back and give her a wave.

CHAPTER 8

The date escapes me right now. I know it's a Monday. Are we in July yet? Times moves by so fast, and I can't keep track. I will update this entry later. Probably not. LOL.

Yesterday Audrey got so mad. Well, she usually gets mad at the most mundane, silly things. I was mowing the front lawn again. The grass is greener now, healthier. We've been blessed with great weather this summer. Proportional amounts of rain and sunshine. The garden loves it, and the grass is growing quickly, maybe half an inch per day. So it needs frequent care, which I gladly do. I like the hum of the mower. Combined with the heavenly smell of the freshly-cut grass, it takes me into a meditative state. I feel closer to Mom, to the power of twenty-seven, to the universe. Audrey doesn't understand my fixation with lawn mowing, like she doesn't understand other stuff I'm doing. It's fine. I'm used to being the quirky one. Nobody's ever understood me, except for a select few.

Anyway, I was mowing the lawn and Audrey felt compelled to bring me a glass of cold lemonade. She always does that, although I've never asked. She was wearing the orange cardigan she sometimes wears at home. It's old and has lost all its shape, but she likes it.

It being a warm, sunny day, I was sweating like a mule, thick drops of sweat pouring from my forehead. So, I said it seemed to be too hot for a cardigan and she was like, "I'm too exposed here."

I don't know what that means. The sun is shining the same way as at the back where she was taking care of the roses. And it's wasn't like she was wearing a bikini.

I took time wiping my sweat, and she got all anxious that it took me so long to take the icy glass from her hand. And while she was grunting about it, old lady O'Toole stopped by on her way to church. She uses a cane and her hands are so sinewy, it looks like someone carved them out of wood.

"It's so nice to see you again, Audrey," she said with her quivering voice. "God bless."

Audrey just grunted. It makes me laugh to see her reactions. Is it so hard to smile and say thanks?

"That's one big, judgmental bitch," Audrey whispered so only I could hear.

"Why do you say that? She's just a harmless, sweet old lady!"

While we were busy with this lovely chat, we didn't notice Elijah from across the street coming right at us while walking his terrier. The little dog began wiggling its tail and barking happily.

"Shut up, Scotty," Audrey said. "Sit down." The dog sat as instructed, whimpering.

"I changed his name. It's Bolt now," Elijah said.

"Is that so?" Audrey asked, all fiery. I didn't get why she would be so upset that Elijah changed the name of his dog. I stood there quietly, breathing only shallow breathes, trying to make myself part of the background.

Elijah handed Audrey a seedling of an English Rose covered in wet tissue paper. "I'm returning the favor."

"No, thank you," Audrey replied harshly. "I might not be able to keep it up to par, and *some* people will accuse me of neglect."

Elijah looked hurt. He kept his hand stretched out with his offering for a few more seconds. "Suit yourself," He began walking away.

The little dog didn't follow. He wiggled his tail and jumped joyfully in place, looking admiringly at Audrey, waiting for her to give him some attention. She didn't.

Elijah came back. He knelt to put the dog on a leash. The dog treated it like a game, running around, stopping and waiting for Elijah to come closer only to run off again.

"Scotty, sit!" Audrey ordered. The dog obeyed. Elijah connected the hook to the dog's collar.

"Would you like to take him back?" he asked softly.

"Will it bring back my Charlie?" Audrey shot in reply.

Elijah sighed and continued with his walk.

She waited until he had gone far enough, then, rolling her eyes, she said, "I gave him a seedling from my own garden to start off his English Rose project." She didn't say anything about the whole Scotty/Bolt situation, and I didn't ask. Some things should be kept private.

CHAPTER 9

 mily

As soon as he's out the door, I call Brenda from the administration, only to hang up quickly when he comes back inside. I hope he didn't hear Brenda's bored "Jefferson High" greeting.

Tom isn't interested in what I'm doing or who I talk with. He just announces, "Took the wrong keys."

I'm run upstairs into Tommy's bedroom—now Tom's bedroom. I peek outside, hiding behind the drapes, and watch him leave before I call Brenda again.

"Jefferson high, Brenda is speaking. How may I help?" she asks flatly.

"Bren, it's me. Now spill the beans."

There's a sigh on the other side of the line. It's deep, coming straight from the gut. And then, silence.

"Come on, Bren, how long have we known each other? I thought we were friends."

"I thought so too," she whispers into the phone, and I imagine her turning her back to the counter, ignoring the sea of students who always knock about the office, asking for staff. "I was expecting your call a long time ago, to be honest."

Now the ball is in my court, I hesitate. Speaking up will mean exposure. Everyone will know Tom and I are having trouble. Brenda won't be able to keep such juicy information to herself—she's such a gossip. I mean, that's the reason I called her. I know she has the information I crave.

"Oh, that's nice," she suddenly says and breaks the tense hush. "Do you remember Yolanda?"

My heart misses a beat; my face is flushed. I haven't thought about Yolanda in years. Nor did I expect to hear that name again.

Brenda doesn't expect an answer, and why would she? Tom is the only one of the school staff who knows about Yolanda.

"She was an art teacher here. I think it was before your time..." I can visualize Brenda's eyes rolled up, her tongue stuck out slightly as she tries to jog her memory and calculate when Yolanda left, and I started.

"Kyle, don't you touch the fax machine! It's not a toy." Brenda's voice is somewhat muted while she's yelling. She's probably covering the phone's mouthpiece with her hand. I've seen her do it a million times before.

"I just got a tweet," Brenda says, "about Yolanda. She won a major award and mentioned our school in her speech. That's so sweet. She only worked here for a short time."

My heart is racing now. Did she mention me in that tweet?

Brenda silences the phone again, her voice blurred as she talks to one of the students.

"Anyways, Em, what's up with you?"

I take a deep breath and shoo away the memory of

Yolanda. There's no time for that now. "Tom didn't tell me anything until this morning. And even now, all I have is Math Nazi. Please, fill me in. I'm going crazy over here, Bren."

"Okay, give me five." She hangs up. I sit by the phone and bite my nails. I haven't been such a nervous wreck since...well, Yolanda. I haven't thought about her in years. After everything that happened, I locked all memories of her in a deep box inside my mind and haven't open it since.

I'm curious. It's been so long ago, I've forgotten why I so desperately wanted to forget. I want to remember, but it's hard opening the rusty old box. Luckily, that's where Google comes in handy.

It finds her in a no time at all. Facebook tells me she has an account, but *I* need to have one in order to see what she shares with the world. I never saw the point of having a Facebook account until this moment. My heart races as I wait for the app to install on my phone. It's not just curiosity that consumes me, it's also a pinch of "what if."

The phone rings and cuts off my wandering thoughts.

"I'm shocked he didn't tell you." Brenda starts off without hello. By the sound of the wind and distant yelling, I guess she's by the bleachers, where it's kind of private at this time of the day. "It's been going on for, jeez, four months now?"

"That's right after his father passed."

"Yeah, I know. I've been meaning to call, Emily. I really liked Tom Sr."

"Thanks." I get up and go to my sewing room.

"So, Zach Laney. Remember that goon? I don't know what he did, but he claims Tom shamed him in front of the whole class, and he has a recording. Allegedly. You know we have that zero-tolerance policy now, so Patrice had to bring it up with the board." While she is talking, I organize the room. Fold some fabric pieces. Arrange the threads by color.

"They sent him off with a warning because, you know, it's Tom. But he wasn't himself after. You know how the kids used to love his classes? Well, now they're skipping." I sit back down with a sigh as Brenda keeps talking. "Apparently, he flunked one of the popular girls. You don't know her, she's new. Her mother was going through chemo at the time. She's fine now. The mom that is. The girl, Esme, she didn't do her homework several times. Tom refused to take her mother's condition into consideration when it came down to grades. Now the freshmen are rebelling."

It's too much information to digest all at once.

Brenda is stomping in place. "It's too cold out here, Em. I'm going back in."

"Brenda? What does Patrice say about the freshmen situation?"

She takes a deep breath. "I think she's waiting for it to run its course. But if it escalates...he already has a warning," She ends the sentence with a whisper. I'm guessing she's back in the office.

I can't believe Tom didn't share this with me. Poor Tom. He must be devastated. Teaching math is his vocation.

"Thanks, Brenda. For telling me that. I appreciate it."

"I'm shocked Tom hasn't said a word. Are you two all right?" And here it is, her ugly snoopiness.

"He's still grieving," I say. I don't know where that came from, but it shuts her up. I'm hoping she'll tell that to Patrice. In fact, I'm counting on it.

I can't get a grip. Can't stop thinking about poor Tom and what he had to endure. On one hand, I feel sorry for him. But I'm also extremely mad. Why has he banished me from his life? It's hard enough to cope with him not sleeping in our bed, but to realize he's been keeping so much to himself...

I've been trying to give him the space to grieve, to heal. And he's repaid me by becoming distant, both physically and emotionally. I grit my teeth.

Tom has always been so enthusiastic about teaching math, insisting that every kid can learn it if taught with the right attitude. He struggled to reach each and every student, inventing new methods and tricks to overcome math anxiety and dyscalculia. The kids loved his teaching methods, the way he simplified complicated topics, making them into games and puzzles.

Most of the students aced the math part on their SATs. Principal Patrice was happy. The school board was happy. Tom got "Teacher of the Year" awards from the state, year after year after year.

I can't believe the kids call him math Nazi now. I shrink into my shell, thinking how offended he must be. No wonder he's having panic attacks. Poor thing. My heart goes out to him, but I'm so angry. Oh, I could scream!

Seeking distraction from my frustration, I go back to stalking Yolanda, telling myself it's nothing but innocent curiosity as I create a Facebook account. When asked for a surname, I type in my maiden one. I don't stop to question it. I just want to see what Yolanda is up to these days.

And Facebook tells me *everything*. She's living in Santa Fe, where she runs a small art gallery named Sweet Pea. She's in a relationship with Sahara, a yoga instructor. There's only one photo of Yolanda. She's smiling at the camera, looking happy and free. She hasn't aged one bit.

I move on to check out her girlfriend—or maybe it's her wife? I don't know what "in a relationship" means. I'm curious to see if there's any resemblance between me and her current lover. But there are no photos.

Back on Yolanda's profile, I find a link to her art gallery's website. She got the NM Governor Award for Excellence in

Arts for her ceramic figurine collection. It's called Team USA and features all-time Olympic gold medalists. The athletes look so real, as if she caught them mid-movement. I recognize Michael Phelps. He's wearing a Speedo and is about to dive into the water. There's Simone Biles in her red bodysuit, doing the splits. And Carl Lewis, wearing golden shoes, about to jumpstart a race. His whole body is tense. It's so genuine and genius. The award is well deserved.

Back again on Yolanda's Facebook page, I study her photo, shivering when I remember how she begged me, her hands pressed over my little baby bump, her dark brown eyes wide like she'd walked out of a horror movie. *Don't leave,* she'd said. *No one will ever love you like I do.*

Sitting alone in my sewing room, I start wondering. Was I wrong to choose the normal suburban path over a life with her? I wipe my eyes. Tom and I had a good life. *Have* a good life, I mean.

But do we really? Why didn't he tell me about his latest struggle? Have we drifted so far apart he doesn't want to share his agony with me anymore? My whole body clenches, lungs included, as I replay his outburst from this morning.

I can take only shallow breaths. Dear god, I'm having a panic attack. I force myself to relax. Outside the window of my sewing room, the sky is clear, and it's already dusk. I wasted so much time on the phone and didn't even turn on my sewing machine. Caught between guilt and daydreaming, I'm startled when I hear the door.

"Hi, Em. I'm back!" Tom's home from school.

"Hi, honey." I can't face him. I don't know what to say. "Kind of busy up here, working on a new project."

I want him to come upstairs, although I also dread it. What will I say? I want him to come clean. Confess. Apologize. I want him to share everything with me. I wait. Ten minutes. Half an hour. I stand by the landing at the top of the stairs. The grandfather clock chimes for the hour and startles me.

Tom doesn't come up. Doesn't even say a word. As the minutes pass, I grow more disappointed. More certain that our life together is quickly reaching its expiration date. If he doesn't come up in the next ten minutes, it means there's no hope for us anymore.

And while I'm waiting, I keep scrolling through Yolanda's Facebook page. I notice the "Add Friend" button as the grandfather clock dooms my marriage with its deep chime. The time has passed, and there's no sign of Tom.

I tap the "Add Friend" button. I could really use one right now.

My palms become sweaty. What have I done?

Not a minute goes by, and I get a message. Yolanda approves my request. Now that we're Facebook buddies, I can see more information about her. There are some photos of Yolanda and her spouse having a fun day at the beach. Sahara looks so different than me. She's blond, tall, and skinny. But still, I can see Yolanda has a type—young. Sahara looks to be in her late twenties, or early thirties at the most. There's something sad and somewhat familiar in her smile. It's a sunny day, and they're wearing matching bikinis and sun hats. They both look so skinny and fit. There's a child there too, building sandcastles. I can't see her face, just some strawberry blond curls. She looks cute.

Yolanda's last words echo in my mind. *No one will ever love you like I do.* My heart pounds so hard, I'm afraid Tom might hear it downstairs.

We've never really talked about my relationship with Yolanda. When we were done, I wanted to erase her from my life, from my memory. Tom respected that. My parents and Katie marveled when I left her. "Emily's phase," they called her. They didn't mind me coming home pregnant, they were just happy that *the phase* was over.

I've repressed Yolanda for so many years, but now, memories float back up. I glance at the door anxiously, certain Tom will be standing there and catch me red-handed, stalking my ex. But there's no one there, just the usual shadows of the hallway. I'm somewhat disappointed, as if I wanted to get caught, to get into a huge fight with him.

My phone beeps. Yolanda. She sent me a message on Facebook. I didn't know she could do that.

Emily? Is that really you?

Yes, I reply. Why would she even ask that?

Wow! What a nice surprise! She adds a bunch of smiley faces.

Congrats on your award. I don't know how to add smiles.

I must admit…

And there's a long pause. I sit on the edge of my chair, biting my nails.

Sorry. Had to deal with something, she types after ten long minutes.

You said you had to admit something.

Oh, yeah. I tried looking you up… But you weren't on Facebook.

I just opened an account.

And I'm your first friend? What an honor.

Yes. I wanted to tell you that I love your art.

She replies with another set of smiles.

I wait for something more concrete, and it comes in the form of a line that takes my breath away.

Art mends broken hearts.

I read it and re-read it several times. I'm aroused. Excited like I'm a twenty-year-old art student who's grabbed the attention of her college professor. I don't know how to respond. What can I say? That I miss her? It wouldn't be true. Or that I'm questioning my decision?

I remember her soft lips and rough palms, stroking me. Crawling under my shirt.

How's Tom, she asks.

Distant. Secretive. Scared.

Are you two still together? She types before I get a chance to answer. *Only on paper*, but I type, *Yes.*

Will he let you come visit? I'm having a small gala in my gallery tomorrow evening to celebrate my award. I'd love it if you could come.

She's sending a lot of smiley faces. I guess that means she's happy. Maybe excited?

I know it's short notice, but it would mean the world to me! She adds an animated photo of a pug puppy with big begging eyes. The caption says saying pleassssse.

Maybe I will. I type it quickly, and my heart races. She sends me the address of her gallery.

I wait for something to happen. Something drastic, like a sudden thunderstorm. Something that will stop me from going forward. I'm begging Tom to stop me, calling out for him silently, like he did the night before. He said he contacted me telepathically, and I came back. I didn't tell him I returned because I was getting tired of roaming the streets. I never intended to go to Katie's—my duffle bag was empty.

"Em, would you like some dinner?" Tom's holler startles me. Did he just hear my plea?

It's been hours since he came back from school. It's already deep dark outside.

"Maybe you can set up that lovely spread you did this morning?" he calls from downstairs. It's the last straw. He won't share his life with me, but he expects me to drop everything I'm doing to cook his dinner?

I've decided. I'm going to Yolanda's gala.

"I'm not hungry," I yell from the railing. This time I *am* packing an overnight bag.

He sits in his favorite spot, hunched over the phone like always, his laptop open in front as his gaze moves between the screens. He looks tired. Worn out.

"Tom," I say. My voice is serious but also a little bit shaky. I don't know what to say. Then I see the glasses on the table. His martini. My rosé. He's fixed a drink for me. And that little gesture moves me to the core.

"Tom," I say again. This time, he lifts his head and looks at me. He takes it all in. My coat. My overnight bag. He's confused— I can see it in his eyes. Then his face crumbles as he understands what's going on. His eyes get moist. I can't look at him. There's so much pain on his face.

"Em," he whispers. I shake my head. My throat closes as I open my mouth to speak. Nothing comes out.

We stand there for a whole minute, the coffee table between us. We stare at each other silently. His phone beeps and his eyes jump toward it, just a little bit. He doesn't pick it up. If he asks me to stay, I will.

"Call me when you get there?" he asks softly.

I nod and close the door gently behind me.

CHAPTER 10

7/27/16

Michelle called at exactly 7:20 p.m.

I was visiting Mom at the time. The sun was soft, the trees casting a nice shade over the stone. Only a few rays of light penetrated through the thick canopy, shining on Mom's name, making it look like it was carved in gold. Already I was elated. And then Michelle.

"Hello?" I answered hesitantly because I hadn't heard from her since I left Berkley, and that was months ago.

"Hey, Seven. It's Michelle."

"I know."

She said, "I waited for this date. For this time. To call you."

"You remembered." That's all I could say. I was overwhelmed by her gesture.

It wasn't a coincidence—the date, the time. That I was at Mom's. That her name was written in gold. It was a sign.

Hearing Michelle's voice again brought back memories from our last day together, back in January. She and I were on her large show bed, viewed by many of our fans when the phone rang.

"We're in a middle of a session," she'd whispered through gritted teeth. But it was St. Helen's. I had to take it.

She got so angry. "It's not just the money I lost," she'd said as I packed my few things. "It's my credibility. I'm a professional, and you hurt my reputation by picking the phone in the middle of the session."

I couldn't care less. Mom's tumor was back, and I knew that meant her days were numbered. I had to go back. Michelle was furious that I was leaving. Harsh words were exchanged. I documented everything in my journal.

"How are you?" she asked.

"I'm fine. How are you?"

"Good. The school year ended fine. I was top of the class again, but that's nothing. You know."

"Yeah."

"Shayleen and Aisha graduated. They got excellent residencies, in case you ever need cardiology or pediatric care in Wisconsin or South Dakota."

"That's cool." I didn't know what else to say. I barely knew Michelle's roommates. They were hardly ever in the apartment.

"Your mother?" Michelle clearly didn't know how to phrase the question.

I took a deep breath. "She passed."

"Oh. I'm so sorry to hear that."

"Yeah. Thanks."

"So..." she said.

A cloud hid the sun, and Mom's stone became darker. A sudden chill made me tremble. "So."

"I miss you, Seven. We had good times together."

"We sure did," I say with a smile. Michelle introduced me to a new lifestyle I never would have thought of exploring online sex shows without the power of twenty-seven.

"Some of the regulars still ask about you."

"Really?" I put my hand against the stone which is now Mom. I told her everything about Michelle. She couldn't wrap her head around it and kept asking me about my sexual preferences.

"You can tell me if you're a lesbian," Mom said, *"I would love you either way."* I smile as I remember how it opened her eyes when I told her people didn't have to pick sides or put a label on themselves. I liked who I liked regardless of gender. Mom had looked at me so warmly.

"That is so logical. How come I never thought about it?" she asked.

The stone was cold. I pulled my hand away.

"When are you coming back?" Michelle asked.

I looked at Mom. Am I supposed to go back? She didn't give me any sign. It killed me sometimes, being so close to her, yet feeling so alone.

"Michelle, I don't think I'm coming back. It was an adventure. And it's over now."

She sighed, and I pictured her for a moment. Her big body. Her braided hair. Was she lying on that big bed of hers? Was this phone call part of he show?

"Thing is, well, I have some money for you. Guys decided to give extra after they heard you on the phone back then. I kept it for you."

"Oh. That's so nice of you. I still have some medical bills to take care of." I was overwhelmed with her kindness.

Michelle chuckled. "I know a way for you to earn some money pretty quickly."

I wanted to tell her about Audrey and Charlie, but she'd be offended to hear I live with someone else now. It wouldn't matter that I didn't particularly like Audrey.

She sighed again at my stillness. "Well, Seven, you'll always have a place in my heart. Take care, baby. Safe travels."

I got the blues when she hung up. I liked Michelle. She was fun and smart. And I liked doing that sex stuff on camera. I probably wouldn't hear from her ever again. I hesitated for a minute. Maybe I should make an exception and go back.

A gust of wind shoved my hair into my mouth, and I understood. Let bygones be bygones. Michelle was something of the past.

mily

Sitting in the driver seat of my Honda, I struggle again with the navigation app on my phone. This smartphone is part of the new crypto coin wealth, as is the sedan. I resent them both.

I'm not even a block away when I need to pull over.

A flashback hits me hard. Yolanda and I cuddle in bed, happy and content.

"Was it love at first sight?" she asks me, and I nod, like I always do when she asks, but I'm not really into our usual after-sex sweet talk.

"What's distracting you, Em-em?"

"Do you know that math teacher? Tom?"

She twitches her face. She doesn't like to hang at the lounge with the other teachers. That's why she brought me in as her assistant.

"Is he the tall one?"

I nod. "He has these amazing lucid blue eyes. They look like a pond up in the mountains."

She chuckles bitterly. "You like him? Is that it?"

I shake my head. "Of course not. I love you."

She kisses me gently, and I lose myself in her touch.

Loud rap music from a passing car brings me back to reality. I try to stay focused as I reach the interstate. I'm thrilled about my adventure, but I'm also grieving my old life. Did I leave Tom for good? What would my life have been like if I'd picked Yolanda all those years ago? Would I have been happier?

It was so different back then. Gay couples were considered an abomination. Today, they're cool. Well, in some places. I'm so excited, yet, I dread the meeting. I feel so heavy, like I ate a large meal and need to lie down to let my body try to digest, yet I'm also famished. I skipped lunch and dinner. That hasn't happened to me for a long time—maybe not since back when I pretended to be an artist. With Yolanda.

There's a flight to Albuquerque leaving in an hour. Feeling bold and daring, I purchase a one-way ticket to New Mexico. I'm so light when I walk to the gate, it's as if I'm floating a few inches above the ground. Maybe it's the lack of food.

Half an egg-salad sandwich later, I rush to the bathroom.

It's a recurring theme that accompanies me throughout the flight. Three and a half hours of pure agony. At some point, the sympathetic fly attendant stops holding my hair back because there are other passengers requiring her attention. So here I am, on my knees in the tiny airplane bathroom, hugging the stool. From my miserable position, I can see ankles and shins, jeans and leggings, pumps and boots. They're tapping on the floor, anxious to use the bathroom. The hum of the airplane and the suction of the flush swallows their angry complaints, although I still sense it. On my fourth trip to the bathroom, which is kind of my own right now because no one wants to use a contaminated stall, the most dreaded question booms over the PA.

"Is there a doctor onboard?"

It doesn't register that I'm the passenger in need of medical assistance, because although I'm crouching on the bathroom's sticky floor and throwing my guts out, I keep visualizing my exciting, new life with my artist girlfriend, and each time my intestine cramps, it's as if I'm getting rid of the old and making room for the new.

"I'm cleansing," I say to the elderly woman who presents herself as Doctor Leary, a retired physician. From my position, I can only see the deep red boots she's wearing. They're kind of youngish, but her voice is unmistakably old.

"You need to keep hydrated," she says in an authoritative voice when I finally manage to get up. She has pale pink hair, probably a weave, and her face has the unnatural waxy look of a woman who's had too much work done. I'm immediately filled with contempt. This so-called doctor is nothing but a Barbie doll wannabe. She's a shallow human being, interested only in her appearance.

While I'm passing judgment, Doctor Leary sweet-talks the crew, and I'm upgraded to business class and seated next to her. She doesn't need to be *that* persuasive since my sickness has caused a huge drop in food sales over in coach. At my new seat, there's a nonstop supply of sweet tea and crackers per the doctor's instructions.

"You need to replenish your electrolytes," she says.

While I sip my tea and take small, hesitant bites of the salty crackers, she amuses with me with tales about her life.

"This is James, the love of my life." She hands me her phone and helps me enlarge the photo. James is a handsome elderly gentleman, probably in his late seventies but still standing tall. He has a head full of silver hair and a radiant smile. By the sparkle in his eyes, I can tell the photographer is a loved one.

"This one was taken in front of my house. I've sold it now. James and I are going to live in a retirement village just outside of Albuquerque." Her age shows in the brown marks covering her slightly shaking hands. Yet her fingernails are painted hot pink. The minutia of Doctor Leary's life distracts me from my physical distress, from the journey I've embarked on.

"He was my high school sweetheart, but then we parted ways for almost sixty years. Can you believe it? We met at the funeral of one of our classmates a few months ago and haven't been apart since."

She demonstrates the diamond on her ring finger. "We're getting married next week." Her eyes sparkle like a teenager in love for the first time.

"It's going to be a secret wedding." She chuckles. "James' daughter doesn't approve. She thinks I'm going to steal her inheritance, but what would I do with the money?" Dr. Leary leans closer to me until her shoulder touches mine. "I'm seventy-six years old. Am I going to buy a yacht? A private jet? The worries of the young," she says with a sigh.

Her eyes move away, her gaze foggy. "I waited for Lionel to ask me about my engagement ring, but he never did. Maybe he thinks his mother is too old for love." She flips through the photos on her phone and shows me a picture of a newborn. "That's baby Kyle. He's my granddaughter Sonia's. My Lionel is a grandfather now. I can't believe it." She shakes her head. "Time goes by so fast. You should make the most of it before it's too late." She closes her eyes, and I follow. Her dedicated treatment has scared the nausea away.

Memories of Yolanda keep me afloat. I see her face in my mind's eye. Not her current face, with the short red hair, the glasses, and the little wrinkles over her lips, but her younger self, as she was when we first met.

It was the first day of achieving my childhood dream of becoming a haute couture fashion designer. Without enough money to get a real college education, I'd had to settle on a few courses at the community college, all condensed into the one day I wasn't flipping burgers.

It was a shame having to keep that high school job two years after graduation, while all my friends scattered out of town and ventured into exciting new opportunities. At the local college, I signed up for all the artsy, hands-on work-shops available that day. Pottery was one of them, although I never liked clay. Gooey stuff that made your hands dirty wasn't my cup of tea.

My first glance at the teacher, and I was ready to leave. She pouted while setting up the workbenches, reminding me of my aunt Gloria, who was always pouting when she set the table for dinner, throwing plates and utensils like this one threw wooden tools, knives, and sponges.

I expected Yolanda to be sarcastic and resentful like aunt Gloria, so I avoided eye contact and sat as close to the door as possible, holding on to my backpack, ready to flee at the first sign of discomfort. It was the end of a long day. I'd had History of Arts, which was more boring than inspiring, followed by Economics 101, which made me feel stupid. Even the drawing workshops were a disappointment—the teacher had made us copy other artwork as if we were a bunch of forgers learning to seamlessly create fakes.

So Aunt Gloria was the last straw. I was ready to quit college altogether.

The memory of that first day is so clear in my mind because Yolanda and I discussed it repeatedly. Of course, that was months later, when we'd became lovers.

I remember the determination and enthusiasm in her

voice as she walked past the students and handed each one of us a piece of clay. She was like the teacher from Fame. "You have big dreams. You want to become famous artists. Well, fame costs." That got us all laughing. "Now, close your eyes. Let your deepest and darkest desires flow into your fingers as you mold this raw material." She walked around the class, her clogs tapping on the linoleum floor.

It was so uplifting. Inspiring. I followed her directions with great intent. "Art comes from the soul. Submit yourself to the creative process. Don't think, just flow." My breath stopped when her paces got closer to me. I felt her next to me, and then, her strong palms massaged my shoulders, releasing my tension. "Relax," she said and held me for just a moment before she moved on. She was *nothing* like aunt Gloria.

Later, months later, lying naked and content next to her while she caressed my arms, we analyzed what it was that got me so hooked on her. She didn't remember that little massage or even stopping by my side. We talked about that day like a couple of ruminants, chewing and chewing on the same piece of weed.

"Did you know I was going to kiss you that night?" she would ask sweetly.

And I would lie. "Didn't you see how I flirted with you?"

And she would giggle. "*Seriously* though, Em-em." And I'd repeat the same lies again and again, frightened she'd know I was faking, afraid she'd learn the truth—that I was clueless.

One freezing night after class, she'd stopped next to me while I waited for the bus.

"Hop in," she said, smiling, "I'll take you home."

I was so grateful to get away from the cold. My teeth were clenched, and she turned the heat up a notch. We chatted casually along the way. Later, when she brought up this ride in our never-ending reminiscing, she said she'd asked me if I had a boyfriend. She said I blushed and mumbled something incoherent, and that's how she knew I was into her.

Deep inside, I knew this wasn't true, but I went along with the story. I admired her. How could I not? She was so talented. So smart, sophisticated, and cool. I'd just turned twenty, and she was eight years older, a woman of the world who'd been to Europe and had pieces presented in art galleries. I'd never gone out of state, and the only things I'd ever made were clothes for my dolls and one prom dress that turned out to be a fiasco. But most of all, I liked the fact that she liked me. It was so flattering. Her, seeing something in me, made me see myself differently.

But I never knew she was going to kiss me.

I made it a habit to stay after class and help her clean up. Several other students stayed late as well. It was a chance to engage the professor in a conversation about her favorite artists—who soon became my favorites as well. The night she kissed me was just like any other night, only all the others had gone to see the game, and it was just me and her. I didn't know what was going to happen, even when she stood behind me and reenacted that scene from "Ghost."

Well, Ghost was released about a year after, so technically, the movie reenacted our moment. When I watched it, I was already with Tom. It was like someone had invaded my privacy. Tom and I were already married, Marni kicking inside my womb. I never told him why this scene was so embarrassing to me.

I had complained about my difficulties with the potter wheel, and Yolanda volunteered to instruct me. Standing behind me, her hands were confident and strong on my slightly shaking ones. Her breath tickled my ear as she leaned forward over my shoulder, our fingers interlaced as we slowly molded the rotating lump of clay. Our palms and the mud became as one, moving together in harmony. The moment was charged with creative energy as we turned the slippery, cool earth into a perfect bowl.

Overwhelmed with the beauty we'd created, I'd turned my face to catch her eye because only she could understand the depth of my emotions at that moment. She misread it as an invitation.

How could I know? I was naive. I didn't understand her sexual preference even after the kiss. It was the late 80s. Lesbians were something of an urban legend, not your local college professor.

"Was it love at first sight?" Yolanda asked me for the millionth time during one of our nightly chats, and I just cracked.

"Actually, the first time I saw you, you kind of reminded me of my aunt Gloria."

She laughed. "You're such a tease Em-em."

Snuggled in my business class seat, I remember the amusement on her face and the softness touch of her lips when I met them. Not really kissing, just touching. "Gotcha," I said into her open mouth.

The memory makes my stomach crumple, and I rush to the bathroom one more time. I'm empty inside. Like a shell ready to create its pearl.

Pearl. That was the nickname Yolanda gave my fetus. The memory makes me flinch a little.

We were sat in the living room, watching a documentary about Frida Kahlo. Yolanda's hand casually caressed my baby bump. It had been a few weeks since I'd said yes to Tom. I was still waiting for the right time to tell Yolanda. I knew she would flip, and I dreaded it so much, I kept postponing, while planning a wedding behind her back. Earlier that evening, I'd tried to tell her.

"Yolanda," I'd said, with my serious face on. She was cooking dinner, something nutritious for the baby. She'd kept me on a strict diet since we'd found out about the pregnancy.

"What's that, love of my life?" she replied absentmindedly.

"Oh, nothing." I retreated.

"Come on, say what's on your mind, Em-em." She kissed the tip on my nose.

"I have a terrible craving for vanilla ice cream," I quickly said. She hated vanilla, therefore I hated it too. She' laughed. "The pregnancy is playing tricks on your mind."

With only half an eye on the TV, I was rehearsing the monologue in my head when there was a knock on the door. Yolanda hit pause. I started shaking.

"What's going on?"

I opened my mouth to speak but nothing came out. The doorbell rang.

"Who's at the door?" She straightened up and looked at me.

I avoided her eyes. As I got up, all I could murmur was, "I'm sorry. I'm sorry." I made a beeline to the door, but she was faster. Her long dark hair curls after her like lava.

"*You!*" she thundered when she noticed it was Tom.

"Yolanda. Emily." He stepped inside.

"What are you doing here?" Her strong palms clenched into fists.

He didn't reply, just examined me with the quiet, blue gaze that made me fall for him in the first place. It gave me strength.

"The...thi...thing is," I stuttered, "I want to marry Tom."

"*What?* No, you don't! You don't even *like* Tom."

Turning to Tom, her heart-shaped face was full of contempt. "You mean nothing to her. You're just a tool. A playmate."

Torn between the two of them, I stood there quietly, desperately wringing my hands.

Yolanda grabbed Tom's shirt. "Did she tell you I had to persuade her to go out with you? Damn. I encouraged her to *fuck* you!"

He took a step back. "Yes," he said calmly although I never said anything about that.

It was his nondramatic calmness that drew me to him. Seeing him, standing tall without even a blink, made me feel stronger. Yolanda turned back to me, her eyes wide as dinner plates.

"You'll never be happy with the math wussperer. You hear me? You'll be just another boring mom from the suburbs. You'll never be an artist."

"I don't want to be an artist," I whispered without looking at her. It was so liberating, telling the truth. Tears of relief trickled from my eyes.

Yolanda embraced me. "It's the hormones speaking, Emem. You're not stable right now."

Tom stood there. A rock of tranquility. He didn't put words into my mouth, nor did he push himself into doing my dirty work. He was so different than Yolanda, who always answered when someone asked me a question. I loved him for standing there, being supportive without intervening.

"I'm sorry, Yolanda. I've made up my mind. My baby needs to grow up with a father." I wiggled out of her hug.

"But what about me? I'm her mother! This baby is mine!" Her face was a mask of agony and anger. She clenched her teeth; her eyes looked crazy.

I took Tom's hand in mine. He rubbed his thumb over my knuckles so gently. That simple gesture made me feel safe.

Suddenly, I miss him terribly. What is he doing right now? Did he have another panic attack? Doctor Leary mumbles something in her sleep. My memories of that dreadful last night with Yolanda keep flowing.

Terrified of her wrath, I asked Tom to accompany me to the police station. I requested a restraining order and had to come up with some serious shit against her, which I did. After being with her for a year, it was so easy for me to lie.

Remembering that moment from so long ago, I'm overcome with shame. Why did I do it? What was I so afraid of? I've repressed these memories for years, and now they're flooding like a clogged toilet. They stink. Why recall those specific moments? The awkwardness of the beginning, the ugliness of the end. We had some good times together. We laughed. We loved. We traveled and marveled. I try to sharpen my memory and retrieve some of the happy moments, but I keep seeing her tormented eyes as she predicted no one would ever love me like she did.

The crew asks the passengers to prepare for landing. Doctor Leary wakes up. She pulls a compact out of her purse and fixes her makeup. Beautifies for her beau.

TOM

The other day, I read an article about a scientist who wanted to prove the existence of the soul. He measured the body-weight of dying people minutes before they passed away, then again minutes after. He noticed they all lost about an ounce at their moment of passing. He figured this was the weight of the soul leaving the body.

When Emily leaves, so quietly and gently out the front door, the house loses its soul. For a few minutes, I still stand by the sofa, facing the door, waiting for her to come back. It's a drag because now she's exhausted this tactic of leaving me.

There was the dramatic exit at Beirut, then she took the whole "going to Katie's" card to the next level, so now, she's like the boy who cried wolf. Chuckling, I sit back down. She's clearly going through some stuff, and for some reason, wants to pull me into her play. But despite me saying this to myself, her absence is a disturbance in the time-space continuum.

My father's old clock chimes for the hour. How I love those sweet bells—the relaxing music of my childhood. I bet she'll be back before it chimes again.

When it does, I give her one more hour. Then another. I try to enjoy the peace and quiet of the empty house after the terrible day that I had, but it's impossible. I'm in a state of limbo. The soul of the house has left the building.

What am I without her?

My mind takes me back to that dire day in September, like it does every time I sit in idle. Driving to the hospital, I chanted to myself. *It can't be right. It can't be right. It's a terrible mistake. All will be cleared up by the time I get there. Everything is fine.*

But everything is *not* fine. Emily's not coming back.

When the realization hits me, I gasp for breath. It's as if all the air in the house followed her, leaving me in a vacuum.

I try to imagine she's still upstairs, doing whatnot in her craft room. But I can't figure it out. Imagining has always been Emily's role in our relationship. My part is to ground her when she imagines too big.

I text her. *You've made your point. You can come back now.*

I wait for the two little blue Vs to appear on the screen, indicating she received the message.

I'm sorry, I add when I see she's not biting. I don't know what I should be sorry about, but it's always safer to start with an apology. She doesn't read that message either.

What is she doing all afternoon in her craft room? She

never came downstairs to say hi or to chat for a bit. It's not like her at all. She's always down here asking how my day was and today especially I didn't want her to come down. How could I pretend everything is fine when I had this meltdown at school? I should have taken her advice and stay home. Is that why she's upset? My panic attacks? Does she think less of me now?

I rush upstairs. Everything looks so normal. Her fabrics are folded on the table, and there's stuff everywhere—pins and ribbons and a whole lot of loose thread. Some of it is caught in the rug. The room is a mess, and it makes me relax a bit because she's *definitely* coming back.

But then I get angry. How could she leave it in such a state? She could have at least tidied up before she left. She was up here all day, what did she do?

There are no clues in the room to explain why she left so suddenly, and I struggle to reason with her behavior. We had a stupid argument this morning. I texted an apology around lunchtime. Was she still cross about it when I got home? Did she expect me to express more remorse? Why didn't she say anything? She always tells me when she's upset with me. even for the silliest things, like the way I put the silverware in the dishwasher. As if there's only one right way to do it. What didn't she tell me? She just stood there with a suitcase like a character in one of those stupid drama series she likes.

The bedroom seems fine too. Most of her belongings are still in the closet. Some are lying on the bed as if she auditioned them for her trip and they didn't make the cut. Sleeveless dresses and light cardigans and flip flops. Pfff, Emily. Were you packing for Hawaii?

But what if she *did* go to Hawaii, and I'm wrongly assuming she went to Katie's? A whole new field of possibilities opens up. She could be anywhere.

The room suddenly gets colder, like I'm being embraced

by frost. My heartbeat races, then there's the familiar burst of sweat, and the pain in my stomach that folds me in two. Oh, no. Not again. I curl up on the bed, on top of Emily's mess. Breathe in and out. In and out.

I forgot how comfortable this memory foam mattress is. I move my fingers over the crisp white sheet. Oh, Emily.

It's cancer, I know it is. Undiagnosed, disguised as a panic attack. Would she come back for me if she knew I was on my deathbed?

CHAPTER 12

Still lucky day, 27th of July

I had to document the call with Michelle right after it happened. I couldn't wait to get ~~home~~ to my private room at Audrey's. I want to be specific about that. Living at Audrey's doesn't make it home. Anyway, I wanted to write while the memory was still fresh. Luckily, I had my journal with me, so I sat down on a random bench close to Harriet Rodriguez, beloved mother and wife who was about 102 when she died—so probably no tragedies there, just normal benign death of old age. I journaled everything, and when I was done, the sun had shifted. It wasn't dusk, but there were hints of the day fading away and I got gloomy. My lucky day was going to end like all things do.

I was too emotional to go back to Audrey's, too lonely and alone. I wanted somebody to hold me, comfort me, say that everything was going to be all right, but there's nobody who could do that. I don't have any childhood friends. I don't have any family. All my relationships, be they platonic friendship or romantic or any other human connection, have ended by death or by me physically moving away.

There's no room for these sorts of feelings on lucky day twenty-seven. So, I wiped my eyes, took a deep breath, and walked out of the cemetery. I had no particular direction in mind. I just roamed the streets, swinging between feeling sorry for myself and telling myself to shake off the feeling.

Eventually, I found myself across the street from Sunjay's. It was already dark by then, not the deep dark blue of the night, but the fairer one just after sunset when there are still some orange patches in the sky. The streetlights were still off, but Sunjay's was lit, and the light poured into the hectic street like a beacon. It was like a sign. I couldn't ignore it.

I ran through the stream of cars, high-pitched beeps following me like the train of a long dress.

Bill was by the register, pouring over an anatomy book. I'm writing Bill, but when I stopped there, I still thought his name is Sunjay.

"Hey," I said, "you look like you could use a hug." Of course, *I* was the one in need of a hug, but I was too timid to say that.

His face lit up into a beautiful smile when he saw it was me.

"I can always use a hug when it's from you." He moved away from the counter and embraced me. He smelled like strawberries. It was dizzying, that hug. It gave me hope.

It was closing time, and I helped him drag in the paper towels and the vegetable boxes from outside.

"There's something I've been meaning to tell you," he said while we lifted and pulled and stacked produce under the register. Then he told me his name is Bill. Who knew? He's from South Dakota. His great grandparents immigrated when India was partitioned by the Brits in the late 1940s. The *real* Sunjay hired him to work in the store and pretending to be Sunjay was part of the job. He's never been to India and he's not even Sikh. He wears this turban just to seem more exotic to the customers, like a uniform.

It's kind of funny, actually. Not fighting racism, but accepting it exists and exploiting it for your own benefit.

Bill is the only one who knows about Mom being a bee. I guess I'm not really alone. I have a friend. It doesn't matter that he's two decades younger than me.

mily

I'm terribly weak when we land. My knees are wobbly, and I walk slower than my elderly neighbor, who rushes outside to the terminal. I see her when I make my way out, breathing heavily from the effort of carrying my bag. She's embracing James, kissing him passionately. A young man passing by me gasps with disgust. And I get it. Because I also used to think that love was a matter for the youth.

"Oh, dear, are you all right?" Doctor Leary asks when she sees me. She detaches from her husband-to-be and comes over. He follows, his hands tucked all the way into his pockets. He's whistling a tune I can't hear, but I see the movement of his lips. There's something rebellious in his stride. He projects self-confidence—but not the arrogance—of an extrovert. It's way more subtle. He's a man who knows what he's worth, regardless of his age, and he's not afraid to show it. His gaze is serious, but there's a mischievous sparkle in his eye as if he's ready to goof around, should the right opportunity present itself. I can see why Dr. Leary loves him.

When he comes to a stop, his posture reminds me of Tom. I pant. It's like an arrow through my heart.

Doctor Leary summons the terminal assistance. As a senior citizen, she's entitled to these kinds of perks. Help comes in a golf cart that glides over the smooth floor with an annoying beep. It startles everyone who walks by, which is exactly what it's meant to do. Doctor Leary asks the tired driver to take us to the car rental counter. He refuses, but she's very persuasive, and he finally caves.

The golf cart drops the three of us by Avis. All they have left is a Lincoln Navigator. It's a luxury SUV fitted for seven passengers. I would feel so much better in a small sedan, but the clerk shakes her head. "You're lucky someone canceled last minute. We literally have A car for you." She chews on her pink gum and doesn't give me a second glance. Doctor Leary and her fiancé stand a few yards away, engaged in conversation. I can't disturb them. They've done so much for me already. I look at the other counters only a few dozen steps away, but in my current condition, it's like climbing Mount Everest.

"I'll take it," I say with a sigh.

After a short but heated discussion with Doctor Leary, they agree to bring the car from the parking lot to the handicapped space by the door. Techie grandma helps me put Yolanda's art gallery address into the navigation system, and once I'm all set to go, I'm invigorated, excited for my road trip.

"Let me give you a lift to your car. That's the least I can do."

They both get in the back, cuddling and giggling like a

couple of teenagers. James instructs me where to turn, and I stop by his car. We all step out. It's time to say our goodbyes.

Holding Doctor Leary's hands, I don't know how to thank her. "I'll forever be obliged to you." I'm choked, overwhelmed with emotion. I can't believe this sort of kindness still exists in our cynical, harsh world. Perhaps it's love. It empowers her to be a better person.

James wraps his hand around her shoulder. "That's my Irene," he says proudly. And he should be proud. She's something else. I can't believe how condescending I was when I first set my eyes on her. First looks can be so deceiving.

Dr. Leary gives me an embarrassed, dismissive gesture when I ask for her address. I want to send a fruit basket. A wedding gift.

"Please, let me show you my appreciation," I beg of her.

She smiles sweetly. "You just take care, dear. Keep that fluid regime I prescribed, and you'll be back on your feet in no time."

She climbs into the Prius like she's Cinderella, off to have her happy ever after with her Prince Charming. I'm so hopeful and inspired.

It's probably not the best idea for me to drive in my current condition, but I do it anyway. I'm high on hope and love. I'm in desperate need of a shower and could probably get a decent one at the Homewood Suites on Sunport Blvd. But I don't stop. Instead, I turn to interstate #25 on route to Santa Fe.

The navigator in my car states it's going to take an hour and twelve minutes to get there. My stomach is pinched with hunger. Each time an exit sign pops up, I'm tempted to get off the interstate and find some place to eat. A shower. And about halfway through, a bathroom.

Each sign of a gas station is a deliberation. Should I stop

here, or should I go on? I keep on driving. Hungry. Filthy. Dying to take a leak. I'm focused on the road. I love seeing the number of miles separating me and Yolanda drop. It's like someone is taking her clothes off.

An hour and twelve turns into forty-seven minutes, which then becomes thirty-two. My bladder is so full, it's about to explode. But I'm not stopping. As the minutes drop, my excitement level rises. I rock in the driver seat, trying to hold my water, and I keep going. Keep going. Keep going.

A sign says I've reached Santa Fe county, and I almost burst out in a holler. My body is going through a storm. This day seems to have lasted a lifetime. When I woke up in a hospital chair this morning, I couldn't have imagined that by midnight, I would be driving across New Mexico.

I'm almost wetting my pants. Jumping up and down in my seat. *Just keep on going.* On and on and on. There are only eighteen minutes left when I find myself take a sharp right into La Bajada Rest Area.

"Bathroom?" I ask as I pass a couple sitting at a picnic table. They're having what looks like a candlelight dinner.

They both point to a building. "Go around," the woman cries. To say that the bathroom wasn't very clean would be a compliment. It's filthy and stinky and in a different situation, I would carry on driving instead of evacuating my bladder in this bacteria-infested bowl. Barely able to unzip my pants before the flood comes, I don't even need my shy bladder app. I'm way past that. I go on forever, crouching over the stool. My hamstrings begin to flex. And when I'm done, it's such a relief on one hand, but on the other, my stomach aches as if I still need to go.

I wash my face and check my reflection. I look tired. And old. There are black bags under my eyes, and my skin sags like someone who's lost a lot of weight in a very short time. I want to look my best when I meet Yolanda—my competition is a young yoga instructor. I see the dread in my eyes, and I bend toward the mirror to examine them up close. A bottomless abyss is reflected back at me. It's brown and spiraling and full of pain. My life has been a total waste. The loss is so excruciating, a pulsating headache blinds me for a second.

Where would I be today if I'd stayed with Yolanda? I certainly wouldn't be bent over in a filthy bathroom in the middle of nowhere. I'm so alone. Pulling my phone out of my purse, I don't even know who I'm going to call. In the end, it doesn't even matter because the battery is dead.

I press my fingertips against the puffy bags under my eyes. I pull out my cheeks. I sigh.

Miserable and frustrated, I walk outside. The air is cold and dry. My energy level has dropped significantly, as if it was all stored in my pee.

"Yo, man, you alright?" the woman from the picnic table hollers.

"Yeah... No." I raise my hand in a gesture I don't know the meaning of. I don't even know what I want to express.

"Want a sausage? Craig made way too many!"

My stomach starts rumbling. I'm not sure sausage is the right thing to be eating right now, but I'm so hungry and tired and feeling sorry for myself. I'm craving human connection—and not just for food.

"Thank you," I whisper.

"Here, sit down," the woman says and scoots over to make room for me. I flinch when I notice her facial piercings. Lips. Nose. Eyebrow. She's practically a walking cheap jewelry store. There's a tattoo of a broken heart under her left eye and a sunflower decorates her right temple, its stem trailing all the way down her cheek, leaves covering her right ear and her nose.

She waits patiently while I examine her, and although the table is poorly lit—what I thought were candles are actually the flashlight app on their mobile phones—I can still see the vulnerability and expectation on her face as she waits to hear what I think. Soft Christian music plays from one of the phones. The man hums with the melody, *praise the Lord, praise his name.*

"You're so pretty," I whisper because she really is. Her face lights up with a smile.

"Pay up!" says the guy who sits across the table and she laughs.

"Craig thought you would be intimidated by my looks," she explains. The man hands me a sausage on a paper plate. His face is hidden under a baseball cap, but I can see a cross tattooed on his neck. If I had met these two in a different scenario, I would have thought they were a couple of gang members and would have kept my distance. They smile when I gobble down the entire sausage in two bites.

"Man, you're hungry," the woman says and taps my back. Craig nods and hands me another sausage. The sky is dark, and the stars are sparkling. It's so grand and beautiful. Suddenly, I'm grateful to be alive to witness this beauty.

"Thank you," I say when I'm done with my third serving. "Thank you from the bottom of my heart."

"A pleasure," he says. And I find myself telling these two strangers, who are probably half my age, that I'm on my way to visit an ex I haven't seen for almost three decades.

"Is he the one who got away?" the woman asks.

I hesitate before I say, "it's a she." They laugh full-heartedly.

"Well, good for you," they say. I help them clean up. We hug. And then I'm in my car again. I'm so grateful for the way the night has unfolded. First Doctor Leary, and now these two. The world is full of goodness. I look to the horizon. A slim crescent of a moon hangs low in the distance. It's just perfect.

I wake up sometime later when the sun rises over the mountains, blinding me. And immediately, I'm inside an Expressionist painting, the golden ball of fire in the east painting the land with sharp, bright colors. Everything around me looks fresh, from the brown-yellowish plains to the vast, blue morning sky. So different than the usual gray overcast sky we get in Michigan. There's a single white cloud floating in the distance, like a little lost sheep. The scenery is breathtaking, and I step outside so I can bask in the sun, only to realize it's a lying illusion. Despite the shining light, it's *freezing*.

There are signs in the rest area commemorating women who contributed to the development of New Mexico. I take the time to educate myself about these brave individuals. Their stories are an inspiration. With peace and serenity, I continue my journey.

TOM

When I wake up hours later, my mouth is dry, and my bladder is full. It's still dark out there, and why shouldn't it be? It's only 3:03 a.m. I'm so weak, dragging my feet to the bathroom. Automatically, I put the seat down when I'm done. Then I remember. I wonder if she came back while I was asleep.

"Emily?" I call. My voice is so hesitant. I hate it. There's no answer, but maybe she's just keeping quiet out of spite. I'm certain she's here, playing a cat and mouse game. Like the one in Beirut, when she grabbed my phone and refused to give it back. Now I'm getting mad again, and the anger makes me stronger. Strong enough to creep downstairs. I'm going to surprise Emily with a roar. Make her jump off her feet. I stop, breathless, in the kitchen. And as my pulse settles down, I take in the soulless emptiness around me. It's like a black hole that gravitates around me, sucking my life force, my energy. And I remain standing by the sink. There's nothing inside me. My skin is like a banana peel dumped by the side of the road.

The pendulum clock makes its ten-minutes-past-the-hour music. It sounds like a death knell, announcing my demise. But as it chimes, I think I hear something else, and I try to listen carefully. Did my phone just notify me about a new message? The clock keeps on with its stupid music, masking all other noises.

Suddenly, I get why Emily hates it so much. In an instant, I shake the pseudo-catatonic state that blights me and rush back upstairs. For a brief second, I feel great. It's like someone has administered a secret potion to my body, eliminating all pain, and leaving me stronger and healthier than ever. I have a plan now. A purpose. An understanding. Emily went away because she couldn't stand that damn clock! She didn't tell me anything because she didn't want to hurt my feelings. Oh, I love her so much. Did she choose this specific moment to text me *knowing* the clock's music would blend with my phone? Oh, she's so smart, my wife.

Excited, I pick up my phone from the charger in the master bedroom.

There's no message.

Nothing, except for some texts in the group chat from a couple of students bitching about the homework being too hard. The usual suspects of procrastination and laziness who think that whining will score them some points. It's my fault. I reward creative efforts expressed in any field, even in the field of whining. If it wasn't 3:13 a.m., I would probably articulate an appropriate response, but right now, I just leave it.

In a fraction of a second, I'm plunging from the rooftop of happiness to the deep pit of rejection. I had a wonderful woman, and somehow, I managed to drive her away. I'm such a failure. I can't seem to do anything right.

And then a new thought flashes through my mind. Maybe she left her phone behind, and *that's* why she's not reading my messages. Of course. She often forgets her phone at home. That must be it.

I call her, just so I can hear it ring. And ring. I'm listening carefully, trying to catch the weak vibration sound, in case it's silenced. I look in the wardrobe and on the nightstands until the line disengages. I go into her sewing room and call again, putting the phone on speaker while I poke around her stuff. Maybe the phone is buried underneath a pile of fabric or in the bucket full of zippers.

It was Einstein who said that only a fool repeats the same experiment over and over again and expects different results. Foolish me repeats calling Emily's phone in the kitchen. In the living room. Even in the bathroom. And each time, it rings and rings until it disengages, and I become more and more frantic.

I drag myself back to the master bedroom, where I get angry with the mess she's left on the bed. Absentmindedly, I plug the phone back into the charger. It's a simple, every day, mundane task I do every night before I go to sleep. But there's a bottle of water next to the charger, and the whole thing sits on a stack of fashion magazines. Something is off. It's like the end of a thread that needs unraveling. I pull it lightly, and then it all falls to place.

This is Emily's phone charger.

Maybe she took the phone, but she certainly didn't take the charger with her.

Bang. Now I know why she hasn't read my texts. Why she hasn't replied. The world makes sense again.

And with this newly earned peace of mind, I can finally go back to sleep. But before I allow myself to doze off, I leave a message with Brenda, the school administrator, telling her I'm sick and she should find a substitute.

CHAPTER 14

7/30, Saturday morning

Last night, Bill came over to dinner as usual. I welcomed him at the door. Audrey was setting the table. She also helped me cook, which would have been a nice gesture, if only she'd confined herself to doing what I, the experienced cook, said. Sometimes she wears me down with her constant need to argue and question everything.

Bill was wearing his turban, so I played the game.

"Good evening, Sunjay," I said out loud, winking at him at the same time. He flashed me a smile. Our little secret bonded us together.

We had veggie lasagna because Audrey said it's only polite to not serve beef to an Asian Indian.

"The Sikhs are allowed to choose if they want to abstain from beef," I said, then I bit my tongue. I'd almost blurted out that he's not really a Sikh. I knew for a fact that Bill appreciated a good steak—the other night, he offered to take me out on a date and suggested a steak dinner. Of course, I couldn't, because of Audrey. Bill and I haven't set the rules on our friendship, but it was kind of insinuated between the lines.

After our meal, Bill offered to help with the cleanup. The three of us were done with it pretty quickly.

"May I interest you ladies in a nice stroll outside? It's a beautiful night. The weather is perfect."

Audrey inhaled deeply. He knew she didn't like to leave the house. And *I* knew he wanted to go for a walk only with me. I kept quiet. Despite all of Audrey's quirks, it was awkward leaving her alone.

"You two go. I have my stories coming up soon," she said and gave us her blessing to leave. At first, we walked quietly side by side. It was embarrassing.

"I really like you," Bill said.

"I like you too."

His hand groped for mine and for a few yards, we walked hand in hand, quietly, before he asked, "Is this all right?" I acknowledged it with a nod.

"Where would you like to go?" he asked. I shrugged. I really didn't care. It was nice just being away from the house, and it *was* a pretty night. Dark, though. The moon hadn't come up yet.

"We could catch a movie," he suggested.

"Nah."

We kept walking quietly past the park. The vast trees were the only disturbing shadows in the blackness.

"Would you like to go to my storage unit?" I'd been meaning to go there since that talk with Michelle.

"Sure," Bill said. After a while, he added, "I can trust you to offer an extraordinary location to hang on a Friday night." He laughed.

We took a bus to the outskirts of town, and then we rummaged through the stuff Mom left behind. There were boxes of vinyl records from the 60s, mainly The Beatles and

The Stones. And there were lots of cooking books and Mom's giant box of recipes. I let Bill wander around while I went straight to the backpack with all my previous journals and pulled out the last one. It's only a few pages long because I was with Michelle only a few short weeks before the hospital called and I rushed back home.

Bill found the photo albums.

"Is that your Dad?" He showed me a photo of Mom's wedding. She was so young. Barely eighteen years old. My father's head is ripped off. He's just a body in an old-fashioned suit.

"Yeah. Mom tore his face from all the photos after he left. Said his face shouldn't be remembered."

He kept browsing. "Your Mom was a real beauty."

"Yeah. She was."

I put the journal in the backpack. I didn't need it anymore.

Bill stopped at a photo of my parents kissing. Well, it just Mom. Her eyes were closed, and it looked like she was kissing a tree, which is, of course, was the photo on the next page peeking from underneath. I thought it was funny, but Bill wasn't laughing. He looked at me kind of funny.

"May I kiss you?" he asked. So sweet.

I smiled and nodded, but he didn't do anything, so I made the first move and kissed him.

He kissed me back so hesitantly.

"Was that your first time?" I asked when he stepped away.

He admitted shyly that his family was very traditional, and they believed in arranged marriages. By coming to study in Michigan, he thought he would escape that. "It's not easy being brown," he finally said. And only then did I notice his color for the first time. Huh.

om

It's the first night I sleep uninterrupted for eight hours since…forever. I don't toss and turn. I don't count sheep. I don't wake in a pool of my own sweat. I just fall into a sweet, embracing state of bliss and wake up naturally around noon, feeling well-rested, rejuvenated. stretching and yawning, I check all my organs for pain or malfunction. Everything feels fine. I have a healthy appetite and satisfying bowel movement, which is a relaxing way to start your day when you're only a hair's breadth from your fifties.

Checking my phone is a reflex. The crypto-coins app Tommy developed sends a daily status at 7:45 a.m. every morning with predictions and trade recommendations, and I usually make notes and set alarms for the rest of the day.

This morning, I'm not in the mood. I'm taking a day off *everything*. School. Emily. Trading. Life. This day is going to be *my* day. I make myself a big breakfast, though it's more of a brunch at this hour. I turn the radio on and hum with the tunes. Maybe Emily should leave me more often. I giggle at the thought. Who knows, maybe we'd have been better off if she had carried through on her threats about going to Katie's.

But did she go to Katie's after all? She should have reached her by now. And Katie must have a phone charger.

While eating my eggs, I get a sudden urge to check on her. Yet, my texts are still unread. So, I make the call to Katie. She answers after one ring.

"Tom? Is everything all right? I'm in a meeting." Katie's whispering voice sounds alarmed. And I know why. We talk only when there's a pressing need.

"Yeah. Well, I don't know. Have you seen Emily?"

"Hang on," she whispers. I hear chairs creaking and her breaths get shorter. I hear muffled voices and then—

"I haven't talked to Emily since Marni's wedding. I'm still waiting for an apology." There's a lot of echo, like she's in a small, confined space.

"Oh. I didn't know you two had a fight."

"Tom? What's going on? You're scaring me."

I take a deep breath.

"It's nothing, really. Emily and I had a bit of a falling out and she left. I thought she headed your way."

"Well, she didn't. Have you checked with her friends?"

"What friends?"

"I don't know. Colleagues from school? Wasn't she friends with the school administrator?"

"Who? Brenda? She wouldn't go there. She thinks she's a hen."

"Yeah. Right. Other teachers, maybe?"

We're both quiet as our brain-wheels turn, seeking a clue. We reach the same horrifying conclusion at the same time.

"Oh no. Tom. Do you think?" Her voice fades away.

"No. No way. Impossible."

We think again.

"Is it possible she went to visit Marni?" Katie suggests

"I don't know. I guess. Or she might have flown to see Tommy. He said just the other night he won't be coming home on spring break, and that's *after* spending his New Year's Eve house-sitting at Marni's."

"She must miss him," Katie says, and I feel the relief in her voice.

But I'm not buying it. You don't consider Hawaiian shirts and flip flops for a trip to Boston in February. "Yeah. That's probably it. Sorry for wasting your time, Katie."

"Keep me posted, Tom, please. I worry."

"No need, Katie. I'm sure she couldn't reach her. I mean, it's been at least five years since last time, right?"

"Right. But she's persistent. You know. We think we've covered all our bases, then she finds a way to creep back in. This scares me, Tom. She's never left you before, has she?"

"She's threatened a lot, saying she'll go to yours for a few days. That's why I called."

"Oh."

We fall into a tense silence again. I know we're both thinking the same thing.

"Well, let me know."

"Will do. Have a good one."

Although I'm certain Emily hasn't gone to visit the kids, I still check in with them.

"Dad, is it urgent?" Marni whispers. She sounds in a hurry.

"No, I just miss you. Wanted to say hi."

"Love you too, Dad," she says and hangs up. Would she have said something if Emily was there? I'm sure she wouldn't have been so casual about it. And I know Emily wouldn't have gone there, with Marni and Marcus so busy with their internships. They're even working on weekends. We've been planning to visit them for some time now, and they're always too occupied to meet. No. Emily didn't go to New York.

It's harder with Tommy because he's so smart and sensitive. I don't know how to ask without raising his suspicions. After contemplating it for a few minutes, I finally send what I consider a neutral text, like those we exchange daily about his algorithm.

Did you check the dailies? Opportunity with Bitcoin!

We almost never get opportunities for Bitcoin, because it's a too big and saturated market.

Tommy replies within a second. *Don't go in*, he types. *Too risky.*

I wasn't going to. It's just a conversation starter. I'm thinking how to ask him about Emily when he types, *AB/BC?*

I don't know what he means, so I just reply with a question mark.

On your calendar. A.P. Calculus Class.

Shoot. I didn't think of that. Tommy and I share calendars. I should be teaching right now, hence, I shouldn't be texting him. Now he knows something is wrong, and I need to come up with a good enough explanation without freaking him out. I just type the first thing that comes to mind.

Personal day.

My explanation must have eased his mind because he doesn't write anything else. Does that mean Emily is there with him?

I don't have time to ponder it. My phone beeps. It's an unfamiliar beep, not like the ones I'm used to hearing with my trading alerts. It's from Facebook. *Facebook?* It's been a while since I rode on that train. I opened an account a few years back when it was trendy, but apart from a few child-hood friends who surface just to say *hi* and *what are you're doing?* I didn't see the point. But there it is. Someone tagged me in a picture. Only it's not me. It's Emily, wearing a straw sun hat, looking straight to the camera and making a duck face. She looks so happy and free. So pretty. And then I recognize the face of the other person in the photo. She's wearing a matching straw hat but also the winner's smile. My heart clenches.

The phone rings before I'm able to recover from the shock.

"I've seen it," Katie says dryly. No hellos are necessary now. I hear the echo down the elevator shaft. *Seen it. Seen it. It.* The dramatic addendum is fitting.

"I can't believe it." I shake my head.

"I know. Me neither."

"That snake. That blood-sucking tick of a woman. She keeps coming back!"

"Yeah. I thought she'd given up by now. Moved on with her life."

"What should we do?" I ask.

Katie's quiet for a moment. My brain turns into a mush. I can't think of anything but the blinding rage. "I'm going to go there and get Emily back. And make sure she never, ever dares to reach out again."

"Tom—" Katie's voice is soft and comforting. I tense. "Emily went there of her own free will, didn't she?"

I can't answer. I don't want to answer. I don't want to even know the answer.

"Here's what I think we should do," she says then pauses. I wait.

"Nothing," Katie says. "We shouldn't do anything. We should sit this one out." Her breaths are short and heavy, and

I can hear her footsteps and the echo of her footsteps. Wherever she's at, she must be pacing in circles.

"But—"

Katie interrupts before I'm able to present my argument.

"Look, Tom, we've been guarding Emily for years. It's time we trust her to deal with this on her own." There's a distinct, loud sound of a metal door closing.

"But she's a monster, Katie! We can't let Emily deal with her on her own!"

"Emily's not as fragile as she once was, Tom. I think she can handle it."

"Really, Katie? Do you truly think she won't get sucked back into Yolanda's vortex? Or are you just saying that because you're angry with her and prefer to keep your silly grudge instead of saving your sister?"

She's quiet for a second. I try to listen carefully, but there's so much noise. She must have gone outside, into the street. Cars are honking, and there's the low hum of the wind. Did I take it too far?

"Tom," she finally says. She sounds tired. "Let's wait a day or two before we do something hasty. We need to be smart about it."

"But we *are* going to do something about it. Promise me!"

"Yes. I promise. Now *you* promise me you won't do anything hasty."

"Fine," I say reluctantly. I know she's right. But I don't want to do the right thing. I want to charge. I want to roar. I want to rescue my woman.

"Find a distraction, okay? I've got to go now." She hangs up, and I stare at my phone. Oh, Emily, what have you done? Why did you enter that lion's den again?

～

EMILY

The gala is at seven, but I arrive early. Way early. There's the apology issue I need to get off my chest, and I think maybe I could help her set up. I've organized a few charity events at school, and I know every helping hand is a blessing.

It's almost noon when I park by Sweet Pea. It's a one-story adobe-style house by the edge of Canyon Road. There are huge bronze statues out front, life-size replicas of Yolanda's award-winning Team USA figurines. A young man with a forklift is moving them around the yard. Clearly, I underestimated the scope of this setup. A man with a work helmet, wearing shorts despite the cold, stands on the porch and directs the forklift driver with hand gestures. I'm just an observer, and no one seems to mind.

A van pulls over with a screech, and a woman with rainbow-colored hair jumps out. She's wearing ear pods, nodding her head to a rhythm only she hears. She pulls out a box full of potted plants and carries it to the yard. Her gaze is focused on the forklift. The driver doesn't see her, and I dread a terrible accident is about to happen.

"Be careful," I yell and wave my hands. She doesn't hear or see me.

The man on the porch runs toward her, his helmet jumping on top of his head. He yells, "Yo, flower lady! Yo!" She doesn't hear him either until he touches her shoulder. The forklift finally stops, and I'm relieved.

"What are you doing here?" The man with the helmet yells. "You're two hours early! We're not ready for you now!"

It's clear that the yeller is in charge of setting up. I'm slightly disappointed that Yolanda isn't there, and mentally berate myself. What was I thinking? This isn't some lame school function. It's on a completely different scale.

I spent the entire morning beautifying myself. I got

recommendations for a local establishment from the receptionist at the Holiday Inn Express where I booked a room for the night. Luckily the salon accepted walk-ins. I had a facial, then had my hair and nails done.

I'm wearing a royal-blue jersey dress which I designed and sewed to my specific measurements. It was the very first item I designed from scratch in my new sewing business, and I'm quite proud of my achievement because it doesn't have that sloppy, homemade look. It could totally pass as off-the-rack store-bought. The dress is accompanied by a jean jacket and a jean cross-body bag, also of my making. Well, the jacket is an upcycle from a thrift shop. It looks kind of vintage, but with a modern touch. I want to show off my creations, just a little bit.

Getting dressed in front of the mirror in my hotel room, I felt comfortable and confidant. But standing at the foot of this chic gallery, I'm a provincial, misfit, weird, middle-aged woman. I'm not a fashion designer. I'm a pathetic little housewife from the Midwest. An art teacher on a sabbatical who plays make-believe with fabric.

It was wrong of me to come here. What's little old me going to do with hotshot Yolanda and her Governor Award of Excellence in the Arts. Yolanda will look at me with contempt. She'll mock my creative efforts. She liked daring. She liked originality. And my entire being shouts mediocrity. I'm about to turn and leave, when someone calls from inside the gallery,

"Hello? Miss?"

My heart rate escalates. It's not Yolanda. She has a slight accent, the remains of her childhood in east Europe. This voice sounds young, chirpy, light. I freeze in place. Was she calling out to me?

A woman steps outside of the gallery. She's wearing an oversized gray cardigan over sweats that are so faded I can't really tell what their original color was. In an instant, I feel overdressed.

"Can I help you?" she asks. There's something familiar about her face, and not just because I saw her photo on Facebook. She tilts her head to the left and focuses her gaze on me. She has gorgeous sea-green eyes and long, straight strawberry-blond hair. I can't compete with that. No way.

"Yeah, um, I'm Em—" The words are stuck in my mouth.

Her smile deepens in response to my stammering, and two dimples add to her currently too-much cuteness.

She stretches her hand out. "I'm Sahara."

"Yeah, I know," I say. She raises one eyebrow. "I'm Emily," I add quickly.

"O. M. G! It *is* you!" She crosses the short distance between us and grabs my hands. "Yolanda is going to flip! I mean, she'll be over the moon!"

It's embarrassing. A hot flush covers my cheeks. She's even prettier up close, and she's also so generous. Jealousy chokes me. I wish she'd drop dead right this minute, and I'm so ashamed at that thought.

"I can't believe you're actually here." She shakes her head. "Can't believe that stupid plan actually worked," she adds as if talking to herself.

"I'm sorry?" I ask. I don't understand what's going on. What plan is she talking about? Why is she so happy to see me? I would have been devastated if I was her.

"Wait here!" she orders and rushes back into the gallery. Despite the order, I follow her, somewhat slower and hesitant. She's on the phone.

"Yol?" she says in a matter of fact tone. It's on speaker and I can hear Yolanda huffs angrily on the other side.

"What?" she barks. I remember this tone. My skin covers with goosebumps. She never used it with me until the day I said I was going to marry Tom. "By marrying this man, you're giving up on all your dreams, Emily. You're going to have a very boring, lower-middle-class life. Always fighting for money. No time for creativity."

I'm shaking. What will she say when she finds out her premonitions turned out to be right?

"Sorry to bother you," Sahara says and winks at me, "but you might want to get down here. There something you might want to see."

Yolanda cusses. It's not in English, but the tone can't be mistaken. "How many times do I have to tell you I don't like riddles!"

Sahara frowns, and I flinch a little.

"What is it?" Yolanda barks again. "Is Dan there? What's he done now? You said you could manage this, Sarah, and now I need to come down and fix your mistakes? Again?"

Sahara shakes her head. She puts the phone next to her chest and whispers, "don't worry, she's always cranky before a big event." She hands me the phone. I don't want to take it. I'm not sure what's going on here, and I don't want to meddle in their relationship.

"Hello? Sahara?" Yolanda sounds very irritated. "Why did you wake me? Tell me what's going on!" She keeps speaking in that angry tone.

Sahara just ignores it. She smiles and pushes the phone into my face. "Go on," she whispers, "say hi."

"Hi," I say. My voice trembles.

There's silence on the other side. I'm not sure if she heard me. Then, "Emily? Is that you?" Her voice is trembling as well.

I'm speechless. Words don't come out of my mouth when I open it to answer her question.

"Sahara, I swear to god, I'm going to kick your butt if you're playing tricks on me—"

"No, it's me," I say before she finishes her line of threats. "Emily. I'm in your gallery. I came to the gala."

She hangs up without saying goodbye.

Sahara shrugs and puts down the phone. "It'll be probably ten minutes. She lives down the road."

That confuses me. "Wait, don't you two live together?"

Sahara shakes her head. "I live here, in the back room. Yolanda lets me stay here rent-free and in return, I manage the gallery."

"Oh." My voice is nothing but a whisper. "I'm sorry. I thought you two were together."

"What made you think that?" Her voice is sharp.

I'm so embarrassed. "I'm sorry, I must have got it all wrong. You see, it says you're in a relationship on her Facebook page."

"Yeah." She laughs. "We are. Only it's a different kind of relationship." She looks straight into my eyes. I'm puzzled.

She sighs softly. "I'm Sarah. Sarah Newton. Don't you remember me?"

I shake my head. Should I know her?

"Sheila's daughter."

I'm still in the dark.

She exhales loudly, looking disappointed. "My mom is Yolanda's best friend from college. I spent that summer with you, and you two stayed with us one time in Brooklyn. We played paper dolls together, you and I. Don't you remember?"

"Vaguely." I look up as I try to recall. "Is it Sarah or Sahara?" I pick one of the confusing details.

"I've had to change my name." She makes a dismissive gesture. "It's a long story."

"And what about the little girl I saw in the photos?"

"What little girl? What photos?" Her tone rises, and she looks tense.

What did I say? "The Facebook photos. You and Yolanda at the beach—" I stop mid-sentence because her face whitens, and she leans against the counter. "Are you okay?"

"She put Apple's photos online." She's getting frantic.

"Well—" I don't know how to continue, and it doesn't matter anyway because she's not listening.

"I can't believe that woman," Sahara murmurs. Her lips are pressed into a thin line. "She has no respect." With no more words, she disappears through the back door and leaves me alone in the gallery.

Only then I'm aware of the workers inside the gallery, hammering and installing, setting dividers and light fixtures. The forklift outside beeps while reversing, and the foreman's voice breaks as he yells through a bullhorn, "st—op, sss—op!"

It's kind of comforting to see the world hasn't stopped revolving because I caused Sahara—or Sarah, whatever her name is—to have a crisis. Yet, I'm not sure what's going on around me. I feel so out of place, so clumsy. I've only been here for a few minutes, and I've managed to do what seems like terrible damage. I don't know if I should follow Sahara and apologize or stay put.

She storms back through the same door merely two minutes later, holding a duffel bag that seems to have been packed in a hurry. It's unzipped, and I see a mess of clothes and kids toys inside. Her shoelaces are untied, and she looks anxious and frightened.

"Tell her—" Her eyes are dark and cold; her nostrils flare. She waves a dismissal and storms out of the gallery. She gets into an old pickup truck parked out front. The tires screech as she speeds away and vanishes.

Puzzled, I stay put. I put my hands in the pockets of my jacket and pull them out again. I glance at the men and women working around me. No one makes eye contact. They're all busy with their tasks. It's like I'm not even there.

"Excuse me," one of them says as he enters with a big wooden board. I step to the side. I try to make eye contact, but he looks at me as if I'm transparent.

Then Yolanda arrives, and I forget about everything else. Like a breathtaking sunrise, she steps inside, takes me in her arms and crushes her lips onto mine. She smells like earth, and sun, and citrus. I kiss her back. Her tongue slides into my mouth. It's so familiar, yet so new. Her hands on my back are fierce and controlling. This kiss, it makes me spiral. I want her so badly. I want her right now.

But then her hands are too tight on my ribs. It hurts. I step back. She lets me detach from her but still stands close. Her forehead rests on mine, and she looks deeply into my eyes.

"Hey," she says softly. When she smiles, the wrinkles around her eyes deepen. They're not new; she had them when we were together. Only now there are more of them, and they're deeper. The mole by her nose *is* new. And so are the brown age marks on her temples. It's clear she hasn't had any cosmetic surgery or Botox, and it's beautiful to see her age reflected in her face. Even her hair isn't dyed. It's still dark, but now somewhat faded, and there are silver and white strands here and there. She looks younger than fifty-six. Maybe mid-forties.

"You look great," I say.

She smiles. "You look..." She takes a step back and examines me from head to toe. "Older," she says finally.

I grimace. That is *not* what I wanted to hear. Especially not after that hot welcome kiss.

"In a good way," she adds quickly.

I laugh, but not full-heartedly.

"I'm so glad you came," she says and hugs me. "I've missed you so much." She emphasizes the "so" and "much."

"Me too." The lie slips so easily off my tongue. Well, it's

not exactly a lie, because I *did* somewhat miss her. It's just that *her* statement makes me feel like she's been yearning for years, and I didn't think about her until yesterday.

It's so easy to slide into old habits. Throughout our relationship, I used to bend reality a little to make her feel good. I've always agreed with her, even when I felt differently. Even when she tried to read my mind and was way off course, I would smile and say, "you know me so well." It made her happy.

It's so different than my marriage. I've never pretended to be someone else just to please Tom. Re-engaging so easily into this old pattern makes me wonder who I really am.

The workers gather around Yolanda like she's the queen bee. Everyone has a question, a favor to ask. They want her to acknowledge their work. They seek her approval. They're buzzing for her attention, but she has eyes only for me.

She waves them off. "Talk to Dan," she says, or "talk to Sahara." Finally, she roars, "Leave me alone!" and everybody disperses quietly. It's so familiar; it's like I'm at college again. Students would gather around her, present their best work and beg for a compliment or constructive criticism. I wasn't part of that group. I never thought I was worthy enough for her attention. And as if nothing has changed, I move backward, distancing myself from the crowd.

Yolanda emerges from the circle of people. "Come!" She grabs my hand and pulls me toward the front door. "Let me give you the tour. I've been dying to do it for years!"

When we are outside in the blinding, deceiving sun, she comes to a halt. Leaving me at the curb, she rushes back into the yard yelling "Sahara! Sahara!" Her sharp, deep voice is heard clearly over the commotion. The foreman yells something, and she waves that she can't hear. He picks the broken bullhorn and reports in a deformed static voice, "Sh— lef—t, dro—aaa her ca—"

Yolanda's eyebrows knit together. She looks so furious, that if she was a dragon, she would have exhaled fire through her nostrils. I'm too scared to mention my contribution to Sahara's sudden departure.

"Okay, let's go," she finally says.

With her hand around my shoulder, she takes me for a stroll down Canyon Road. She has a plan of handpicked galleries I *must* explore.

"Is someone dead?" she asks casually as we walk down the picturesque narrow street.

"What?"

"I figured someone must have died because that's the only reason they'd let you pop back into my life."

"What?" Her explanation just makes me more confused.

She guides me to a two-story adobe house. "This is Monica's. Her current exhibition features some great pieces. You're going to love it. It's all very contemporary."

I don't like any of it, but I nod enthusiastically as we stand for long minutes in front of each exhibit, sharing random thoughts I think she would like to hear.

After the third contemporary art gallery, I'm tired. It's overwhelming, but Yolanda is just getting started. I realize she's been planning this for years, and I let her carry me on. We don't talk about the past—she's just too eager to share her life with me. When her phone rings, which happens quite often, she looks at the caller ID but doesn't bother to pick up.

"They know they shouldn't bother me. There are Dan and Sahara to manage everything," she says when I ask if she doesn't need to take those calls. "Being here with you is way more important." Her hand doesn't come off my shoulder even for one second, and it's embarrassing. She's parading me like I'm fine cattle on market day.

A sharp memory hits me, fresh as if it happened only yesterday. Yolanda and I were on a field trip to check out galleries in New York City, which was a great experience for an up-and-coming artist like me, she'd said, although I knew it was just an excuse for us to spend the night together. We didn't go to MoMA as I expected, nor the Met. My 'education' included visits with fringe aspiring artists, friends of Yolanda's who'd agreed to open their studios for her and her young protégé, as they all insisted on calling me—not that I minded.

Some of them were high on amphetamines, which they kindly offered to share. Yolanda refused and steered me away from them. "Real geniuses don't need a boost to get their inspiration rolling," she'd said, and I wrote it in my notebook, a notebook which I left later at her house with the rest of my things. Although Katie retrieved a box with my clothes and accessories, the notebooks and sketchbooks with numerous fashion designs were not in it. I took it as part of Yolanda's revenge, taking away everything she'd ever given me. I grieved the loss of my creative efforts for a long time, but life went on, especially the life looming in my body. And so, I'd let go.

I air draw a design of some sort of fancy dress. Then I remember drawing it at the basement apartment in Brooklyn where we spent the night. There were roaches everywhere, and I couldn't sleep, so I took out my sketchbook and designed a line of Barbie-doll dresses. That was Sheila's house. Her sweet little child was my inspiration. "I remember little Sarah!" I call out.

Yolanda doesn't hear me. She's preoccupied with purchasing matching straw hats for both of us. I remember fondly how she used to dress us up in matching clothes when we went cruising art exhibitions outside of town. My costume was a burgundy pantsuit, the jacket worn without a shirt underneath. She would wear a burgundy dress and beret. Sometimes she would draw a little mustache over her upper lip. It was cool to have fluid sexuality in the art scene.

"Perfect." She smirks as she puts the hat on my head.

There's a collection of antique American Indian art across the street, and thrilled, I rush over to check it up close. I'm immediately drawn to some colorfully embroidered hand-made clothes and boots. "Come over, Yol!" I gesture for her to join me. I'm thinking of how I could segue the conversation from this exhibition to my recent endeavor.

"Nah." She steers me away to the next gallery, which features a full-size sculpture of an obese human being made of candy wraps.

"Isn't it amazing?" Yolanda says as we circle the piece. I find it quite offensive, but I just nod quietly. She's lecturing me about the artist, Steven something. I pretend to listen, but my mind is elsewhere. Inspired by the quick glance at the Native American clothing, I'm thinking about incorporating some of the features, like fringes and feathers, into my work.

"Are you listening to me?" She stomps her foot.

"Of course!" I repeat her last line, and as I do, I realize this is another old habit—listening just enough to be able to repeat after her but without paying attention to the meaning of the words.

She doesn't seem satisfied but quickly shakes off her disappointment. "Let's take a selfie." She holds her phone at a distance and turns her face to kiss me. It takes a few trials until she's happy with the outcome. It's all very amusing. "That'll go straight to my Facebook page!" She's tapping her phone, taking her time.

"Do you want to make your girlfriend jealous?" I say with laughter in my voice, teasing. She doesn't respond; she's too busy with her phone. Oh dear. But then she puts it down, and we continue our stroll.

"This is me."

We stand in front of yet another adobe-style house. There's a white picket fence and a gate that screeches when we enter. She looks at her phone then at the sky. She smiles at me.

"Let's go inside, I want to show you something special." She curls a piece of my hair around her finger as she speaks.

I shiver a bit. Does that something special include me taking my clothes off?

August 15th, 2016

This morning, Elijah stopped by while I was tilling. Audrey was pruning the honeysuckles.

He held a bowl full of cherries. "Morning ladies," he said in a sing-song voice. The little dog barked as if joining in his greetings. "These are freshly picked. Enjoy." He put the bowl on the grass.

"And this is for you, young lady," he said and handed me a fragrant New Jersey Tea flower.

I was touched.

"Thank you, that's so nice of you!" I said. Audrey scoffed behind me. She kicked the bowl and the cherries scattered everywhere. Elijah stood there with his mouth wide open. That was so rude of her.

"Find a different charity case," she said. I couldn't believe it. Here's a grown woman, acting like a disturbed teenager. I couldn't keep my big, fat mouth shut. Although, in retrospect, I should have.

"What was that about?" I asked.

"He's a nosy, snotty old man," Audrey said, grunting. "Thinks he knows best. Tells everyone how they should live their life." She worked hard with the pruners, taking out all her rage on the poor shrubs.

"Why do you say that?" I wondered. All I saw was a sweet, caring, neighborly person who tried to brighten her days.

"I know what he's thinking," she said. "I'm that mother who killed her only son!"

"*What?*" Her statement was so out of context.

"Yeah. He couldn't stand my constant nagging and preferred enlisting than living with me!" She was shaking like a leaf.

"Wow. Audrey. This is so farfetched. He could have done a million other things to keep his distance. And you didn't tell him to go to war, did you? You didn't put that mine there, did you? You didn't tell him to step on it, *did you?*" I went on and on, raising my voice higher and higher. In the middle of my speech, she dropped the pruners and went inside, slamming the door behind her.

I've seen these full-on guilt trips in movies, but I'd always thought it was Hollywood make-believe. It *was* actually kind of funny. I mean, does she *really* think she's responsible for Charlie's death? That's so random.

mily

Yolanda's studio could have doubled as a laboratory, it's so clean and pure. The floors, walls, and high ceiling are all painted a blinding white. She'd always liked her workspace clean and scarce without distractions. Back in the day, she took me on a tour at Pierce Hermitage's studio. It was cluttered and dirty, stiff brushes and empty paint tubes lying about. Even the floor had dry paint stains all over it. Yolanda had looked around with disgust, "I don't know how you could get inspired in a place like that." I nodded in agreement, although I liked the mess. I thought there was beauty in it.

There's a skylight in the middle of the roof and when we enter, the sun is shining through, illuminating the entire room. It looks like it's raining gold. I'm so impressed. I look up and down, following the rays with my eyes.

"It's beautiful, isn't it?" she whispers next to my ear. The movement of the air against my face while she speaks is hot and cold at the same time. It's so sexy.

She presses a button, and the skylight is partly covered with a shutter. As soon as my eyes adjust to the new darkness, I see the canvases stacked at one end of the room. Some of them are placed for display on easels.

"That's my latest work. I call it, *Biographies.*"

My legs carry me toward the display, but she leads me in the other direction. It's her workspace, separated from the rest of the room with a translucent plastic curtain. It has the feel of a shower curtain, and it blends perfectly with the walls—I didn't see it until we were a few inches away. The space behind it is as clean and white as the rest of the studio. A piece of transparent plastic covers the floor where Yolanda's easel is set. There's a white bench next to it, with a set of various brushes and mixing knives, a jar full of beads, and several packs of adhesive. Her paints are neatly organized on a shelving unit, sorted by hue. The easel faces the white wall. Next to it, there's an orthopedic chair and a small desk with a laptop and a projector. Yolanda turns on the computer and it projects an image on the wall. It's a closeup of an old man.

"This is Doctor Randell Eaton, MD," Yolanda says.

There's nothing special about him. He looks like a regular Joe. Glasses. Bald head. Serious gaze into the horizon.

She clicks a button. The photo is minimized, and there are a few lines of text arranged in bullet points: Cycled to work. Loved to surf. Served in Vietnam. Married three times. Worst cook ever.

Yolanda gives me a few minutes to read the data. The excitement on her face when I look at her puzzles me. What does this everyday stuff have to do with her art? She doesn't say anything, just points at her work-in-progress.

It's abstract. One of the corners is plain black, and there's a curve of blues in the middle, like a huge wave. I get closer to check it out and realize the blues are made from tiny glass beads. It's meticulous work that requires a lot of patience. Yolanda always was patient. She could work for hours curving one line on a clay pot.

I move further away to let it all blend. There's a section of the work which is made of gray circles. Small circles, big circles. They come in pairs. It reminds me of something, but I'm not sure what it is. Then a woman's face suddenly emerges in what I thought was a red smear. And then a second face emerges and a third. Another section of the painting is white and gold. It looks like broken eggshells.

And then everything clicks. It's a visual representation of Randell Eaton's life. The blue wave for his love of surfing. His three wives. Cycling to work.

"That's genius! You're such an amazing artist."

Yolanda's face lights up. She grins. "I knew you'd get it without me needing to break it down for you."

"I love it! What's the black part? Oh, that's war." I'm asking and replying at the same time. Understanding an elaborate abstract piece of art is always so rewarding. The combination of the aesthetics and the deep meaning behind it is like an explosion for the mind.

Yolanda comes closer and gives me a strong embrace. Her smell drives me crazy, and the way she nibbles my neck makes my knees wobbly. The way she touches me, just flicks her hand over my breasts, my torso—it takes my breath away.

"Would you like to see yours?"

The question takes me by surprise. I realize my mouth is wide open.

She walks over to the shelving unit and pulls out a canvas. It's a mandala. The entire painting is so detailed and colorful, it looks like a piece of a kaleidoscope. The center is bright yellow trimmed with circles of darker yellows and golds with rays of the brighter yellow separating the radials. Moving out from the center, each circle has a different color, and together, they form a rainbow. I come closer to examine the details. There are flowers and delicate ornaments in greens and purples. It's so perfectly balanced. I'm in awe. She awaits my verdict, looking at me eagerly.

"It's so... Is that how you see me?"

She raises her eyebrows. While I'm struggling for words, she picks several tubes from the shelf and sits by the easel. She mixes the colors, adding some white, then a smear of blue. I barely dare to breathe, but it doesn't matter. She's in a world of her own, so concentrated in her work, it's like I'm not even here.

She takes her time. Mixing, and remixing until she reaches a combination that pleases her. Then, with the thinnest brush possible, she paints a line. Only then do I notice the background of the mandala. It's black and bleak. She draws a line in the middle of it, as thin as a hair, but it brightens up the black. She turns to look at me, and I nod to assure her I understand what she's doing. The black is our time apart. And the brightness is right now, this moment in time, captured forever.

"We always understood each other without words," she announces quietly while rubbing the brushes clean. It's not completely true but saying that out loud would be ironic. It would collapse the declaration altogether. So I don't say that it's more of a one-way understating, and it's related only to her art.

A memory flashes. We're in pottery class and she's working on a teapot, carefully engraving a complicated motif. The usual clan of fans is gathered around her, trying to guess what it is. They're all so stupid, and I'm sick of it. "It's an African symbol, dummies." It was the first time I'd spoken in class. No one paid attention but her.

"Who said that?" she asked and stretched her neck to look at the crowd. Frightened of her wrath, I didn't identify myself. Someone else pointed in my direction, and she complimented me with a smile. I realize now why she fell for me in the first place. It's because I get her art.

"Would you like to go upstairs?" she whispers in my ear. Her whisper is so breathy it makes my hair dance. It's like she caresses me with her voice. Her words touch my skin and light a fire inside me. Yolanda smiles deviously. My arousal must be written all over my face. Now I'm blushing with embarrassment like a twenty-year-old.

"I'm so glad to see your reaction." She puts her hands on my shoulders and kisses me softly. Her hands are firm on the small of my back. I lose myself in her touch.

We're so close, I can feel the phone vibrate in her pocket. "Just ignore it," she utters. Her hands slide on my spine. Up and down. Up and down. The phone keeps going, and finally, she detaches and picks it up.

"What?" Her voice is sharp.

There's a high-pitched voice on the other end. I can't make out the words.

"Can't this wait? I'm in the middle of something." But then she frowns. She turns away from me and signals with her finger that she's going to be a minute. She walks out of the studio, but I can still hear her. Well, I can hear both of them. Maybe she doesn't realize she's on speaker, or maybe she doesn't mind me listening to her conversation.

"I *specifically* told you not to put Apple's photos online!"

"Calm down, Sahara."

"Don't, Yolanda. Just don't. You exposed me."

"What do you mean exposed you? Where are you? Sahara? Where are you right now?"

"Why? Do you want to tell Richard?"

"Geez. Calm down, sweetie."

"Don't patronize me. You used me, Yolanda. You abused me, even. And now my life is ruined."

"A smudge overly dramatic, aren't we?"

"He's going to find me. He's going to take her."

Yolanda peeks through the door and gestures she needs some more time. I nod, understanding. She moves away from the studio toward the gate. I follow her quietly because the drama is gripping. Sahara sobs on the other side of the line.

"Sahara. Sarah. Listen to me. Richard is in jail. He can't hurt you. You're safe."

"He could send one of his buddies to finish me off." Sahara's voice sounds so small.

"Do you think his criminal friends know my name? Do you think I've friended any of them on Facebook? You know it was only meant for Emily." She says that last bit way quieter than the rest.

I can't wrap my mind around what I've just heard. What did she mean by that? She keeps moving further away from me, and I follow her as quietly as I can.

"Listen to me, I've just looked on my page. There's one photo, and you can't see a face. Just the back of her head. And I've taken it off. I've taken off *all* your photos. You're off the grid, Sarah."

"Don't call me that!"

"Sorry. You're right. Sorry, honey. You're safe. Apple is safe. Come back. Please, I need you to take care of everything for tonight."

Sahara's sobbing stops.

"Please? I don't want to go down there now that Emily is here."

"Yol? Can you call your friend? The security guard?"

"Sure thing. I'll call her right now and make sure you're covered 24/7."

Sahara sniffles. "Thanks, Yol. You're the best."

I sense the conversation is about to end and turn back quietly. I'm afraid Yolanda will catch me eavesdropping.

"Sure. Are you coming back?"

"Yeah. I'm making a U-turn as we speak."

Yolanda turns and starts walking back. I freeze in place. She's caught me red-handed.

"Isn't it sick that Emily came? I can't believe it finally worked," Sahara is saying.

Slowly I turn back and face Yolanda. Now I've caught her too. "Care to explain that?" I ask when she hangs up.

She inhales deeply. "It's not what you think."

I don't know *what* I think.

"I'll explain everything later. I need to go and take care of things." She waves her phone hopelessly. "Promise me you won't leave?" She comes closer and grabs my hands. "Please, Emily, I've waited so long."

"Okay," I say. My mouth is dry.

"Walk with me." She grabs my hand and leads me back to Canyon Road. We walk in silence, but when she finally speaks, she says, "Sarah also married a douche. It's the same story. She got pregnant and married the father of her child. As if it matters." She scoffs. "So what if he donated genetic material? It doesn't mean he can be a parent."

"Tom isn't a douche. He's a great dad."

"Is he? Really? Sarah said the same thing about Richard even after he got into the habit of beating her."

"Tom never hit me," I say. She doesn't look convinced.

"Poor thing, she finally left when he threatened to hurt the baby. She filed for a restraining order."

Her nostrils flare, and I'm not sure it's Sahara's ex she's mad about. This would be a good moment for me to apologize for *my* restraining order. But I don't. I'm too mad about her innuendos concerning Tom. I pull my hand from hers. Now we walk next to each other.

"He tracked her down, though. In complete violation of his court order. Even after she found shelter at a friend's house. He made a huge commotion. The friend had to go to the hospital. Broken jaw."

"Tom has never done anything like that."

"So she had to run away. Change her name. Well, she just moved the 'H' from the end to the middle." She doesn't make eye contact, and I remember she used to do that back in the day on those rare occasions where I put my foot down and refused to agree with everything she said.

"Tom would never do something like that. He's sweet and kind and loving."

"I took her in, of course. Lucky for me, she's good at managing the gallery. Not so good with men, though. I told her she should switch teams." Yolanda giggles.

She's not acknowledging my words, and I can't take it anymore. "Why are you telling me this?"

"He's a manipulative son of a bitch." She has a crazy look in her eyes when she faces me.

"Who? Tom?" I'm confused.

"Yeah, Tom. Who do you think I was talking about all this time? He kept you locked away from me, didn't he? "

"He never locked me away!" I claim passionately in his defense.

"Yeah right, Emily. Wake up already. Gee. He got a restraining order against me. *Me*. He made sure I wouldn't be able to contact you." She continues walking, and I follow her like a berated toddler.

"Yeah. I wanted to apologize for the restraining order. It was a bit too much."

She halts abruptly and turns to me. Her face looks scary, the anger and hurt so clear in her eyes.

"It was you? All these years—" she yells and shakes her head in disbelief.

"I'm not proud of it—"

She slaps me across the face. It's so unexpected. So violent. My cheek throbs. I lift my hand to touch the wound as she covers her mouth with her palms. We face each other, speechless.

Something flashes in the back of my mind. A tip of a memory. It's not exactly a deja-vu, because I don't remember her ever hitting me before. It's the shame and humiliation that tickle my mind. The answer floats from that deep, closed chest of Yolanda's memories. It speaks in her voice.

"It means I love you, silly."

The memory unfolds itself. We're in pottery class. It's close to the year's end. Yolanda and I are already an item, but it's very hush-hush. The night before, I didn't agree with something she said, so she retaliates by humiliating me in front of the entire class. She degrades my work. She mocks my personality. Her criticism is known to sting, but this is something else. It's brutal, pure cruelty. It's murder. She went on and on until finally, Elvira, a classmate who I'm friends with, tries to speak up in my defense.

"Shut up," Yolanda shot back at her, "or you're up next."

Later, when I asked why she did it, she said, "it's because I love you." It was the first time she said the L-word.

"I forgive you," she finally says. "You're here now, aren't you? We can go right back to where we were." She taps on my stomach, and I flinch in fear. "we need to put a baby inside you ASAP. You're not getting any younger."

She grabs my hand again and pulls me as she starts walking. I let myself be dragged along as the flashback continues. I remember now why she shamed me. It was because I didn't want to have a baby. We'd had a huge fight about it the night before. She wanted me to get pregnant so we could start a family. I thought she was joking. I laughed. She was hurt. Then, I refused, saying I was too young to be a mother. Saying I didn't even know if I wanted to have kids. It was the only time in our relationship I put my foot down. I changed my mind after that cruel public shaming to "maybe someday when I'm ready." Destiny intervened and made that day come only six months later.

We're almost back at the gallery when she lets go of my hand. The foreman hollers through the broken bullhorn, although there's too much static in the message to understand the words. I slowly veer away from her, though not too far. I still want her. Desperately. But I'm bothered by the slap, and the crazy talk, and the fact she hasn't shown the slightest interest in my life.

When we pass my rental car, I quietly slip inside and before she notices, I drive away.

∼

TOM

Full of rage, I open my laptop and hammer the keys. Being a numbers guy means I have the code to tap into Emily's credit card account.

And there it is, black and white. She purchased a plane ticket to Albuquerque. One way. It breaks my heart. I read the charge over and over again, but it doesn't lose its sting. I know Yolanda's based in Santa Fe. I've known it for years. She's sent letter upon letter. I have a discreet arrangement with the postmen servicing our area. I pay a small retainer and in exchange, any mail from Yolanda Auchenko is returned to sender. Emily doesn't know about it. When she was a blushing young bride, I vowed to protect her from Yolanda's claws. And I've kept my promise ever since.

The charges keep piling up. Car rental at Albuquerque's airport. A motel in Santa Fe. Nicky's beauty salon. That last one makes me mad. She beautified herself for that freak.

Browsing through her expanses, I look specifically for one item. It's the purchase she *didn't* make that breaks my heart. She never got a phone charger.

I get up and pace about the house. Distraction, Katie said.

I gallop up the stairs then rush down, then up again. Then down. And again. My heart is racing; my blood is boiling. Again. Again. My face is dripping sweat. Again. Again. I stop by the laptop to catch my breath. I'm still angry and hurt.

I click some keys and hesitate before I hit the Enter key—and tap into Emily's phone account. Checking her credit card charges is one thing. I mean, she knows I do it all the time. She gave me permission. But getting into her phone, that's a breach of trust. I close the laptop. I can't do it.

Distraction, I think. Distraction I seek.

There are dishes in the sink. Will they be distraction enough?

Part of me says I shouldn't respect her privacy when she went willingly to see Yolanda. Another part says I'm responsible for her being with Yolanda. It says I'm the one to blame. Because I'm weak. Because of my panic attacks. If I was more of a man, she wouldn't have run away to an old flame.

And yet another part of me says it has nothing to do with me. She always liked women. Our marriage was just an interlude. I've heard lately about men who were married happily for decades before coming out as gay. But then another part of me wonders, why now? Why didn't she run off to Yolanda's when I moved into Tommy's room?

I try to distract myself by clearing Emily's mess. I fold her clothes and hang her dresses. Then I take care of the laundry basket. Did she intend to go to Yolanda when she left me a note about going to Katie's? There aren't enough dirty clothes for a full load, so I take mine off to put them in the washer. Did she mean to send me a message that I completely missed?

As I'm undressing, a business card falls out of my pocket, and I squat to pick it up. It's the sex therapist's card. I hold it for a few seconds. That guy. He seemed smart, put together. Why didn't I set up a meeting? I need help now. Should I do it? I take out my phone, flinching a little at the photo of Emily and Yolanda. It's my screensaver now.

Then I find myself by the laptop, typing away. And I'm in Emily's phone account. There was a surge of data usage yesterday, almost half her plan in one day. I scroll back and back, checking her activity over the last few months. There's nothing irregular.

So now I know. It happened yesterday.

I still don't have a clue about how it started. Did Emily search out Yolanda, or did Yolanda find a way to creep in? Now I'm going into full spy mode. I look for Yolanda's phone number in Santa Fe. I call it. What will I say if she picks it up? My heart races. A woman's voice.

"Hmmm... Sweet Pea?" she half-says half-asks as if she's not sure where she is. It's not Yolanda. I would have recognized her accent anywhere.

"Emily?" I ask, puzzled, although I know it's not her.

"Just a second," she says, and this time she sounds surer. I hear her yelling, "is there an Emily here?" And then, "Sorry, sir. Sahara is out, and no one knows an Emily."

CHAPTER 18

8/20/16

Audrey didn't get out of her bed for two days. Well, she probably did the essentials. Eat. Drink. Poop—although I didn't see her do that. I made soup. Brought a tray to her bed. When I came to pick it up, the plate was empty but that doesn't mean she ate it. She could have spilled it into the toilet.

She lay completely covered every time I entered the room. I didn't say anything. I didn't think it was my place. She needed to work things out, so I let her.

On the third day, she was finally ready to talk. I came into her room with a PB&J sandwich. She was lying with her eyes wide open.

"I knew I shouldn't have gone out of the house. Bad things happen when I leave the house!" She slammed the words in my face as if I'd made her come out to the garden.

"Well," I said calmly, "if you want my opinion, I think you've just made huge progress."

She gave me a condescending look like she was asking if I was thick.

"The way I see it, you've just slept in your bed for three nights in a row. After sleeping on that recliner for how long now? I think that's quite an accomplishment."

She scoffed.

I left the sandwich and went outside.

An hour later, she joined me. She didn't say anything about her outburst, nor did I.

I could feel Mom's smile from Heaven. When the leaves rustled, it was like Mom applauding me, although I didn't completely deserve it. After all, I didn't mean to cheer her up. It just happened.

I told Bill about the ways I connected with Mom, now that she was dead. He said it was cute and kissed me. We kiss *a lot*. Just that. So sweet!

mily

A noise pulls me out of an elaborate dream that escapes me the minute I open my eyes. At first, I don't know where I am. Dim light crawls through the slit between the closed curtains and lights the geometric pattern on the cream wallpaper. The TV is on, playing an old black and white movie. I'm wearing my good jersey dress. My left cheek is pulsing with pain. I remember.

That noise again. "Police! Open up!" It comes from the door. I jump up and open it. Yolanda is on the other side, accompanied by two police officers. They march into my room. Yolanda's a feast for the eyes with her long, silky evening gown and complicated hairdo which consists of multiple braids in a tiara over her head and the smoky makeup that makes her eyes pop and her cheekbones look high.

"What's going on here?" I mumble as they dump out my suitcase and go over my stuff.

"You're not the only one who can call the police," Yolanda whispers in my ear. She pulls her phone out and pretends to be in a conversation.

"You found it? Really? That's great!" She winks at me. "I've decided to spare you," she says for my ears only.

Addressing the officers, she changes her tone. "Orson, Jacob, guys, Sahara just found it in the gallery. It wasn't stolen after all. Must have fallen through the cracks. I'm so sorry to waste your time." She slips a fifty to each of them as they roll out of the room.

"What?" She raises her eyebrows mischievously. "I had to come up with something creative since you left me, *again*, and you don't have the common decency to answer my Facebook calls."

"My phone died," I say, confused. Because it's the only thing that makes sense right now.

"Yeah, right." She lifts her hand and gently touches the bruise on my cheek. "Does it hurt?"

I wince. "Not so much," I lie.

Yolanda's wearing silvery sandals, which show off her pretty feet. She checks the pile of clothes the policemen poured out of my suitcase. She picks up one of my jumpsuits. It's a mild one, made of geometric black and white fabric. I've removed the hood—zebra, of course—but the zippers that adjust the fitting and all the rest of the details are still there.

Yolanda scoffs as she examines it. "One of your little creations I presume." She drops it back onto the pile.

I was already pregnant when I finally gathered enough courage to show her my fashion design sketchbook. She gave it one condescending look and began criticizing my choice of pencil colors and my drawing technique. "You can't be serious," she said. "This is not art."

I was shaken to my core. Here was this woman who I looked up to, dismissing my deepest dream as if they were some childish caprice. I grabbed my sketchbook and shut it.

"Why are you so offended? I'm actually doing you a favor."

"This is not the way you treat the mother of your child!" I yelled. "I shared something with you, and you pooped all over it."

"Pooped. As if. If you can't stand the heat, get out of the kitchen, Emily. Really."

"You're not listening to me!" I cried. I stomped the floor like a child having a tantrum. I couldn't articulate my feeling into a coherent sentence.

"You're acting out, Emily, and it's not good for the baby."

Angry and frustrated, I just screamed my lungs out.

"I don't like it when you shout at me," she said and left the room. Not only did she degrade my work, but she also disrespected my feelings and somehow turned herself into the victim and forced me to apologize.

Now that we're both confined in this small space, most of it occupied by the unmade bed, there are butterflies in my stomach. I'm eating her with my eyes, and she's doing the same. Examining me from head to toe and back up again. I touch my hair in a desperate attempt to fluff it. Under her scrutiny, I'm suddenly aware of all my flaws.

"Well?" she finally says, "aren't you going to apologize?"

"I'm sorry?" I suggest while lifting my hand to touch the swelling over my cheekbone.

"For?" Her eyebrows are knitted together.

"For?" I repeat after her like an echo.

"For ditching me in the street, for heaven's sake. For forcing me to call in a favor with the police. For making me look for you while I need to get ready for my gala. Really, Emily, when will you grow up?"

"I'm sorry," I say, this time more genuinely. But I don't feel sorry. Well, not for the things she said. I am sorry for coming here and disrupting her life. I decide to do all I can to make her night special. It's the least I can do.

"That's better," she says as she leans in and gives me a peck on the lips. I know that peck. It says *I want to kiss you, but I'm afraid it'll ruin my makeup.* We've been through it so many times before, and although it's been almost three decades since, I still know how to decipher her signs and gestures. It's like muscle memory. I let my arms drop as I close my eyes and inhale her sweet aroma. I'm so turned on.

Yolanda shoves a package in my hands and orders, "Put this on." It's a burgundy pantsuit like the one she got me ages ago when we went on that notorious NYC trip. I laugh as I look at her, expecting to see a mischievous sparkle. She's dead serious, one eyebrow raised in anticipation.

But I'm no longer that slim 20-year-old who could put on anything and look great. I pick up the jacket and check the seams. It's not a just-off-the-rack suit. It's couture, and it's beautifully made. I realize she must have had this suit with her for a while. She couldn't have just purchased it today. It's weird.

"This is gorgeous, Yol, really. Thanks. When did you get this?" The fabric has a nape to it, and I can't stop caressing it.

"Hurry up. We need to be there in a few," she says.

"I can't wear fitted pants anymore."

"Don't be silly, Em-em. You can wear whatever you want. And I can see just how much you want this."

My heart misses a beat when she calls me by my old nickname.

"Okay," I accede. Picking up the outfit, I head toward the bathroom to change.

Yolanda laughs. "Don't be a prude, Emily, it's unbecoming." I freeze. "I've seen you change a hundred times before. You were never this shy."

Well, I've never had the figure of a middle-aged women before either. But I don't say it. I don't say anything. I stand with my back toward her, and although I've done it hundreds of times before, it still feels weird undressing in front of her.

I can sense her piercing eyes on my bare back. I take comfort that the motel's dim light doesn't shine on my flab. I'm vulnerable about my upper back fat, my stretch marks, my chubby underarms. But at least I'm able to hide my stomach bulge and most of the dimples on my thighs.

I'm aware of the way the air moves around me as I pull the dress above my head. I take up so much space that each movement creates turbulence. I'm torn between moving as slow as I can to create the smallest disturbance possible, to feel petite. Yet, I also want to do it as fast as I could and get it over with.

I try to listen to Yolanda's breathing. I can tell what she's thinking if she gasps. Or if her breath gets shorter. But all I can hear is the pounding of my heart as blood rushes through my veins, reddening my ears. I can sense her eyes, like two laser beams up and down my back. Checking me out like I'm a piece of meat. I dread her ruling. Is she going to find me repulsive?

The carpet mutes the clack of her heels. My breath is taken away when she faces me, catching me in the most unflattering position possible—trying to pull the pants over my thick thighs. The effort has made my panties roll down and my stomach sticks out more than usual. It looks like I'm five months pregnant. I freeze as she examines me.

Her face becomes pale for a second as she stretches her hand toward my belly. Horrified, I realize what she must be thinking. I quickly pull my panties up, hiding my bump. She pulls herself together, shaking her head like someone who wants to shake off bad memories. Then she twitches her face.

I'm devastated. My whole body tenses in preparation for a nasty remark. She wriggles her hand between my legs and rests it over my panties. Her hand is cold against my crotch, and I shiver. I'm moist. It's mostly sweat from the struggle with those pants.

"I see that Tom let you slack around," she whispers. "But now that you're with me, I'm going to take care of you. A few more weeks, and it will all go away."

With her heels, she's about an inch taller than me, and she's leaning over to whisper in my ear. "You're still sexy, though." Her hand tightens. All the blood in my body rushes to that point. She can certainly feel my arousal. Panting, I close my eyes. She always knew how to touch me. I spread my legs a bit, as much as the tight pants allow. It's an invitation. But she doesn't bite.

"Later, babes. We're in a hurry now." She moves away from me.

"Here, use these." She throws high-waisted Spanx at me.

"I hate wearing shapewear. I wore it for Marni's wedding and—"

"Chop chop, Emily. Less talking, more dressing."

So, I take off the pants and put on the damn thing. It smooths my muffin top but makes it hard for me to breath.

"Marni? Is that her name?"

There's so much pain in her voice, I hesitate before I answer. "Yes."

"And she got married?"

"Last summer."

"Tom must be proud," she adds after a few seconds of silence.

"Well, he's prouder of our youngest. Tom Junior. He's a

computer whiz. Got a full scholarship for MIT." I'm babbling. As if words could cover the shame.

"Pfff," she scoffs, the jealousy dripping.

It was a mistake to mention the kids. Desperately trying to change the subject, I ask casually, "What's with Sahara? Did she come back safely?"

Yolanda doesn't reply. She gives me a harsh look and another wave of shame washes over me. I concentrate on getting the damn outfit on. Only when I'm done do I dare give her a glance from the corner of my eye. She's looking right at me, as if she was waiting for me to make eye contact.

"Are you set on ruining me completely?" she asks with a soft tone that doesn't match the harsh words. I flinch. Here it comes, I'm thinking, *this is it.*

"I was kind enough to invite you to an event that is very important to me. I was willing to let bygones be bygones for everything you did to me back then, although I'm still hurt. And what do you do?" She counts my felons on her fingers. "You arrive hours early. You scare off my manager—"

"It was a mistake," I say, interrupting her mid-sentence. She ignores me and continues with her speech.

"Which makes me take care of things on my own while I needed to rest. And then instead of helping me out, you make yourself scarce without a word, and I need to chase you. Call every sleazy motel in town like I'm in a fucking rom-com. I need to focus on *you* instead of getting ready for my big night!"

My lips are shivering.

She shakes her head. "And now, you're worried about stupid Sahara! You didn't even bother to ask how *I'm* doing!"

"You're right, Yolanda. I'm so sorry. How *are* you doing?"

She rolls her eyes, and I feel stupid. And small.

"I'm sorry. I shouldn't have come," I say. I unzip the pants and take off the jacket. There are two sweat circles in the underarm area. It's cold, nervous sweat.

"What are you doing?" she yells, and I jump up. "Put it back on!" she orders. And I do exactly as she says. I'm extremely uncomfortable in the suit. The fabric clings to my hips and pressures my waist. It's synthetic and doesn't allow my sweat to evaporate. I pull it in all directions but there's not much stretch to it.

"I'm sorry, Yolanda. I'm sorry for everything." I wring my hands, bite the inside of my cheek.

She gives me a fiery look. "Are you sorry you left me? That you threw me away like a piece of garbage?" Her nostrils flare.

I nod miserably. "Yes," I whisper. "I'm sorry for everything."

I feel so awkward. These clothes. This behavior. It's not me. I miss Tom. I miss him so much.

"We'll continue this talk later," she says. "I don't want to be late because of *you*." She angrily mutters the last word.

"You can go at the gallery. Come On! Let's go!" she raises her voice when I head to the bathroom.

"I want to fix my hair. Put on some makeup."

"No need," she says so I puff my hair without even looking in the mirror and groan as I bend down to put on my boots. The suit is pressing against my internal organs.

"You really should take the stairs," she says when we reach the elevator. "You need the exercise." Her eyes rest on my heavy thighs. The pants seem like they're about to explode. I nod quietly and head over to the fire exit. It's not easy navigating in the fitted suit. I'm one story down when I notice she's not behind me.

"Yolanda?" I call, tilting my head up.

"I'm already here," she answers. Her voice comes from downstairs. She took the elevator. Of course. I don't say anything when we meet. Not even when she announces we're going to take my car.

I need to unbutton my pants in order to get into the driver's seat. She grunts when she sees me do it.

"Sorry," I whisper.

"That's alright, Em-em. You're still attractive." She slides her hand over my knee.

I almost go off the road. She laughs and moves her hand up, almost to my crotch, and we drive quietly until we reach Sweet Pea.

Her mood changes. I'm still tense, though.

The gallery is jaw-droppingly amazing. Christmas lights drape from the roof like a curtain of stars, sparkling in blue and white and making the yard look magical. The bronze statues are illuminated from the bottom with colorful spotlights, changing from purple to green to yellow, each color emphasizing another feature of the piece. Sometimes it's the eyes that pop while the figurine looks like a creature from a horror movie, but then the light changes, and the nose is highlighted, and it looks so real it triggers my olfactory sensors. All the potted plants scattered between the exhibition pieces are sweet peas, and they fill the air with their delicate, spicy-sweet aroma. Soft classical music plays, completing the setting.

"Yolanda, it's…wow. I'm speechless. I mean, what a show for all senses."

She caresses one of the statues. "It looks like bronze, doesn't it? But it's plastic. 3D printing."

I'm properly impressed, considering the way the space looked only a few hours ago. Everything is elegant and chic. Compared to this, the charity events I've produced are dull and inept.

Decorative dividers close off small, intimate spaces in the gallery and create a walk-through maze that guides visitors through the exhibition. The award-winning figurines are placed on little transparent shelves at different heights along the partitions. There are glasses of white wine and trays of finger food concealed in the corners. I reach out to grab a glass. Yolanda slaps my wrist. It's like a reflex.

"I'm not underage anymore," I laugh.

Squinting at me, she says between gritted teeth, "You don't need the empty calories."

Is she pissed again? Her rapid mood swings puzzle me. I don't know how to react, and the moment passes. There's already a small crowd inside. They cheer when Yolanda enters. She looks absolutely radiant with happiness. Her hand is casually wrapped around my waist as she guides me through, showing me off like I'm a trophy wife.

She directs me toward an elderly lady with big hair.

"India, dear." Yolanda air kisses her. "And this is my...Emily."

"Hello." I stretch my hand out with a smile. Her eyes glide over me from head to toe. I'm embarrassed about my ridiculous look. I caught a glimpse of my face in the rearview mirror while driving and was horrified to see my swollen eye.

"Oh my," the woman named India says when she finally takes my hand. "I've heard so much about you."

"India was my first patron in Santa Fe. When I moved here, I was heartbroken and devastated, of course, and she was consoling and supportive. She is a great advocate of the arts."

India nods. "Yolanda has always spoken so kindly about you, Emily, despite everything. You're the one who got away —as the youngsters say. I'm glad you found your way back."

I can hear the doubt in her voice and see it in her rolling eyes. She must have pictured me differently. I smile nervously. It's flattering to know Yolanda never got over me, but it's also nerve-racking.

And that is what I say to Sahara when I can finally escape Yolanda's grip.

She's standing by herself at the back, holding a glass of white wine and not even pretending to mingle. She's wearing a light-pink tutu skirt and a black bodysuit. Her uncombed hair falls wildly over her face. She's not wearing any makeup, and she looks tired. glazy stare in her eyes it's obvious she's drifting, daydreaming. She's miles away, probably in a dark place. Only when I get closer, do I notice the child concealed behind her, sitting on the floor with a unicorn coloring book and some crayons. She's shading a horn with dark pink.

"Sahara, hi."

She's startled. "Oh, hi." Her face is glum, and it gets darker when she sees me.

"What happened to you?" She looks terrified.

I touch the bruise. "Oh, that? I fell." She gasps. I don't know why I said that. Why am I covering for Yolanda? It's the ultimate excuse of the battered woman. Is that what I am now? Is that how Sahara acted when her husband abused her? Horrified with this version of myself, I lean forward and touch Sahara's shoulder.

"I'm sorry. For earlier. I didn't mean to cause a kerfuffle."

She waves a dismissal.

For a minute we just stand next to each other. It seems like both of us don't belong in this artistic gathering.

"Love your outfit," I say finally.

"Oh," she looks down at herself, "I didn't have time to shower. I put the skirt over my yoga gear. Hope it's not too noticeable."

"Mommy? Mommy, who's that?" The child points at me coyly.

"That's Emily. She's auntie's Yolanda special friend. Remember she told us about Emily?"

"And you must be Apple," I say. I try to squat down to her level, but it's impossible in my outfit.

Apple examines me with her pretty round eyes. "No, mommy. That's is not Emily. Emily isn't old and fat."

"Apple! That's rude. Apologize to Emily," Sahara's snaps.

"Sorry," she says reluctantly and picks the pink to color the unicorn's tail.

I shrug. "She's right, though. I am old. And fat." After a moment of silence, I add, "Yolanda forced me into this ridiculous getup. Since it's her big night and all, I didn't want to disappoint."

"Really?" Sahara raises an eyebrow. "Because I'd have thought by now she's pretty used to being disappointed by you."

"I guess I know where your daughter gets her rudeness from," I mutter.

"Excuse me?" Sahara opens her eyes wide as she looks at me. With that astonished look, she resembles the little girl she once was.

My heart mellows. "Do you remember that summer you spent with us? I think you were about six or seven years old."

"Of course, I do. It was when my parents split up. I stayed with you guys for a week." Her voice is softer, and her eyes have a dreamy, nostalgic gaze. "You taught me how to sew," she reminisces. "We sewed clothes for all my Barbies."

"I remember we drove all the way to Lake Eerie on the weekend. You were in the back seat, asking if we were there yet every five minutes."

She laughs. "Yolanda says when she saw you playing with me, she knew you'd be a great mother." She frowns. "The next summer, you were already gone. And I was so looking forward to spending it with you."

"I'm sorry." I touch her forearm.

"You never said goodbye," she whispers. The area under her eyes gets moist. "I thought I did something wrong. I thought you left because of me. That you didn't want me to play with the baby."

"Of course not! I'm so sorry you felt that way." It's the first time I realize there were deeper repercussions of my sudden departure from Yolanda's life.

"Come, Emily." Suddenly Yolanda is there, dragging me to meet and greet more of her friends. I shake hands and say, "Nice to meet you, too," while smiling my fake smile. Inside, everything rumbles. Does Yolanda feel that? She looks somewhat mad and gets madder as the introductions continue. I forget the names and faces the minute they're out of my vision.

And then I make the mistake of saying, "Nice to meet you," to someone who I was already introduced to five minutes ago.

Furious, Yolanda drags me to the caterer staging area, which is separated from the room with another decorative divider.

"Are you deliberatively embarrassing me?" Yolanda says through gritted teeth.

"What? Of course not. Quite the opposite."

She grabs my elbow forcefully.

"Ouch! Yolanda, that hurts!"

"Good." She mutters.

A waiter carrying a tray full of wine glasses passes by. We both force a smile and wait until he's out of hearing distance.

"Stop acting like a stupid cow, Emily," Yolanda orders and storms away. I stay put for a few seconds while waiters come and go and frown at the sight of the huge obstacle standing in their way. Then I go back to being a wallflower, standing a few feet away from Sahara. I don't want to engage in a conversation anymore. I don't want to be presented and paraded anymore. I just want this night to end.

I try to gather enough courage to confront Yolanda. A serious talk is due. She's mingling in the crowd, holding a glass of wine just for show. She talks to a middle-aged man wearing orange pants. Her head is tilted to the side as she listens, and then she bursts out in laughter, pats him on the shoulder and moves on to the next guest. She's like a queen bee at this event. In between small talk, she scans the audience nervously. Her eyes meet mine and in an instant, her shoulders relax. Sahara leans over. "Do you see what an impact you have on her?"

I nod.

"Maybe she put you in this outfit to reenact your trip to NYC, if you know what I mean." She raises her eyebrows.

"She told you about that?"

"Yep. Amongst other juicy stuff."

My face reddens.

Sahara chuckles. "It was a part of a crash LGBT course she gave me when I hit puberty."

"Didn't she—" I don't know how to ask without being rude.

"Didn't she what?"

"I get that she was hurt after we broke up, but after a while, I mean, we were together for a year, which is not that long comparatively."

"She had other relationships, if that's what you're asking. But she's a tough woman to be with, as you must know. And you're her soulmate. You were The One."

I shake my head.

"She's been sending you messages for years. Tried to contact you through different channels, never fretting when it failed. She was certain that one day you'd pick up and you'd be in sync once more." She knits her fingers together.

"What do you mean? What channels?"

Sahara shrugs. "I don't really know."

After a moment of silence, she adds, "Yolanda says you were always on the same page. On everything. Until this man muddled in the middle."

"What man? Tom?"

"He stole you from her. Stole her Sweet Pea. Forced you into marriage."

"He didn't force me to anything."

She shrugs. What has Yolanda told her? Some kind of twisted version of our relationship?

"And how could he have stolen her gallery?"

"Your baby. Sweet Pea," Sahara says.

I'm confused for a second. "Oh, do you mean Pearl?"

"Is that what you named her?"

I smile. "No. Her name is Marni. Yolanda referred to her as Pearl when she was a fetus."

Sahara twitches her face. "I'm pretty sure it was Sweet Pea. She said she named the gallery after her."

Looking down I say, "Maybe I'm mixing things up. After all, it was a long time ago." But I know my memory is intact. Sweet Pea doesn't bring any physical reaction, while Pearl makes my stomach twist and turn. I wonder what else Yolanda's twisted. All these people in the room, the ones she's been proudly marching me around to meet. What version of the truth do they know?

"Yolanda is so good with kids," Sahara says. "It's a tragedy she can't have any of her own, isn't it?"

"Can't she?"

"Well, duh." She rolls her eyes and shakes her head as if this is common knowledge.

"What do you mean?" I'm perplexed. Did I know Yolanda couldn't conceive? Did we ever talk about it? My confusion is probably showing.

Sahara's quiet. Then she turns to her kid. "Come, Apple. It's already past your bedtime." And they stealthily disappear to the apartment at the back.

~

I stalk Yolanda from my corner, changing places as she moves through the maze of the show. I keep asking myself why I came here in the first place. What did I want to achieve?

I check my memories from the early years of my marriage. We worked hard, Tom and me. We both had our side hustles. We needed them to make ends meet. With Tom doing the taxes for other teachers and keeping books for Windy's dry cleaning and Sela's bakery. And me, sewing Halloween costumes until the middle of the night on the dining room table. Warm nostalgia fills me up. Despite all that, we had some good times. We were happy. It was challenging getting a graduate degree while working part-time and raising a baby, but Tom was there to support me. He shared my happy moments and comforted me when I was down. He listened. We were a team. I remember Marni taking her first steps, Tom and I yelling in excitement, encouraging her. Then she fell asleep, and we made sweet, tender love on the rug in the nursery.

With Yolanda's big ego, there was room in the relationship only for her. My wishes and ambitions were never taken into consideration. She would have never encouraged me, like Tom did, to take a sabbatical and pursue my long-life dream. She wouldn't even have bothered to ask what that dream was. I made the right choice when I picked Tom. My heart aches with my love for him.

But it doesn't quench my desire for Yolanda.

Her throaty laugh pulls me out of my contemplations.

She's flirting with a young, curly-haired woman, who gazes at her with adoring eyes. Is she doing that just to make me jealous? It's working. The knot in my chest tightens. Yolanda gives me a quick glance. She expects me to interrupt, to erupt, to make a public scene that will expose my feelings in front of her friends.

She did that on our New York trip when we ran into one of her exes. I recall how miserable I felt when she threw herself on Nora, fake laughing while stealing glances at me. When I couldn't stand it anymore, I went outside to cry. She came quickly after me.

"Why didn't you fight for me?" she asked. And I just shrugged. I'm not going to leave in tears this time. She can flirt if she wants to. It doesn't humiliate me more than my ridiculous suit. Am I attracted to her? Sure. But other than that, I don't feel any deeper connection.

It's 9 p.m. when the crowd begins to disperse. Sahara emerges from the back room, all cleaned up and wearing a golden satin dress that emphasizes her petite waist. A baby monitor is attached to her belt. She approaches me at my wallflower post and hands me an object. It's a doll-size denim jacket with a few embroidered embellishments. I recognize it and raise my eyes with a smile.

Sahara is grinning. "I kept this piece of art because it's so pretty and delicate," she says. I hand it back to her. "Like you," she adds while gently caressing the fabric.

"Thank you," I mumble. My mouth is full of saliva. This is the first time anyone has called my handy work art. People used to say I was talented. Some described me as a gifted seamstress. But no one has ever called me an artist. My heart goes out to her.

"Listen," I begin to say, without really knowing how I want to continue, when Yolanda interrupts our private moment.

"What's going on here, ladies?" The jealousy is spread all over her face. It makes her look grotesque. She also seems somewhat drunk. Not going-to-throw-up drunk, but more than tipsy. She drops her hand heavily on my shoulder. Leaning in, she sucks on my neck. That's going to leave a mark.

"Ouch," I say.

She laughs. "Oh, darling Emily. I knew you'd come crawling back. I just knew, didn't I?" She faces Sahara on that last part.

"Yes, you did. Never gave up faith." Sahara smiles. "It was the Twitter tag that got your attention, right? Tagging the high school where both of you used to work?"

"Was it?" Yolanda's tongue is heavy in her mouth.

I have no idea what they're talking about. I don't have a Twitter account. Yolanda sways on her heels. I wrap my hand around her waist to keep her balanced. Touching her makes me dizzy as well.

"Oh," she says.

Looking in her eyes, I can spot the passion in her enlarged pupils.

Without dropping eye contact, she says, "Emily and I need to go and take care of a pressing matter." She grabs my hand and pulls me to the apartment at the back. Once we're inside, she locks the door behind us.

In a matter of seconds, Sahara tries the handle then knocks on the door. I'm leaning against it and can feel the strikes pulsating on my back. Yolanda crushes her lips onto mine. Her hands are mussing with my hair. I want it. I want it so bad. Slipping my tongue deep into her mouth, I press my hands on the nape of her neck.

"Yolanda, open up! Apple is asleep there."

"Go away," Yolanda growls when she stops for air. I don't know if Sahara walks away, but the banging stops.

Well, on *that* side of the door. On this side, we're just starting.

Yolanda tears my jacket open and releases my breasts from my bra. She spoons the girls in her palms as if she's trying to estimate their weight. They used to be perky and small. Now they sag heavily, but that doesn't seem to bother her. She moves her thumb over my hardening nipples. My eyes are half shut. It's been so long since I've been touched like this. I get goosebumps.

When we kiss again, I crush my body against hers. I lift her dress, take it off. She's not wearing a bra, and when our skin touches, it's electric. I suddenly realize *this* is what I came for. Sex.

Yolanda looks deeply into my eyes. "Are you ready to betray your marriage vows?" she whispers hungrily, as if she takes pleasure in the idea. Tom's face floats before my eyes. I flinch.

"No." I push her away and force myself to cool off.

I don't know if Yolanda doesn't hear me, or if she just isn't taking no for an answer. She unzips my pants, and they fall to my ankles. She relieves me of the tight shapewear. My first response is to breathe out with relief.

"No," I say, somewhat louder. "Please. Stop."

She slides her hand between my legs. My knees get wobbly. My eyes are shut, and a groan escapes me. It's so good. But it's also so wrong.

I grab her hand. "No, Yolanda. Stop."

She ignores me. Her hand is down my underwear, her fingers searching, spreading my labia. I want it, and I don't want it at the same time. I'm too weak to resist. Behind shut eyes, I see Tom's lucid blue ones. I imagine it's his index finger massaging my clit. She's moving her finger too fast, too strong, it's actually disturbing. But I'm so aroused.

I try to fight it. I don't want to climax, but she pulls it

out of me, forces my orgasm. My knees turn into butter, and I collapse to the floor like a puppet whose strings are cut. It's a physical reaction I can't control. I don't enjoy it, not even one bit. And while my analytical self is still blurred by this veil of bodily relief, a sharp, terrible insight consumes me.

She's never going to let me go.

She grins at me when I finally open my eyes. I'm slouching on the floor next to the door and she sits on her hills across me. I don't smile back.

"What?" she asks, puzzled. "That was good for you, wasn't it?"

"I asked you to stop."

"But you liked it!"

"It doesn't matter. I told you to stop." I'm overcome with sudden exhaustion.

She leans forward and rubs her nose on my neck. My skin gets itchy again. My breath shortens as she licks my cheek.

"See, your words say one thing, but your body is telling a different story." She nibbles my earlobe. Her hand is back between my legs.

I push her away. I don't use a lot of force, just enough to create some distance between us. She falls on her butt.

"Em-em. Come on. Don't tire me with your juvenile games."

I don't respond. I don't even gift her with a look. I'm bewildered with shame and guilt, trying to collect my thoughts.

"My turn," she says. Kneeling on all fours, she turns her rear toward me and starts crawling back. She's wearing a Brazilian-cut pantie, and once again, I'm amazed at how fit she looks. She comes to a stop very close to my face.

"No," I say firmly.

She squeezes her butt over me. It hits my collarbone.

With her legs spread apart around my waist, she brushes her slit against me.

"You were always such a taker, Emily. You need to give something back."

"No." I push her. She falls on her nose. I get up and put on my clothes. One of the buttons on the jacket is torn. I hold it closed with my hand.

She puts on her dress. When we face each other, we're both fully dressed. She has crazy eyes. It's as scary now as it was three decades ago.

"I'm not a piece of clay, Yolanda. You can't shape me to your every whim." I don't know where it comes from.

"No," she thunders. "You were this beautiful, rare flower I groomed and nurtured and when you finally bloomed, someone else picked you and stole you away."

I shake my head.

"But now you've come back to me." She puts her hand on my cheek, just under the bruise. It still throbs. Her hand shakes, and I can see the pleading in her eyes.

I take a deep breath. "Tell me about Sweet Pea. I know she wasn't my daughter."

For a moment, a vulnerable woman stands in front of me. She doesn't need to tell me. Sweet Pea was her baby. She's never recovered from her loss.

"I'm so sorry," I whisper.

She shakes her head, and the tough Yolanda is back. "Sweet Pea is the baby your husband stole from me."

She's too deep in denial. I can't help her with that. All I can do is give her some closure. Maybe it'll give her the strength to move on.

"I *chose* Tom, Yolanda. He didn't force me into anything. We have a good life together."

"Yeah? Then what are you doing here?"

"We may have hit a rough patch," I admit, "but I'm going

to mend it. I'm a great seamstress." I smile. Because I know it's true.

She scoffs.

"When I met you—" I stall for a second, trying to find the right words. "I adored you. You were this amazing artist, and I was a naïve, provincial child. I'd never met anyone like you, and the fact that you liked me..." I stop for some air. "It meant the world to me. Truly." I look her in the eye with compassion.

She flinches.

"But our relationship—" I ditch the eye contact because it's too damn hard to say what I need to say. "It was a fake. I was never your soulmate. I lied the entire time just to make you happy." I look at her again. Her face is a mask of agony and pain. My vision blurs with tears.

"I gave you everything," she whispers. "I handed you the world on a golden plate."

I nod. "You did. And I'm grateful for that." I want to touch her forearm, but I don't dare. "But it was *your* world. It was never mine, as much as I wanted to be a part of it." I put one hand over my heart. Speaking the truth is so liberating. "I tried so hard to please you, and in the process, I forgot who I was."

"You're lying," she hollers "You're *lying*."

I shake my head.

"You loved me! It was love at first sight. You said so."

I shake my head again. I pity her.

Her fists clench. I'm scared she's going to hit me again, but I don't even wince. If she needs to hit me in order to let go, so be it. "I'm so sorry," I say. "You deserve to be with someone—"

"I gave you faulty condoms! On purpose!" she yells. Then, realizing what she's just said, she puts her hand over her mouth.

I'm in shock. How could she do that to me? For a second we just stare at each other.

"Then I should thank you," I finally say. My voice is so little. "You gave me the best gift I ever got." I turn the key and open the door. Sahara stands guard on the other side. By the look on her face, she's heard everything.

"Goodbye, Sahara." I grab her hands. "You're so pretty." I pass her, waddling. Behind me, Yolanda's screams. It's a scream of a wounded animal. I don't look back.

CHAPTER 20

The forecast predicted a thunderstorm. I invited Bill to stay the night. He's so young and sweet. He snuck in after Audrey went to bed. I didn't know if she'd approve. We'd never discussed the option of me having an overnight guest—there had been no need.

He came for dinner as he does twice or thrice a week now. Audrey *still* hasn't exhausted the subject of the Sikhs—she's done some research and expanded on the subject. Now she talks about other belief systems in India, mainly Hinduism. She's into yoga too and exercises in the living room every morning at sunrise.

Bill told me he needs to educate himself every time he comes over. He started reading books about India and has reconnected with his family for the sole purpose of gathering enough authentic information to share with her. I appreciate his dedication. He's an impressive young man.

He told his parents about us, he said. And they object, not because I'm double his age, but because I'm not Indian. The fact that I come from different origins disqualifies me as his partner. It's very upsetting. Bill said I should ignore it, which I try my very best to do.

Anyway, we were having dinner. The storm hadn't started yet, but the air was humid and heavy. I could feel it in my bones, and I was very anxious when I asked, "Bill, would you like another piece of pumpkin pie?"

It was made from the first pumpkin of the season, harvested only the day before. Bill gave it to me so I could make my famous pie.

"Bill?" Audrey asked, curious.

Only then did I notice what I did. Bill and I looked at each other, and then, in a poor attempt to fix it, we spoke together.

"It's my name," Bill said.

"It's his nickname," I said.

Audrey looked at both of us, a wrinkle forming in the middle of her forehead. "Which one is it? Your name or your nickname?"

We spoke together again.

"It's my nickname," Bill said.

"It's his name," I said.

That got Audrey even angrier.

Bill sighed. "It's my given name, but I don't use it anymore. You can keep calling me Sunjay."

Audrey pushed her chair back, making a terrible scratching sound, and walked away from the table, carrying her plate. We looked at each other, horrified. Was she going to throw me out?

She returned a minute later. "I'm not so fragile, you know. You don't need to hide things from me just because I'm a grieving mother."

Bill nodded, and I followed his lead.

"Duly noted," I said. That wasn't the reason we didn't tell her. She's simply not the nicest person around.

She went to her room and slammed the door. Bill helped me clean up. Did I mention how sweet he is? The thunder began when we were almost finished. I started trembling.

"What is it?" he asked.

And I told him. "I'm afraid of thunder."

"But there's nothing to be afraid of. You're 100 percent protected when you're inside."

"I know," I said. My voice is small, like I was a child again. "It must be genetic. I got it from Mom."

He held me as the storm got stronger and closer, and we spooned in my narrow twin bed. I was shaking like a leaf. He kissed me gently on my neck and shoulders and made me forget my fears. He's such a tender lover, maybe the most delicate I've ever had. He always makes sure I'm comfortable, asking for my consent before every move. That's so nice.

We didn't get much sleep last night. When the storm cleared out, he snuck away. I'm not sure if Audrey noticed. She gave me a look in the morning and asked how I handled the storm. I'd told her about my inexplicable fear of thunder during one of our first talks. Surprisingly, she remembered.

I said I handled it with care, which was not a lie.

om

The clock chimes for 6 p.m. and my stomach replies with its own music, composed by hunger. I grab my keys and go to where it all started falling apart. Beirut.

The restaurant has just opened. Nasim is pouring olive oil from a huge jar into the small table containers. The entire space has a pungent, fruity smell. I inhale it deeply. It's comforting.

He puts down the jar and comes to greet me with his big smile. "Hello, my friend." He takes my coat. "Welcome, welcome! We did not expect you so early, but Leila will be pleased. She had made all your favorite foods."

I make an effort to laugh at the stale joke.

"And where is the lovely Emily?" he asks.

I shake my head. "She's not here today."

"Oh, so sorry," he says Clearly embarrassed, he disappears into the kitchen.

Then I see *him*. The therapist. His jacket is crinkled, and his tie is stained. He's sitting at the dark corner table, feasting on pita bread dunked in olive oil. He nods slightly when he sees me, and I nod back. He pushes the chair across from him with his legs, distancing it from the table. Gesturing toward the chair with his head, he invites me to sit with him.

I accept.

With a sigh, I sit down and check my phone. It's a reflex. There aren't any alerts. I haven't traded since Emily's quiet exit.

The therapist wipes his oily lips with a napkin and says, "I do have an office, you know."

"Excuse me?"

"You didn't have to come here hoping to meet me."

When he puts it so bluntly, I realize how desperate I am. "I don't believe in therapists."

"And yet, here you are," he says and smiles. Looking stealthily toward the kitchen door, he pulls out his flask, takes a sip, and offers one to me. I take it. Apple juice this time.

"So, let me guess. The feud with your spouse has escalated. You're miserable and lonely, and you want to get her back."

"That's pretty much it," I say, astonished at the accuracy of his guess.

Nasim comes out with our firsts. Quietly, he spreads the salads on the table. I miss his usual show where he explains every dish, declaring its ingredients. Suddenly, I lose my appetite. I poke the salads, eating a tiny, shiny leaf out of one, only a drop of hummus from another.

"Don't feel bad about it," the therapist says while munching on his kebab. "We men are educated to conceal our emotions. To not show even the slightest weakness and never seek help."

He's got it all right.

"It's all bullshit," he says. "Maybe it was like that in the twentieth century, but not anymore. See young men now? They're much more in sync with their feelings."

I think about Marcus and the way he cried when he and Marni exchanged vows. I felt so sorry for him, but Marni looked at him lovingly and cried with him.

Nasim brings the coffee and baklava for the therapist, who doesn't say a word while he enjoys his dessert. The only sounds are slurping as he drinks the hot black beverage and crunching as he chews the sweets.

I'm looking at him, waiting for his next pearl of wisdom. He gets a small planner out of his pocket. Browsing the pages, he says, "How about Monday morning? 8 a.m." He pushes the table as he gets up.

I don't reply. He starts to walk away.

"You didn't give me an address," I shout after him.

He smiles when he turns back, and I realize it was a trick and I took the bait. He scribbles something on a clean napkin, taps on my shoulder with empathy and takes his leave. Now I have something to look forward to. Monday at 8 a.m. I write it in my phone. I 'll have to be late for the first period.

I'm back at home, again in search of distraction. Looking over my phone, I reread the daily mail from Tommy's app about the rare opportunity with Bitcoin. Too risky, Tommy said, don't get into it. Bitcoin exchange rates are known to change rapidly. Currently, one Bitcoin equals almost $20 grand.

But what if I monitor it 24/7? It would be quite a distraction. *And* I could even make a big win. Would Emily be pleased if I earned enough money for our retirement?

My hands shake when I open a credit line in the bank. It's a lot of money.

I call the school. I need to clear my schedule for tomorrow. I plan to leave a message, but Brenda picks up. Shoot. I forgot there's a school board meeting tonight.

"Hi, Bren, it's Tom." I do my best to keep it casual. "Just letting you know I'm going to be on another personal day tomorrow."

She sighs. "Are you sure, Tom?"

"Of course I'm sure," I say angrily.

"Please, reconsider. You're already on edge, and we got another complaint about you yesterday from David O'Keefe. Says you were impatient with him and at class yesterday," she lowers her voice on that last bit.

"He came unprepared for the second time this week and I was somewhat unforbearing. So what?"

"The board is discussing your matter right now," she whispers.

"Fuck them," I say and hang up. It's so unlike me that I shake all over. I can't believe I said that.

And then, my whole future becomes clear. It's like I've been walking in a thick fog and have reached a turn after which the sky is clear, and the path is bright.

I'm going to quit my job, go all-in on this transaction.

I'm going to take Emily on her dream trip to the Appalachians or wherever she desires. I'm going to win her back, even if it means no more teaching. My heart clenches a bit at the thought, and I try to rationalize. I can retire at fifty-five years old, and that's only five years down the road. And this generation of millennials, they have no respect. They don't want to develop their analytical thinking, they want everything served to them already chewed, like they're little birds.

No. I've made up my mind. After this deal, I'll go to Santa Fe and do whatever it takes.

I make the transaction. And then I wait and watch. I've set up alarms to ring when a threshold is reached and another alarm to wake me up every hour in case I fall asleep.

With the Bitcoin exchange rates flicking on the big TV screen, I use my laptop to make some smaller transactions. I get a few dozen dollars here and there. I'm quite content.

The first text comes just after midnight.

You took her from me, now I'm taking her back.

It comes from an unrecognized number, but I know who it is. Why is she so eager to gloat? The next comes two hours later.

Your wife likes to eat cunt.

I flinch. It's so crass. And uncalled for. I stare at the text for far too long. It's already early morning when another one comes in.

You'll never be able to give her that you dirty old cock.

My finger hovers over the delete button. These texts pick at an open wound. I'm bleeding inside. Well, metaphorically. But then again, sometimes there's pleasure in picking at a wound, slowly peeling off the fresh pink scab. I keep the texts but block the number. I can't have any more distractions right now.

I monitor my phone all day long. Around noon Prices reach the tipping point where I should sell according to Tommy's predictions. But then they recede back. I need my full concentration on it. Yet, my mind keeps wandering. What is Emily doing right now? Is she in bed with Yolanda? The nasty texts flash before my eyes and bring a wave of cold sweat. I know it's my fault. I've been off my game for too long, and now I miss her so much. I'm such a fool. I should have gone to a therapist a long time ago. I should have taken better care of myself.

The price is cruising again, so close to the threshold. I'm going to have an enormous gain. I don't stop to check how much, but it's going to be huge. I need my full concentration now. My finger is on the button. I need to press it any second now.

Any second.

I'm tense and focused on this one thing, on the one specific moment that will change the trade momentum, when another text message comes in. It's Katie.

Emily's here.

A few seconds later, she sends another text with a crucial, one-word addendum. *Alone.*

But it's already too late. I've missed my cue. The alarms I've set are ringing and ringing. The numbers are spinning, down, down, down.

CHAPTER 22

Today was the 27th of October.

It was a glum and gray day. I didn't feel any cosmic twenty-seven energy rein on me like I usually feel on the twenty-seventh of each month. Maybe it's the fall. We had the first frost about ten days ago, and since then, the garden has been in hibernation.

I don't feel Mom inside the house, and now she's not in the garden either. I miss her so much.

It was windy most of today, and I sat outside all morning and tried to connect with Mom. I couldn't feel her presence at all. Not in the wind. Not in the falling rain. Not in the low-hanging clouds. It's the first time since she died that she's acting dead.

Did I do something wrong? Why did you leave me?

Bill called around noon, cheerful as usual. He asked if I'd like to come and help him set the store up for Halloween. "Sunjay agreed to distribute free candy from the soon-to-be-expired pile," he said, chuckling.

"Well, isn't it a bit too late to start now?"

He turned quiet. My glumness killed his enthusiasm.

Ever since that thunderstorm, he's been sneaking into my room every night. We no longer have dinner with Audrey. She's super busy with a secret project she works on in her office, and I barely see her. Only when she needs something does she come out to bark at me.

"Better late than never, right?" Bill said. "And speaking of Halloween, isn't it the night of the dead? Maybe your Mom would come."

I sighed. Mom won't come just because it's a holiday. She hated Halloween with all its sugary-rushed kids roaming the streets for their next fix, being rude and demanding.

"I'm not really in the mood for Halloween," I said.

I could hear him breathe. "Okay," he finally said, "tell me what I can do to cheer you up. I hate to see you like this."

I sighed. "There's nothing you can do." Which was true, because he couldn't roll back time.

Audrey was getting ready for trick or treaters too. She set up some decorations on the outside and prepared a huge basket full of candies by the door. She even got herself a costume. Well, a unicorn jumpsuit. I watched her from the living room, where I sat in the La-Z-Boy watching re-runs of *Friends*. Maybe it was me, but I didn't find the show funny like I used to.

CHAPTER 23

mily

By the time I reach the motel, my whole body is trembling. I stumble to my room, chain the door behind me, and collapse next to it. The events of the last hour flash in my mind over and over. At moments I feel violated, victimized. And then I remember the words I said, and I feel stronger.

I wish I could talk to someone. I want to hear Tom's voice. If only I could remember his number. When I try to hug myself, my sleeves tighten over my upper arms. Angrily, I take off the jacket. The pants. The Spanx. It makes me feel a little better, but then I smell Yolanda all over me, and I rush to the bathroom. As the water warms up, a little voice in the back of my head tells me I shouldn't shower. *You'll destroy evidence. You should go to the police,* this voice says. *You should go right now.*

So I grab my stuff hurriedly, just push it into the bag as quickly as I can. At first, I plan to leave the clothes Yolanda gave me behind, but then that little voice says I must take those too. Scanning the room for something to wrap them in, I finally undress a pillow and stuff the suit and Spanx inside it. Then I stand by the door, trying to visualize what's outside. I'm afraid Yolanda will be standing there, lurking in the dark. I'm anxious to leave, yet too scared to go outside of the safe shelter of my room. When I hear footsteps and voices in the corridor, I quickly take my leave.

At checkout, the receptionist asks if something is wrong with the room. "Is that why you're checking out?" she asks while processing my bill.

"No, no. It's—" Uncontrollably, I move my hand up to touch my bruise.

"Ouch," she says. And then that little sane voice inside my head speaks again.

"Can you please take a picture?" I gesture to my eye.

She agrees. "Would you like me to email it to you with your receipt?"

My email address escapes my mind. Luckily, it's already in the system from when I checked in this morning.

"I'm afraid I'll have to bill you for the night," she says, and I agree. I'll pay anything just to get out of this place.

Then I'm back at the rental car, inhaling deeply. Trying to calm my shaky hands before I hit the road.

There's a police station a few blocks away from the motel. I pull over with every intention of reporting Yolanda when a patrol unit stops by and an officer jumps out. He looks like the policeman that visited my room earlier this afternoon. I remember how Yolanda paid them off, and I drive away.

"And then I just drove." I'm completing the story of my impromptu adventure in Land of Enchantment.

I didn't plan on driving all the way to Anaheim, California. Not even when I saw the sign *Welcome to Arizona*, or when I passed the Mojave Desert. My hands were glued to the wheel, my foot hard on the pedal. I followed Route 40 like a fanatic follows a guru. And when the road ended, I felt lost. I blinked against the road sign like a blind person seeing for the first time.

I'd driven all night. It was full daylight when I stopped at the junction, blinking against the sunlight. It was the way the sun shone on me that made me realize I was in California.

It's like there's a love story between the sun and the Golden State. It's not the harsh, direct light of New Mexico or the scarce, remote winter light of the Mid-West. The winter sun in California is soft and caressing. *It's probably time*, I mumbled to myself and set the car's navigation system for Katie's. Good thing I'd memorized her address.

She wasn't home. I knocked and rang the bell and called out her name until the next-door neighbor gave me a terrified glance. I could see her silhouette hiding behind the light curtains. I waved at her hoping she might call me inside. She didn't. I sat back in the car, and the next thing I knew it was dusk, and Katie was leaning against the window with a worried face.

"It's a wonder you arrived here safely after what you've been through," Katie says. "I'm so sorry, Em." We hug one more time. We wipe our eyes. Then we sit in silence.

"I'm sorry, sis," I finally say and put my hand on the back of Katie's hand. It's full of age marks. Being twelve years older than me, she was like our mother's deputy as we grew up, always taking care of me.

"It's fine."

"I meant sorry for sitting you next to Aunt Gloria at Marni's wedding."

She waves a dismissal. "It's water under the bridge. It was stupid of me to get so angry about it in the first place."

And just like that, our feud is over. That's all it took. We smile at each other, and I look deep into her eyes, like we're having a staring contest. It's something we've played ever since I was a toddler. And as always, she out-stares me. I laugh my heart out. And here I was, only minutes ago, thinking I would never laugh again.

"I'm so proud of you. The way you stood up to her."

I shake my head. "Can I use your phone? I need to call Tom."

She slides me her mobile phone.

"Also, I need his number."

Katie chuckles. "It's listed under Tom." She slips away from the kitchen, mumbling something about setting up the bed in the guest room.

"What now?" Tom says when he answers. His aggression overwhelms me.

"It's me," I say dryly.

He doesn't say anything. I can hear the clock chiming, driving me crazy even thousands of miles away.

"I'm sorry I didn't text you earlier. My phone died. I forgot the charger thingy at home."

"I know," he says. He sounds so distant and cold. "I found it on your dresser."

There's a pause. A weird one.

"I miss you," I say softly.

"Emily, I'm in the middle of something right now. Can I call you later?"

"Sure," I say. The rejection kills me. I don't know if I have a home to go back to.

I'm still sobbing when Katie returns.

"What's going on?" she asks.

I fall on her shoulders.

"It's Tom. I think we're done."

She shakes her head. "No way. I don't believe it."

I take a deep breath. "When we came back from Cambridge after we dropped Tommy at college, he said he needed some time and moved into Tommy's bedroom. I figured he was emotional, you know, I was overwhelmed as well with the empty house and everything. But it's been months now, and it's just getting worse."

"I'm so sorry, sis. I had no idea." She has tears in her eyes. "I should have called."

I wave a dismissal. "Water under the bridge." We smile at each other from beyond the tears. Her eyes are brown like mine, but hers are almond-shaped while mine are rounder.

We sit together at the kitchen counter as the shadows elongate. It's been a year and a half since we last visited. I'd accompanied Tommy on college tours of the west, and we'd stayed with her for two nights. Everything looks the same, except for the cat. Alfonso was a spoiled Persian she brought in after her divorce more than a decade ago. Now a striped American Shorthair is snuggled on her lap, purring. It hisses when I try to pet it.

"Careful. Natasha is very sensitive to new people."

I tell her about the math Nazi. About Tom's recent panic attacks.

In the dim light, I can see the crease on her forehead deepening. Until our latest stupid feud, Katie was my confidante and best friend. We used to talk daily, filling each other in on the latest happenings in our lives. She always had good advice for me or a kind word that helped me find comfort in difficult times.

It's almost dark now. The streetlights turn on, the only light in the room. The darkness suits our conversation.

"I shouldn't have left him in his state. I'm such a fool."

"I can't believe you went to see her of your own will,"

Katie says. She gives me a pack of frozen cauliflower to put on my eye. It helps with the swelling. She doesn't say anything about the hickey on my neck.

"It's like she puts me under a spell, K."

"There are no such things as spells." It's the scientist in her that says that. The same scientist that told me to toss the clothes I'd kept as evidence and take a shower already. Without semen, there's no DNA proof.

"I know. It's just..." I swivel the empty mug. "I was wondering what it would have been like if I had married her instead of Tom."

"So? You visualize. You fantasize, Milly! You don't go poke the demon."

"You're right. I know. I repressed all my memories of that year with her. Forgot how narcissistic she was."

"She's nuts," Katie declares. "Like all artists."

"Don't say that!" Sahara called me an artist. My stomach flickers. Does Katie mean to say I'm crazy too? I shiver.

"Like that guy, Van Gogh. Cut off his ear because someone said he had a nice one. Would a sane person do that? I sincerely doubt it."

"That's only one example," I say defensively.

"Come on. All the good ones have quirks, to say the least. I've done my research. Picasso was obsessed with women. Drove some of his models to insanity."

"She's hardly a Picasso." I chuckle at the comparison.

"All I'm saying is that this woman is obsessed with you. She's been trying to reach you throughout the years. Sending letters. Messages. Tom was so happy when you weren't interested in Facebook or social media in general."

"Did she? He never said." I wonder about all the secrets he keeps from me. It's as if I don't know him at all. There's a knot in my stomach. Am I like Yolanda, who thinks she loves me but doesn't know the first thing about me?

"We made a pact, Tom and I," Katie says after a moment of silence. "To shield you from her. Guess we've done well so far." She chuckles bitterly.

"You did that for me?" I whisper.

She gives me a look. It's not a judgmental look, yet it's not a loving one.

"Remember the day you left her? I was working at Belvia and you stopped by. Tom was with you. Remember?"

I nod. "Vaguely."

"That's the thing with you. Your memory has always sucked. You got it from Dad." She crosses her legs. Natasha meows in protest.

"Anyway, I liked Tom for you. He was stable and smart and seemed to love you like crazy."

"But not Yolanda-crazy," I say.

She smiles. It's a bitter smile. "When you went to the bathroom that night, we decided we needed to guard you against her. We knew she wouldn't give up on you so easily. Little did we know... Anyway, the next day I went to her place to retrieve your staff. Remember that? You were too scared. You had a restraining order."

"I remember the restraining order."

"Well, amongst your things there was a letter from her."

"What did it say?" My voice quivers.

"I don't know. Never opened it or any of the other messages she sent throughout the years. Tom sent all the letters back with an address unknown stamp." She shrugs. I can barely see the movement of her shoulders, it's so dark now. "Tom loves you, Emily. I know that for a fact."

I shake my head. "He was so cold when I called earlier. I just can't take it anymore."

Katie holds my hands. "Do you still love him?"

I chuckle. "You know, this horrible experience just made it clearer to me. He is the love of my life, Katie. These past twenty-seven years— I mean, it wasn't always a smooth ride, but it was good because we were together."

"Oh, yeah. Congrats on your anniversary," Katie says.

I smile. It's a crooked smile.

Katie gets up. "Don't tell him I went to see her," I say quickly before she turns on the light.

"Not my story to tell," Katie concludes. As she turns to leave the kitchen, she stops in the doorway and turns to me. "Don't keep it a secret though, if you want to fix your marriage. Keeping secrets in a relationship will only drive you apart, take it from my experience."

I take a deep breath and call Tom again. I'm all for second chances.

"Emily?" he says when he picks up. "I'm so sorry." His voice sounds so full of pain.

"What's going on? Tom?"

He doesn't answer. He sobs. And in between, he keeps saying how sorry he is. Over and over again. My first thought is that he has another woman. All this time I thought he was grieving, he's was actually having an affair.

"Do you have someone else?"

Now he starts laughing. I know that laugh. It means I couldn't be further from the truth.

"Are you having a stroke? Should I call 911?" I've never heard him sob before. Even at his father's funeral, when everyone else broke out in tears.

He sniffles. He gets a grip. "I'm fine. It's just—" And then he sobs again.

"Oh, baby. I'm catching a flight and will be with you shortly, okay?

"No! Stay the weekend," he orders and hangs up without giving me the chance to reply.

~

Katie's guest room bed is so soft, and I'm exhausted, both physically and mentally. My phone is all juiced up, and there's a new text from Tom.

Sorry for being such an eggplant emoji. I need a minute to figure out some stuff.

I smile at the eggplant emoji. Instead of adding the pic, he literally wrote the words. My heart goes out to him. Apparently, I'm a sucker for witty wordplay. But I also heard this exact phrase months ago.

I write back. *Maybe we can figure it out together.*

The reply arrives in no time.

I've made a mistake, and I need to do some cleanup.

Now I feel even worse. What did he do? He refuses to give me more details.

While I wait for more texts, I browse the other messages that have accumulated on my phone over the last two days. There's the usual spam about my close relative who died in Africa under mysterious circumstances and left me a fortune, and a newsletter I'm subscribed to showcasing new sewing notions on sale this weekend. There's also the receipt from the motel with my photo enclosed.

I've been looking at it for some time when I notice the little floating head on the right side of the screen. It's Yolanda's. When I tap it, my previous conversation with her opens. There are many new messages starting from yesterday afternoon when she repeatedly typed *where are you? Why don't you answer me?* And then a little bit after midnight, *You have ruined my life, now I will ruin yours.*

There's a small picture enclosed. I enlarge it and see it's me, trying to fit myself into those tight pants. She must have taken it when I didn't notice. I look horrible. Fat and ugly.

My face flushes and I'm scared for a second. But looking at the photo again, I realize that although I do look ridiculous, I fail to see how it's going to ruin my life. I'm not naked.

I'm photographed from the rear, and only a part of my face is showing. It's a photo of a middle-aged woman with some flab. My teenage students might have a quick laugh about it, but that's it.

Realizing that makes me angry. How dare she threaten to ruin my life! And what was my crime? Not fitting into the box she's created for me? Refusing to bow to her every whim?

I need Katie's help with my reply. Together we manage to extract the photo of my black eye from the email and move it to the Facebook chat. We phrase a clear message to accompany it.

I also have a volatile photo I can send out to everyone you know. Wouldn't the Governor like to know how the winner of a prestigious award behaves?

Her reply comes in a matter of seconds, like she's monitoring her phone.

You are nothing but lowlife scum. No one is going to believe your lies.

Katie grabs my phone. *They don't need to believe me. I have DNA to prove you molested me.*

She adds a photo of the suit.

"But you said this DNA was useless," I say.

"Yeah. We're bluffing," Katie says with a smile.

It's probably working because Yolanda turns quiet. I re-read. our last exchange. This poor, pitiful woman has been hooked on delusions for most of her adult life. I think about the people I met on my trip. Doctor Leary. The tattooed Christian couple. Sahara. Those people, they had to make tough choices in their lives, and they came through. They had to let go of their past. I hope Yolanda will be able to do that as well.

I won't press charges if you move on with your life, I write.

I want to add an emoji that reflects my feelings and I go

through the entire set on Facebook before I find what I'm looking for. It's a black circle. *Emily's biography,* I caption it and hit send.

I don't know if Tom and I can patch things up, but I do know the Yolanda chapter of my life has come to a complete and utter end.

~

TOM

Friday evening, there's a knock on the door that wakes me up. I've spent the last twenty-four hours on the couch in the living room, desperately trying to come up with a solution for the deep deficit I've created, with no avail. The Bitcoin rate exchange plunked about 40 percent in a matter of seconds, and 40 percent more since then. I lost so much money, there's no escape but to sell the house and everything else we own. And even that won't be enough.

I stroke my scruff as I approach the door.

"Welcome back," I say as I open it. I'm certain it's Emily, ignoring my request to stay away for the weekend.

It's Patrice. Brenda, a foot behind her.

They flinch when they see me. No wonder. I haven't showered for god knows how long. And of course, all the scruff. I see myself through their eyes, and I also cringe.

"Oh, sorry." I'm the first one to get a grip. "I thought you were Emily."

"Where is she?" Brenda snoops.

"She's out and about," I say lightly. "Did we schedule a meeting for tonight?"

"We were just checking on you," Patrice says. She sticks a casserole in my hands. It smells like cabbage. "Can we come in?" she asks in her matter-of-fact tone.

I don't want them to come in.

"For Christ's sake," Patrice says and rubs her hands against each other. "It's freezing cold out here."

"Of course, sorry." I clear the pathway. "I wasn't expecting company," I say as I lead them to the kitchen. It's somewhat more organized than my living room cocoon, with all the printouts of our savings and my financial calculations. Brenda sniffs the dirty dishes in the sink and catches a few crumbs from the breakfast counter on her finger. The smugness on her face is dreadful. I know what everyone at school will be talking about Monday morning. Emily would be devastated. I try to wipe and shove everything into the dishwasher at the same time.

"There's coffee in the cabinet," I say, and Brenda makes herself useful.

"Not that one. I try to point her in the right direction, but of course, she must open them all before she gets to the right one.

"No need to clean up on our account," Patrice says. She sits carefully on the edge of one of the breakfast stools. Her voice is sharp and drips bad news. I take a deep breath and prepare myself for what's coming.

"Where did you say Emily is?" Brenda asks sweetly. She sets up the coffee maker.

"She's at her sister's." The words slip off my tongue. Only when I hear myself say them, do I realize I've said it out loud.

Brenda gives me a fierce look. "Her sister? Really? She didn't tell me she'd planned a trip when we talked the other day."

Now it feels like I'm being interrogated. "Well, she doesn't need to consult with you prior to visiting a family member, does she?"

Brenda's neck turns deep red. I bite my tongue. Mistake after mistake after mistake. I'm such a loser.

"I mean, because she's on sabbatical," I say quickly, attempting to fix it. There's no use. The verdict has already been decided upon, and now all that's left is to deliver it.

Patrice clears her throat. Right then, I notice she's wearing a suit. This is not a social call. And it's come at the worst moment ever.

"Look, Patrice," I say while at the same time, she speaks.

"Tom, you're clearly not well," she says.

"I'm well enough to come back to school on Monday."

She clicks her tongue and tilts her head a little. I've seen her give this look to troubled kids who are sent to her office.

"You can't fire me."

Brenda begins to chuckle. She sounds hysterical. What is she doing here anyway?

"No one is going to fire you, Tom." Patrice stretches her hands in my direction. "You're one of our most valued teachers. We're just worried about you." Now Brenda nods vigorously. I get it. She's Patrice's wingman.

"I appreciate your concerns, but I'm doing just fine. I'm eager to get back to my students." It's no use. Nothing I say will change Patrice's mind. I see it in her rigid posture.

"The school board has decided to give you a leave of absence until the end of the school year."

"What? No!"

She lifts her hand ready to block any objection. "We would like you to take this time to rest, heal, regroup, and we hope that you'll be able to return stronger next school year."

"No, Patrice. Please, I'm sorry for what I said. You can't let me go right now. I desperately need the money!" I look at Brenda and Patrice alternately. I don't care anymore about my own humiliation. I beg and plead like a student who just got expelled. "Brenda, we've known each other for so many years... Please, tell her."

Brenda lowers her gaze to avoid eye contact.

"Patrice, I beg you. Please, anything else. I need that paycheck."

She shakes her head. "I'm sorry, Tom, it's out of my hands."

"I thought you were making big bucks with that app?" Brenda treads lightly.

"I did," I admit. "But I recently made a mistake, and now I'm in huge debt. We have to sell the house." I don't care anymore. It's all going to be out soon anyway.

"Is that why Emily went to her sister's?" Brenda leans toward me, her eyes sparkling. It's disgusting.

"Emily doesn't know yet, and I'd appreciate it if you'd keep your mouth shut and let me be the bearer of bad news, thank you." She turns red again. I don't apologize.

"Tom, your plea is very touching," Patrice says without real empathy. She's struggling to stay detached. "Let me see what I can do, okay? I don't want you to starve."

"Thank you." I move in to give her a hug and stop midway. This is, after all, an official call, not a Christmas party.

"I can't have you teaching again before you're cleared with a counselor, but we'll hold a fundraiser for you," she says.

"I already have a therapist appointment scheduled for Monday," I say quickly.

"Really? You're going to a therapist?" Brenda twitches her face, "I thought you didn't believe in them." Ouch. So *that's* why Patrice brought her—so Brenda can be the bad cop. After all, she knows everything about everyone, ready to pull out the dirty laundry with glee.

"Well, a person is entitled to change his mind, isn't he?"

Patrice raises her hand before Brenda replies.

"I'm sorry, Tom, for upsetting you in this time of need. I wish things were different."

"Yeah," I agree. "And if I may ask, next time you need to bring such joyful announcements, please come on your own." Brenda blushes. "Or maybe call me in for an appointment in your office."

Patrice nods. "Brenda's here to take the minutes because it's an official school matter. I thought it would be easier for you in your domestic environment. Maybe I was wrong to assume that."

"I see. May I please get a copy of the minutes before you distribute them to the board?"

"Of course," Patrice says and gives Brenda a sign. They head toward the door.

"Give Emily my regards," Brenda says sweetly as she slips on her coat.

Patrice waits until Brenda steps outside before leaning in and whispering, "I truly am sorry, Tom. Really. I'll try and think of something, okay?"

CHAPTER 24

November 7th

So, I spent Halloween night in the cemetery. I camped out next to Mom in the hope she would appear. She didn't. It was silly of me to listen to Bill. *And* I got a terrible cold. I stayed in bed for a few days. Audrey said it was fine, that I get to have sick days. Or at least I *think* I heard her say that. She's quite impatient with me lately.

Today was warmish, so I sat outside for a while and tried to reconnect with the higher power. Mom was nowhere to be found.

Audrey stepped out at some point. She brought me a cup of tea and asked if I was hungry. I knew she meant that *she* was hungry and that I should go inside and cook her dinner. After all, that's my job. I could sense her agitated energy.

"I'll go inside in a minute," I said. She lingered by my side then she bent down and gave me a hug. I leaned into it. Fibers from her wool sweater tickled my nose. She smelled like lavender and mold. Mom wasn't a hugger until she got

188

sick for the first time. After that, she couldn't get enough of it.

Audrey's hug was long enough for me to feel her pulse. I heard the rush of blood through her arteries. Boom-boom. Boom-boom. It became slower as the hug continued. Finally, she let go with a sigh.

"What was that about?" I asked, looking up to catch her eye.

"Did you know I used to be an inspirational speaker?" she asked after a long pause. It was a rhetorical question. Of course, I didn't know, because she never told me.

"I've been working on a new piece. Would you like to hear it?"

I nodded. "I could use some inspiration."

She gave me the whole spiel. First, she stuffed herself into a suit. She did her hair and makeup and wore black pumps. I'd never seen her look so smart. She plugged her laptop into the TV and played the presentation. It was polished and well-rehearsed. She was fluent in it, like one of those TED speakers. It started off with a photo of Charlie as a little boy. She told a funny little story about him, how he was a rascal, a curious young boy who one day dug up the entire back yard because he saw a rainbow that seemed to end there, and he was looking for the pot of gold.

There's a picture of him, holding a jar full of chocolate gold coins. His father buried it during the night and encouraged Charlie to do some more digging in the morning. Audrey also appeared in the photo. She looked radiant, her head tilted back as she laughed full-heartedly.

She went on to say how Charlie became a lazy teenager, and how she, as a divorced single mom, couldn't contain it. The way she said it, so open and honest, wasn't the same person I'd met a few months ago. She said how the military service turned Charlie from an undisciplined young man into someone with purpose and meaning. And then she paused for a second with a photo of Charlie's tombstone.

"And it made me lose all purpose and meaning," she said. It was profound. "I made myself a pariah. I neglected myself. Didn't leave the house. Insulted my neighbors who were only trying to help. I gave up on life."

The next slide was a photo of me, working on the vegetable patch in the back yard.

"This is Seven. Seven Twenty. An angel sent to me from above, disguised as a housekeeper."

My cheeks flushed. I was no angel nor housekeeper. And it was my mom who directed me to Audrey, for my sake, not hers. I was so infuriated, I missed the next slide or so and heard only her final words.

"The same way as my Charlie, I have found meaning through discipline and hard work. Thank you."

I straightened up in my seat, not sure how to react.

"So, how was it?"

"It wasn't true. The thing you said about me."

"It's *my* truth," she said and unhooked her laptop. She seemed angry. "Look, Seven," she said as she sat next to me. I hate it when people call me by my name when there are only two of us in the room. "Whether you meant to or not, the truth is, you helped me deal with my grief."

I scoffed. Because she was lying. Maybe not to me, but to herself. Grief can't be dealt with. It's always there. She was the one who'd told me that when we'd first met.

"I'm going to start a charity in remembrance of Charlie. It's going to be for troubled teenagers who struggle to find meaning in life. And I want you to be my partner."

The house turned silent. I hoped to get a sign. Nothing.

"Think about it," she said but I felt her disappointment. She wanted me to say yes.

om

Tommy calls minutes after I list the house on Craigslist.

"Dad?" He sounds worried. My heart misses a beat. He calls only in case of an emergency. I'm so overwhelmed, I can't handle a Tommy problem right now. "What's going on?" he asks.

"You tell me."

"I don't want you to be alarmed, but I think your identity has been hacked."

"What? Really?" I can't believe it. It's not just a misfortune events piling up anymore. It's like I've been cursed.

"Yeah. I just got an alert from Google that someone listed the house for sale."

I gasp. I forgot he has a series of alerts regarding family matters.

"Dad?" he asks when I don't reply.

"No. Yeah. It was me," I finally say. "I put it there."

He turns quiet. I don't know how to break the news. I mean, he advised me against the investment, and I did it regardless. It should have been the other way around, him making mistakes despite my warnings, and me rebuking him for disobedience.

"Dad," he sounds choked, "are you and Mom getting a divorce?"

"What? No! Where did you get that idea from?" Did he find about the Yolanda fiasco? Did that bitch tag him as well? His sigh of relief makes me realize he's just a little boy worried about his parents. Then again, maybe he senses something. Maybe we *will* get a divorce after Emily finds out what I've done.

"I've— I did something I'm not proud of." He's going to find out about it eventually, and better sooner than later. "Your mom doesn't know about it yet, so please keep it to yourself."

"What is it? You're scaring me with this long exposition."

"Okay. Here it comes. I'll tell you." I take a deep breath.

"Spit it out, Dad. Just say it. Are you gay?" he asks when I take another minute to ponder.

"What? Of course not! Where are you getting these ideas from, Tommy?"

Maybe he *does* know about Emily. Maybe this is his subtle way of approaching the subject. but again, his sigh of relief makes me realize he's just making wild guesses. Tommy was always a whiz kid when it came to numbers, but people and relationships were never his strong suit.

"It's about money," I say. "I went ahead and did that risky Bitcoin deal." My voice breaks.

I hear Tommy click frantically on the keyboard.

"Dad," he finally says," when did you get out? I see it sank by about 40 percent in a matter of minutes."

"I..."

"Dad!"

"I thought it would go up again. I was monitoring it the whole time. I lost concentration for one second, and it all went spiraling down like crazy."

I hear him breathe. He's grinding his teeth. "How much damage?" he finally asks.

I hesitate for a few seconds. "Enough to put the house on the market."

"Mom is going to be mad."

"Yeah." I agree with a sigh.

"But Marni," he gloats, "she'll *freak*."

"Yeah." I close my eyes. I've ruined everyone's life.

"Well, at least you're not being hacked," he says joyfully. I don't know how to respond to that.

"Got to go, Dad, take care."

"Love you," I say, but he's already hung up. I sigh. He needs to process, I think. And it'll be hard once he realizes the extent of my debt.

My phone is still close to my ear when he calls back.

"Dad, I'll sell the app."

"What?"

"We were going to sell someday, right? You were just beta testing it. Figured we could wrap it up nicely, sell it on the Apple store."

"How much will it cost to get it wrapped up nicely? And how much will you charge for it? And what if someone makes a mistake like I did? Aren't we liable?"

"Oh," he says. He drums on something while he thinks. "I know! We'll sell to one person."

"Who?"

"I dunno. Rich dude. It must be worth like, I dunno, a mil?"

I sigh.

"Tommy, I truly appreciate you trying to help, but you

keep your app. Don't sell it in a rush. I'm going to figure it out."

"But the *house*, Dad!"

"Well, maybe it's time for us to downsize now that you're in college and Marni's married." I'm choked. It's the end of an era.

"Okay, Dad. Let me know if I can do something."

"Will do. Now don't do anything stupid, son. Don't hack some bank account on my behalf."

He chuckles.

"I mean it, Tommy! Promise me."

"Geez, Dad. Don't be so dramatic. I promise not to do anything until you tell me to. Happy now?"

"Yeah." I heave with relief. "Thanks."

"And you don't do anything foolish, either. Maybe I should tweak the app, so it won't mention too-risky operations." He says the last bit as if to himself. And then he hangs up without a goodbye.

～

EMILY

The flight back east was even worse than the flight to Albuquerque, although this time, I didn't spend half of it in the bathroom. Sitting in the middle seat between two punks got me pretty irritated.

The dirty-looking teenager sitting by the window pretended to be asleep underneath huge headphones. His stinking breath seemed to be directed exactly at my nostrils, no matter where my head was turned. On the other side was a tall man, folded into a fortune cookie, his legs barely squeezed into the narrow space between the rows. I don't know how he managed to get himself into that seat, but once he succeeded, he fell asleep with his chin on his chest. Twice I had to wake him up when I needed to use the restroom, and we danced the weird airplane dance, full of *sorries* and *excuse me.*

Between the crying baby two rows ahead and the toddler kicking the back of my seat, I had barely minutes to relax and prepare for the serious talk I planned on having with Tom as soon as I arrived. He'd ghosted me for the rest of the weekend.

"Let him be," Katie had said when he'd rejected yet another one of my calls. That time, I'd tried to outsmart him and used her phone.

"He's not well, Katie. I'm worried."

"Stay for a few more days," she said when I asked her to help me purchase a flight ticket.

But I was too anxious to go back and Katie, sighing, helped me with the process on online purchase.

"That's weird." My credit card was rejected.

"Here, use mine," Katie drew a black card out of her purse. "Please reconsider," she said as I typed in the digits. "Tom's clearly going through some stuff but whatever it is, you need to let him deal with it on his own. He'll talk to you when he's ready."

Standing next to me, she slams her palms against her thighs with frustration. The sound brought back an intense memory of the time I'd told her I was going to move in with Yolanda.

"It's a mistake, Em," she'd said. And when I kept packing my staff, she added, "I'm not saying break up with her, I'm just saying take it slow. It's your first adult relationship—don't rush into it."

I hesitated for a second, my finger hovering over the Enter key. Ignoring her advice back then led me to this point.

Yet, if I had followed it, I would probably never have met Tom.

I complete the purchase. She exhaled loudly.

"I do plan, though, to follow your advice about being honest and open with Tom," I said as a peace offering.

She grabbed my shoulders and leaned her head on mine. "I trust you know what you're doing," she whispered.

I chuckled ironically. "Oh, Katie, I wish I knew."

"Yeah," she said and gave me another hug. "Don't be a stranger, sis."

I nodded. It was so good to have her support again.

It's pouring angrily when the flight from hell finally lands at Detroit Metro. Within one minute of stepping outside the terminal, I walk into a puddle. Cussing, I run to the Ground Transportation Center. The shuttle bus departs seconds before I arrive at the bay, then a passing car splashes me with muddy water. I'm still wet when I arrive back home forty-five minutes later.

I'm relieved yet troubled to see Tom sat in his usual position, hunched over his phone.

"I'm home," I call without waiting for him to acknowledge my presence. I still don't know how to tell him about Yolanda. All I've got is, "I'm sorry," and I plan on using that as an opener and seeing where it takes me.

Then Tom's by my side. "Emily!" he yelps. There's so much joy in his voice.

The hickey on my neck cleared during the weekend, but my eye still looks funny. I used makeup to disguise it, but Tom sees right through it.

"What happened?" He points at it.

"Oh, it's nothing." I crouch to take off my soaked

footwear. My feet are two blocks of ice. It'll take hours to get warm again.

"Let me help you with that." He kneels and easily helps me out of my boots. "Poor baby, you're shivering. Go ahead and warm up by the fire. I'll bring your slippers and make you a hot drink."

"Careful." I smile when he comes back with my fluffy clogs. "Don't spoil me too much, or I'll go to Katie's more often."

He chuckles and gives me a peck in the middle of the head. I want more.

"Why didn't you park in the garage?" he asks casually from the kitchen. I follow him there. I can't stand not seeing him, not even for a moment. I hug him from behind. He doesn't flinch, and I consider that a win.

"Did you park your precious in the street?" I can't believe he cleared the space for me. It's so thoughtful of him.

He freezes in place. Leaning over the counter, he exhales deeply. "There's something I need to tell you," he says, and there's so much pain in his voice.

My hands fall and I retreat. Disoriented thoughts buzz through my mind like a meteor shower. *He's got someone else. He knows about Yolanda. He's going to leave me.* And then, out of nowhere, I just know that something happened to the car. Poof! Everything clicks. *That's* why he was remote, why he didn't want me to come back.

"Tom," I ask softly, "did you ding the car?"

He doesn't respond.

"I don't care about the Infinity, honey. Tell me what happened."

Tears fall from his eye silently. "Did you total it?"

He shakes his head.

"Was it stolen?"

"No. No." He can't look me in the eye.

I grab his hands. "Tell me," I whisper.

"I took it back to the agency," he finally says.

I'm confused. "But you love that car."

He's sobbing again. I reach out to hug him, but he kneels and hugs my legs.

"I can't hear you, Tom. Get up!"

When he doesn't, I lower myself to him. We sit on the kitchen floor, leaning against the cabinets as he tells me the news.

I don't really get it. "What do you mean by *everything?*"

He takes a deep breath. "We have to sell the house and cash out some of our 401K."

"Sell the house," I repeat after him like a fading echo.

"I'm so sorry. I'm such a fool." He's weeping.

I can't stand it. "Tom." I hold his face and wipe out his tears. "I don't care about the money. Never did. Never will. So, we'll sell the house. I don't care if we live in a trailer, as long as we're together."

He holds on to me like a scared child. I caress his back. Soothe him. "I'm so sorry, Em."

"That's all right. Guess we'll have a story to tell our grandchildren, if we ever have any." He chuckles, which is exactly the response I was after. I grin. This is the right time to tell him about Yolanda. I hesitate for a minute.

"Was it hard for you to part from your precious?" I finally say.

He shrugs. "They gave me half of what I paid, but it's better than nothing." He gets up and leads me to the garage. The old elliptical machine is gone. So is the old fridge and the power tools. "I made a swoop sale over the weekend. That's why I needed the time," he says. He looks me in the eye. It's like an invitation to come clean.

Inhaling deeply, I find myself asking, "So how much money did you gather?"

"Not enough for the first payment—which is due tomorrow."

I inhale deeply. "Tom. I have a crazy idea. I know what you're going to say, but we're in a deep hole anyway, so getting it deeper won't change a thing, I mean, if it does end like that."

"You're scaring me, Emily."

I start pacing the garage. I'm excited. "I want you to put all the money we have right now on the crypto market."

"*What?*"

"Yeah. Buy. Sell. I don't know how it's done."

"Are you crazy?"

"Maybe I am." His eyes sparkle. "But up until this stupid mistake you had it working flawlessly. You clearly know what you're doing. It's been, I don't know, six months since you picked up this hobby? And this is the first time you've lost, am I right?"

"Well, it was a learning curve at first, but lately I was able to score big. Yes."

"So, you can do it again. Don't you see? This is the quickest way to get out of debt."

"I don't know—"

"Tom. This is just a bump in the road. You need to get back on the horse."

"Are you sure?" He twitches his nose.

"Yes, I'm sure. Go on. Do it. Right now."

We don't go to sleep. I buzz around fetching printouts, extra strong coffee and sandwiches while he sinks into spreadsheets and formulas. Working on both of our phones and the laptop, he mumbles quietly to himself as he trades.

"When the alert pops off click the red button," he instructs me.

My eyes are almost closed when the beep wakes me, quite horrified I click something on the screen.

"Good one, Em." He smiles. "You just made a 0.2 percent profit."

"I just pressed the button like you told me. A trained monkey could do it."

He laughs for the first time since I got home. I guess things are looking up.

"Hey, how about this being our activity?" he asks.

"What?" I look at him like I'm a dimwit.

"You're always looking for stuff we can do together. You know. Ballroom dancing and such. Maybe this can be it?"

What on earth is he thinking? How could this boring thing be our activity? I grit my teeth. *At least he's trying.* At least I know he's heard me and my desperate search for a fun couple's activity. "I'll try," I finally say.

It takes about four pots of coffee and intense staring at Tom doing his thing before I realize. Tom! Where's the clock?"

He shrugs and looks at the empty space on the mantle. "Sold it," he says. "Thing was driving you crazy."

Washed with a wave of love, I run over to hug him. "You're the best husband ever."

He goes rigid under my touch, and I let go. We still need to work on that.

It's early morning, and the birds have started their happy morning chirp routine when Tom finally lifts his head up, yawning and stretching. He has gray scruff all over his face. His eyes are red. He sighs. "I think we'll be able to keep the house. For now." He scratches his chin. "We'll have to take a second mortgage and borrow against our pensions. I'll do accounts for more businesses. Maybe I'll go Lyfting." his gaze becomes blurry as he brainstorms future jobs, "And you'll need to really up your business, Em. Find a way to make a quick profit or postpone it for a while. I'm sorry. I know it's been your life's dream, but maybe you need to go back to teaching."

I acquiesced quietly although deep inside, I'm quite terrified.

His phone beeps. He looks at it and twitches his face. "Oh," he says.

"What's that?" I straighten up. I'm exhausted. This week was too much. I'm not sure I can take another piece of bad news.

"It's a reminder of an appointment I have. Remember that therapist from Beirut?"

I nod. It seems like ages ago.

"Well, we clearly can't afford it now."

"No." I put my hand on his arm before he has a chance to cancel. "It's too important, Tom. You need to go."

He gives me one of his looks. His eyes are red and puffy from lack of sleep, but they're still beautiful. He nods, just slightly. "All right," he says and goes upstairs to shower.

Only after he leaves, do I realize the discrepancies in his schedule. Doesn't he teach eleventh-grade A.P. Calculus on Monday mornings?

I'm too tired to dwell on it. We've had enough honesty for one day.

CHAPTER 26

Bleak Friday

'm still **exhausted** from cooking Thanksgiving dinner yesterday. Audrey is certain hard work is going to heal me. What a pile of rubbish.

She decided to revive an old tradition of hers and invited lots of people from the neighborhood, plus some of Charlie's old friends. I was supposed to cook for twenty-seven. Bill brought in a crate with all the produce she ordered. Three turkeys? How could I roast three turkeys in one oven? Twenty pounds of sweet potatoes? Pumpkins and pecans and potatoes enough for a whole platoon.

Well, I made it. I started Wednesday evening and pulled an all-nighter. Everything was great. Cooked to perfection. But I didn't enjoy it so much, especially when I found out there were only about ten of us, including Elijah's dog Bolt or Scotty or whatever. Audrey used the twenty-seven against me. She laughed at my face when I said she'd mocked my beliefs. I think she's still mad because I didn't want to become her partner in that charity.

There was so much left over that after dinner, Audrey and Elijah roamed the town looking for hungry homeless people who wanted a nice hot meal. They left the dog behind, and I had to walk it. Bill could have done it I guess, but we'd had a huge fight.

Audrey warned me a few days ago that he was going to propose.

"Oh," I said. That was so unexpected, and I needed Mom's advice more than ever. But she was nowhere to be found. In the graveyard, I kicked her stupid stone so hard, I thought I must have fractured my ankle. But it was fine. I was able to limp back to Audrey's.

Bill popped the question right after desert which was a pumpkin carrot cake with cream cheese frosting. Everyone at the table was half passed-out, digesting, but when he knelt down, they woke up, cheering and clapping with excitement.

"Can I think about it?" I said because I didn't want to upset him in front of everyone. They all turned quiet.

Bill knew I wasn't going to accept.

Later, in the kitchen, he said his parents were pressuring him to have an arranged marriage, and he wanted to get married to put a stop to all the nagging.

"I'm sorry, Bill. You're very sweet, but I don't think marriage is for me. Not even a fake one."

"Why are you being so negative lately?" he asked angrily. "You turned down Audrey's kind offer, now you reject my proposal. What's wrong with you?"

He left through the back door. Didn't answer when I called him later and hasn't talked to me since.

What IS wrong with me?

om

Exhausted but hopeful, I arrive at the old soap-factory-turned-clinic. Emily would probably say it's chic or something, but I see the sad story of our times. Factories being closed, people losing their jobs. I see poverty and misery. A new lick of bright paint won't change the fact there were hardworking men and women laboring in this building. People who had dreams and hopes. Where are they now? Drained away, like soap remnants in the bathroom?

The receptionist is a middle-aged woman with a lovely smile. I can't help but smile back.

"You must be Tom," she says, and I nod.

"Oh dear, you've got to help me here. The therapist said you'd be paying with digital money. I'm afraid I don't know the first thing about it."

I swallow hard and almost choke on my own saliva. "I would like to pay with cash, if that's all right with you," I say when I stop coughing. There's a couple of hundreds in my wallet from the low-scale yard sale I held on Craigslist this weekend.

"Oh no," she rejects my money. "He said digital for a reason. I probably should learn how to deal with it. Twenty-first century and all that." She smiles again.

I check the app's daily report and select the currency with the best exchange rate. Then, I help the receptionist with the process of opening a digital wallet. "Press here," I say.

She follows my lead without a shred of hesitation. I expect her to be a little dim, considering her previous show of technophobia, but she's quite competent. I'm sure she's only pretending to be stupid, and it bugs me. I've seen too many girls diminish their scientific disposition in order to be cute. It might be forgivable when you're a confused teenager, but not when you're a grown woman.

"Take a seat, please. The therapist will be with you short-ly," she says when we're done.

I'm too anxious to take a seat. I just nod and start pacing the small reception room, from the elevator back to the receptionist's station. The tiles are black and white, like a chessboard. I step only on the black. The somewhat good mood I arrived with is starting to fade away.

This isn't the place for me. How could a therapist help? I don't need someone to ask me about my childhood and if my mother hugged me enough. It's just a waste of time. I should be at home, working on getting our money back. Looking at my phone, I see that photo of Emily and Yolanda again. I wonder why she didn't mention it. Is she staying with me just out of pity? Is she going to leave the minute I'm back on my feet?

I'm on my way toward the elevator. I'm going to leave. Maybe he'll reimburse me, maybe he won't. I don't care. I'm nothing but a soap bubble carried away in the wind. I'm at the mercy of thin air, like the brave individuals who used to work in this building. I'm just another link in a long chain of men who failed to provide for their families. I summon the industrial elevator, which comes to life with a roar.

As it climbs up, I close my eyes and see Emily's face. She was so helpful last night; we were such a great team. I still haven't told her about getting fired from the school. Maybe she doesn't care about losing the money, but she won't be so cool about that specific piece of news.

I lean against the metal doors. I don't know how to break it to her. She'll be so disappointed. The doors open with a clink. I'm about to step inside when the receptionist calls my name.

"Tom? The therapist will see you now."

I hesitate for a second, one leg in the air. Should I stay or should I go? The door closes, slowly. Am I really going to leave? I've told Patrice I'm seeing a therapist.

Before I have the chance to press any buttons, the doors reopen, and the therapist is there. His eyes are red and puffy just like mine. He examines me for a second. It's as if his eyes are searching deep into my psyche. I can't look him in the eye.

He clears his throat. "Okay then," he says, "you can come back when you're ready." There's no judgment in his voice.

The doors begin to close again, and only then do I dare look back up. I sense something. I don't really know what it is. Maybe it's just a wrinkle getting deeper, but I see an endless empathy reflected on his face. He's on my side. And I so desperately need someone to be in my corner. Someone with a clean towel that will wipe away my sweat and blood.

"Wait!" I call as I frantically press the button to open the doors. He's still there. Silently, I follow him to his office.

. . .

This is the first time I've been inside a therapist's practice. Other than our school counselor's office, I've only seen practices in movies and TV shows. It looks nothing like them. There's no heavy wooden bookcase. There aren't any knick-knacks. No family photos. It's a clean, minimalist space, only bare brick walls. A small sofa sits at one end of the room, and a desk with a few chairs stands by the windows. He waits as I take it all in.

"Come in," he finally says. "Sit wherever you like." He plunks onto the sofa, which makes a *swish* sound as he touches it. He sighs with relief.

In the movies, it's the patient who sits or lies on an uncomfortable sofa while the therapist relaxes in a comfy chair. Seeing him take the sofa destabilizes me. Well, I'm like a shaking leaf to begin with. Every little gesture rocks my world.

I take the plunge and step inside. Sitting lightly on the edge of the couch, I face him. He nods. "Rough night?" he asks.

I sigh. "Lost all my money," I say glumly. Then, I bury my face in my palms. I'm not going to be the guy who cries two minutes into his first therapy session.

"Sorry to hear that," he says. I expect to hear gloating in his voice, but there's nothing of the kind. He sounds genuinely sorry for my bad luck. Now the ball is back in my court. What am I going to say? That my wife went to visit her deranged ex, who by the way, is a woman? That I'm afraid she's going to leave me?

Then I hear myself say, "It's not about the money. I always feel like something is missing in my life."

"Always?" he questions.

I'm safe enough to leave the haven of my own hands. Staring at the ceiling, I contemplate the "always" issue. "Now that I think about it, I recall being quite content in the past.

You know, it's funny, we always struggled financially, Emily and I. We're both teachers." I chuckle bitterly. "Well, we *were*. And we used to have side hustles to help us stay afloat. We busted our ass off, but we had fun. The kids were little and we just, I don't know, goofed around in the back yard, and played board games. Their friends traveled, but we rarely did. And lately, with all the money, I don't know. I'm only now realizing life is less fun."

I look him in the eye. He doesn't say anything, but I know he heard my speech. "It's pointless, you know what I mean?" Frustrated, I hit my thighs.

"Do you find meaning in your cryptocurrency trading?"

I hesitate. Do I? Shaking my head, I say, "No. It's just a means to pass the time. I like the action, I think, the challenge of it all. And the money, of course." I chuckle. He nods. "But when I think about it, there's nothing really satisfying about it."

"What gave you satisfaction in the past?"

I straighten up. "Do you mean sexually?" I ask anxiously. After all, he *is* a sex therapist.

"Aren't you satisfied with your sex life?"

"I don't have a sex life anymore," I admit.

"Do you mean that sex is pointless as well?" he asks calmly, as if we're talking about the weather.

"Yes. No. I don't know. I just lost interest, is all."

"Just with the wife or all together?"

I shift uneasily in my chair. I've never mingled with the guys who talk bluntly about their porn. For me, sex was an intimate business I kept to myself.

He's waiting for my answer.

"I guess I don't have the urge anymore." I shrug. "Getting old, I guess."

He nods. "How does the wife feel about that?"

I wriggle my fingers. Dropping my head, I whisper, "she

doesn't like it." My eyes tear up again, and I swallow hard. "She's losing her patience, actually." Is *that* why she went to see Yolanda?

"Sex in its purest form is life energy," he says, cutting through the deep silence. I dare to look up at him, crushing the wet tissue in my hand.

"Sometimes there are physical reasons, diseases and such, that make a man lose his libido. We can check those to rule it out if you want."

I shrug. "I've been kind of sick lately. The doctors don't know what it is. They say panic attacks. But I think it's just a label they use when they don't have a specific diagnose."

"In my experience, most of the times it's connected to mental distress. Depression. Anxiety."

"Oh." I reach for another tissue, and a little movement catches my eye. There's a grey spider web dangling from the corner of the ceiling.

"I miss my kids," I say finally. Quietly. I surprise myself because I didn't know it until this moment. After saying it out loud, I feel that crushing pain in my chest. I groan and lean forward.

"Breathe through it," he says. "You'll be fine. Pain is good. It's not your enemy. Welcome it."

I breathe in and out for a few seconds, concentrating only on that simple task. After a while, the pain fades a little, and I can sit up again. "I miss having family dinners. Coming home after a long day at work, everybody sitting at the table, talking about their day. We used to joke all the time. And now...it's quiet. Just Emily and me. It's empty, like there's an echo. Our voices echo."

He leans over and touches my knee. "You did good, Tom. This is a breakthrough."

"Is it?" I wonder out loud but deep down I know it is.

He's quiet, waiting for me to talk.

And boy, do I talk. I tell him about September 12th. About sleeping in Tommy's room. About getting sacked from school.

He's a good listener. Most of the time, he lets me talk uninterrupted. Sometimes he comments wisely, just to acknowledge he understands my babbling. I don't really need the comments. It feels good just talking about what's troubling me.

There's only one issue I keep to myself. Emily.

Our time is almost up when he suddenly asks, "How would you feel about having a lodger?"

I laugh. I can't believe he's being so obvious. "To replace my kids? Nah, I think I'll pass." I'm extremely disappointed. Everything was going so well.

"A lodger can be a lot of things." He smiles a mysterious smile. It's not even a smile, just a slight movement at the corners of his lips. "You don't have to, of course, but it's the medicine I would prescribe. You do know I work with unconventional methods."

I hesitate.

"Here's another incentive for you. Since you're broke at the moment, I'll waive my therapy fee if you take in this lodger rent-free."

I don't know if it's generosity or a scheme to bring a mentally disturbed person into my house. "I'll have to ask my wife about it."

"You do that."

Getting up, I button my jacket.

"I noticed you didn't say a word about her."

I don't know how to respond to that. He walks me to the door.

"I would like to meet with her. Privately."

On my way home, I contemplate everything we talked about, trying to take mental notes. He recommended nothing even remotely related to intercourse. That puzzles me.

~

EMILY

"I don't get it, Tom. A lodger?"

He shrugs. He doesn't know the reason behind the bizarre barter deal the therapist has devised—we've already established that.

We're in the living room, having our evening drink. The only thing that's changed is the absence of the grandfather clock and good riddance to it. But now there's a thick, tense silence between us. Things I haven't told him. Things he hasn't told me. It was Brenda who informed me about the latest escalations that occurred while I was away.

"I thought you left him, Emily," she whispered into the phone, her voice hoarse. "And I wouldn't blame you for it. I mean, excuse my French, but he looks like shit."

"Yeah, Brenda. He's dealing with grief. I've told you so," I say tiredly.

"Thing is, he's *not* dealing with it. That's why Patrice had to let him go." She lowers her voice even more when she says those last three words. I'm not sure I've heard her correctly.

"What?" I ask frantically.

"Oh, didn't he tell you?" She takes pleasure in it, faking dread in her voice while enjoying my misfortune.

"Of course, he told me about it, Brenda. And I'm not leaving him when he's on the ropes. Some of us support our spouses when they're having a hard time."

"Steve was a drug addict, Emily!"

"Yeah. I know. Sorry. So, tell me everything. I bet you have more details than what Tom gave me..."

. . .

Tom's fingers fly over his phone, as quickly as always, without making any sound. And now I can't even complain about it because it's "our" activity. My part in it is to follow instructions, bring printouts and deliver coffee. Yay. So much fun. I look at him as he drinks his martini.

"So, how was the rest of your day?"

"Fine," he blurts.

I wait. He doesn't say anything else.

"Tom, what aren't you telling me?" I ask as softly as I can. It takes a lot of effort to restrain my impatience.

"What do you mean?"

I give him a fierce look. "Come on, Tom. Don't pretend like you don't know. Just say it!"

He sighs. "He wants you to come to see him."

I'm confused. "Wait. Who? What?"

"The therapist," Tom says, somewhat angry. "Isn't that what we're talking about?"

He moves closer, leans over, and grabs my hand. "Please, Em, will you give it a chance? Just this once?"

"What has he done to you, Tom?"

He shifts uneasily in his seat. Wordless.

"Fine," I say reluctantly, with a sigh. Just so he knows how much I'm willing to sacrifice for his wellbeing. "I'll go." I get up and go make some sandwiches.

"Tell me more about this lodger," I say when I come back. "Who is he? Can you be certain he's not a serial killer?"

"It's a she."

I gasp. *She?* Are we going to lodge the therapist's secret lover? Are we turning our house into a brothel? "Women can be serial killers too."

"Highly unlikely, Emily."

I get mad in the name of all women, but Tom stops me

before I erupt. "I'm sorry. That was poorly said. Let's not stray off the subject, Em."

"I just find it weird, that's all."

"I know, me too. But I want to give it a try."

"Why? Why do you trust this man?"

He scrunches his lips tightly before answering. "I dunno. Gut feeling, Em. Please."

"Fine," I say for the third time. What else can I do? I wonder if I'm treating it all wrong. Maybe we're beyond repair. Maybe we're just done. I go off to the printer to bring another set of graphs.

"We've just made a grand." He's smiling. Oh, he's loving it.

"We." I scoff. I've had nothing to do with it. But he's not listening, already working on the next transaction.

"So, what's her name?" I ask after a few minutes of quiet.

"Who?"

"The lodger."

"Dunno."

"When is she coming?"

Tom shakes his head. He has no idea. "She'll be sleeping in Tommy's room. He was very specific about that."

I look at him. I dare not ask.

"I'm coming back to bed," he says coyly. "If that's all right with you?"

My hearts thumps. If that's all right with me? I miss his presence by my side. It's not just the sex, but the intimacy. It's hearing his breathing while he sleeps. It's feeling his warmth. It's waking up next to him and falling asleep feeling safe and sound with his arm wrapped around my waist.

"You should have started with that." I smile.

I don't expect him to take apart his man cave so quickly, so I'm surprised when he slides into our bed sometime after midnight.

"Tom?" I ask drowsily.

"Shh... go back to sleep." He gives me a little peck on my forehead. I'm so tired, it takes enormous force to open my eyes. He's lying with his back toward me. I pull myself closer and spoon him. I make every nook and every cranny in my body fit his. He flinches a little, but I don't budge. I bury my face in the nape of his neck and inhale his scent. It's a mixture of mint and orange and Old Spice.

His aroma has an arousing effect. I tell myself to be patient. After all, I've waited so long already, I can surely give him a few more nights to adjust. And he still wants me. I remind myself of the way he reacted to my touch in the ambulance a few days ago. Casually, I let my hand slip down as if by mistake. Oh, dear lord. He's so hard.

"Em!" he reproaches me, and I withdraw.

"Sorry, sorry," I murmur. He's trying to shake me off, but I cling on to him like a tick.

The next thing I know, the sun is shining. We've made it through the night.

His eyes are puffy, and there's a thread of dry spit on his chin. He looks at me and I melt into a big lump of sweetness.

"Morning," he whispers. His face is so close. His breath is sour. But so is mine.

"Morning," I murmur my reply.

And then, it's like magic. He crosses the abyss between us —only a few inches, but still—and he kisses me.

We must have kissed a million times before. Sweet kisses, passionate kisses. Even sour-breath kisses. But there's never been a kiss like this before. A kiss that says, *I love you*. A kiss that says, *you're my soulmate*. A kiss that says, *I want you so much*. It's a kiss that says, *welcome back, you've been missed*.

And what starts as a sweet gesture, turns passionate.

Tom strokes my skin with the tips of his fingers, runs them up and down on my torso. I can't get enough of his touch. It feels so new, although he's touched me a bazillion times before. I wrap my legs around him. He's firmer and thinner than I remember. I don't know if I like it, but there's no real time to dwell on it.

Things flow naturally, as they always have, and pretty quickly, our bodies are entangled. We're a bunch of legs and arms and heaves and groans, and it's so good to feel him inside me. We fit. Always did. And as we ride together on the waves of pleasure, the last months are erased, deleted. I've got him back.

I've got him back.

CHAPTER 28

Bday

The day started off when Audrey woke me up. I almost didn't recognize her with her new hairdo. She looked so much younger. And happier. Sometimes I envy her.

"Wake up, Seven," she said and handed me a box of chocolates. "Happy Valentine's Day!" Her cheerfulness sounded fake. I knew she was putting on a face just for my sake. Depressed old me. Forty-two years old today.

"And these are from Bill." She handed me a bouquet of red roses. I inhaled their sweet scent but doubted they were from him. He'd left before Christmas. Last I heard from him was a text saying he liked the girl his parents picked for him, and that he was going to go forward with the wedding plans unless I changed my mind. I never replied.

It was snowing terribly, but I still went out to Mom. Can't think of anywhere else I'd rather be, or anyone else who I'd like to spend my birthday with. On my way there, struggling with the howling wind, I calculated that forty-two was six

"

times seven. I figured since I'm in my sixth adventure, that must be a sign for something.

For a while, I've felt I should move on. I've failed at my housekeeping tasks lately, but Audrey doesn't have the heart to let me go. I've heard her whisper it to Elijah. "Poor thing," she said, "she didn't get out of bed until noon." She's certain I'm depressed, but that's not it. I was on a strike, thinking it would be my way to give the higher power a little shake. It didn't work and I don't know what else to do. I'm so helpless without the signs guiding my way.

I asked for Mom's help. Her stone was freezing cold. I cleaned off the snow with my mittens on, didn't dare touch it. And I was waiting for her reply when someone touched my shoulder, freaking me out. It was an old man. Well, oldish.

He handed me a flask. "Here, it'll warm you up." It was pure gin. I coughed my lungs out.

"You hungry?" he asked. I was.

"Come," he said, and I followed. Did Mom send him to me? Was he a sign?

He drove an old Chevy. It reeked of cigarettes and alcohol. Empty bottles covered the car floor like a wall-to-wall carpet.

"Are you in a position to drive?" I asked.

His eyes sparkled. "Well, and here I thought you were ready to give in on life." He threw me the keys and guided me through the white streets to a small restaurant with a flickering sign that was half-missing. All I could read was "rut." A Middle Eastern guy rushed over to welcome us and take our coats. It was nice and warm inside.

"Might I ask what you were doing in a graveyard on a day like today?" he asked.

"I could ask you the same question," I said.

He laughed. "Touché."

"I was visiting with an old friend of mine," he said. "I visit every year on Valentine's."

I shrugged. "I was visiting my Mom. It's my birthday today. I miss her." I don't know why I said it.

"Well, Happy Birthday to you. We need to celebrate." He stealthy looked around before pulling out his flask. I refused to take a sip, so he took one for me too,

We sat quietly for a while before the food came. Salads of some sort. The server made a whole show about each and every one of them, but. I couldn't have cared less. I was famished. I shoved food in like I was bulimic. At some point, I caught his staring.

"Do you have a safe place to stay the night?"

"This night, yes. The next one? I don't know." Only after the words were out in the open did I realize how that must have sounded. "I'm not homeless, if that's what you're thinking. Just not pleased with my current living arrangement."

He nodded. Of course, that's what he'd thought. I mean, he dug me up half-frozen in a graveyard, and I was eating like someone who hadn't seen food for days. It didn't help that everything tasted so good. Again, I thought it must be a sign. Taking a good look at him, something seemed familiar.

"Were you visiting my Mom?"

Instead of replying, he just pulled out a card and slid it over the table. "Maybe I can help you find a better place to live."

The card said sex therapist. I looked at him funny. "No thanks." I slid the card back.

"I'm not offering to put you in a whorehouse." He smiled as he read my mind. Leaning forward over the table he added, "Well, only if you want to."

I get up to leave.

"Wait!" It was the server. "You hadn't had your main course yet!"

"That's fine," I say.

When I get to the door my rescuer yelled after me, "If you're ever hungry again, come here. You'll get a hot meal for free!"

And then I was out in the blizzard. A fancy red car almost ran me over when I crossed the street. That would have been fine ending for the worst birthday ever.

mily

Full of resentment, I go to the scheduled appointment with the sex therapist on Friday morning. I wear one of my jumpsuits. It's made of leopard-print fabric and has a deep V-neck. It's not your usual attire for a visit to the shrink, which is exactly why I wear it. Like my other jumpsuits in this line, it can be worn loose or fitted using a smart zipping system which I designed as part of the garment. It has a hood too, with whiskers and those mesmerizing green tiger eyes. To tone down the predator look, I wear one of my fabric necklaces. It's made of wooden beads covered with red and yellow scraps. I'm so completely out of my style that when I look at the mirror, I don't even recognize myself. I look like I'm ready to go on a hunt.

The therapist's clinic is located at the edge of an industrial zone in what used to be a factory, maybe a warehouse. It's an old, kind of neglected building. I expect the smell of mold and mildew that usually takes hold in old spaces like this, but it smells like lavender. There's an old elevator, which looks kind of flimsy, so I take the stairs. They're dark. I use the torch on my phone to light my way. The staircase is stained and broken. It's only one story up, but I'm breathless when I get there.

A pretty receptionist gives me a look. I guess it's my outfit. I pull the fabric and lift my head high.

"I've never seen anybody take the stairs before," she says with wonder.

"Well," I begin to say, but lose my train of thought when an obese woman steps out of the office at the end of the corridor.

She makes her way heavily toward me, breathing noisily.

"Goodbye, Louise," the receptionist says to her back. "Have a good one!"

Louise walks into the elevator. She's very brave.

"Emily, you can go in now." The receptionist directs me to the office.

I take a deep breath. *Here goes nothing.*

The office is exposed brick. No decorations, no pictures on the walls. There's a desk, a few chairs, and a little sofa. Very basic. Big windows bring lots of light into the room. One of my quilts would look great hanging on the wall. It would make the office look warmer, more welcoming.

"Before we begin, I need to clear the air." No hello or other pleasantries. I look him in the eye. There's a sharp mind behind those frameless glasses.

"I'm listening," I say harshly, determined not to let him affect me with his directness.

"I don't know if Tom told you, but I misled him that night you left him at Beirut. I insinuated you might be depressed, knowing quite well that he's the one who needs cheering up."

I scrutinize him through squinted eyes.

"I apologize for being manipulative. I try to be honest, but sometimes a bit of deception is required. It's part of the healing. Like a placebo effect."

"Okay," I say slowly. I'm still cautious.

"Please, sit." He points to the sofa. I sit on the edge, alert.

"Relax. This isn't going to be painful. I just want to get some background about you and Tom. How did you two meet?"

That only makes me tenser. My foot begins to dance, uncontrollably. I inhale deeply. "We're both teachers, as you might already know. And we met in the teacher's lounge." I allow myself a little smile. "When asked, we usually say we know each other from high school. Note the *from* instead of *since*."

"You're an art teacher," he declares.

"Yes, I am." Now I lean back. The sofa is comfortable. It's soft, but not too soft like those seats that make you sink inside. It holds its firmness quite well.

"And this year, you took some time off to do…what exactly?"

"I design and sew clothes and home decor."

He checks my outfit.

"Yes," I reply to his unasked question. "This item is one of my creations." I cross my legs and stretch my chest. I'm proud of this jumpsuit, despite it being so bold.

He examines me quietly, and I get uneasy. I've heard about therapy tricks meant to make people talk. I sit quietly too, looking at him with half a smile.

"Are you happy?" he finally asks, and I flinch. I didn't expect *that*.

I think about it for a minute before realizing my mouth is wide open. "Well, my daughter is already married. She's a junior editor at Scissors, Paper & Rock— a big publishing house in New York. And my son, I don't need to worry about him anymore. He's got a full scholarship for MIT and is on his way to becoming a very successful young man."

"I didn't ask about your kids," he says quietly. "I want to know about *you*, Emily. Are you happy with your life right now?"

My palms are sweaty. I sit on them. "Is this a trick question?" I finally ask.

He lifts the corners of his mouth. "I just want to establish a baseline here. Sometimes when a spouse is depressed, the other one gets very unhappy and begins to question their life choices, especially those regarding their spouses."

I look him in the eye, quite alarmed. Does he know that I've been going through exactly that process lately? "Well, it is a struggle, I can tell you that. I'm trying to be as supportive as I can."

"But sometimes you just snap, like that night at Beirut," he says. It's a declaration, not a question. I think about it for a few moments.

"Well, yeah. I guess. It was our anniversary. Did he tell you that?"

The therapist nods.

"I didn't want to go out at all. It was very last minute."

"And he was on his phone the entire time," he adds.

"Exactly!" A flush of anger flares up as I recall the events of that night. "I get that he's depressed with everything that's been going on lately, but why bother going out if you're not going to spend time with me?" I give him a glance. Does he know about the whole Math Nazi thing? About being suspended from school? Tom still hasn't told me any of that. He keeps leaving home every morning as if he's going to work, coming back in the afternoon at the same time he usually would.

What does he do in those hours? I have no clue. I ask him sweetly how his day was, and he sighs and says, "The usual,

Em, you know." And that's all I get before he gets back on the phone with his quest to bounce back.

"It's so frustrating. Like he's left me in order to have a relationship with his phone."

"So *you* left," he says.

I'm alert again. Have I shared too much? "But then I came back. Did he tell you that? I called 911. It was a panic attack."

He nods. "Then you left again."

I shift uneasily in my seat. I feel like I'm being judged for my actions. "I went to my sister's, didn't he say?"

He lifts one eyebrow. Does he know I didn't go straight to Katie's? Does Tom know? Dread overcomes me. I can't look him in the eye. I'm certain the lie is written all over my face.

An old cobweb dangles from the far corner of the ceiling. It's silvery-gray and deserted. The spider left long ago.

I should be happy. Tom is back in our marital bed. We even had that morning delight a few days ago. I shouldn't be complaining, yet, I find myself beginning to cry.

"So, let's go back to your meet-cute. That's a happy memory to reminisce about, isn't it?" He pushes a box of Kleenex toward me. Now my tears turn into a sob.

"I was an art teacher's assistant when I met Tom," I say between cries. "It was supposed to be a temporary job." I take a minute to wipe my nose, my eyes. "But then I got pregnant with Marni, so we got married, and I stayed at the school. And then we had Tommy, and I kept at it because we needed the money." Another wave of sobs breaks me. This is the official story Tom and I tell whenever we get asked, the laundered version that eliminates every mention of Yolanda and the part she played in our early acquaintance. As I repeat the story I've told so many times before, I keep looking at him to see if he detects the lie. Did Tom tell him the truth?

"And now you finally get to live your lifelong dream," he says.

I nod.

"And then Tom loses all your money and you have to give up on your dream once again." I don't know if that's a question or if he's just stating the facts as he sees them.

My throat is choked. When I finally get a grip, I ask with such a little voice, "Is that why you wanted to see me?"

"Partly," he says. He straightens up in his seat. "But mainly just to see if you're on board with the lodger."

I sit quietly, waiting for him to elaborate. I let my face show my discomfort, my unwillingness to host this mysterious lodger.

He smiles at me. "You're a smart woman, Emily."

"Thank you." I don't let my guard down.

"You don't trust me, and that's fair. You don't know me and my methods. I can guarantee that everything I'm doing is in your favor." He puts his hand over his heart.

I wait quietly for him to continue. I don't even nod.

"You're a tough one." He smiles. "I would like to ask you to keep an open mind regarding the lodger. She's a wonderful woman, and I'm sure you'll like her. She has her quirks though, and she's quite sensitive about it, obviously, so I'd like to ask you to be patient with her."

"What do you mean *quirks*?" I lean forward anxiously.

"She's not going to harm you or your property, if that's what you're afraid of. She has some beliefs and has made some life choices that aren't mainstream. Some people find it hard to accept."

A heatwave crashes over me. My face turns red. I'm not sure what he's accusing me of. Being unempathetic to people different than me or making questionable life choices? Is there even a lodger, or is this just an elaborate scheme to make me confess where I've been? Judging by the look on his face, he knows, which means Tom knows. I've had so many opportunities to confess since I returned, but each time I shied away.

My eyes are about to pop out, and I start coughing. He brings me a bottle of water and waits quietly for me to calm down.

"Tom and I, we're fine now." I lie.

"Are you?"

"He moved back to our marital bed like you told him to. We're having sex again."

"Oh?"

We did, but just that once. I cave. I'm doomed anyhow. "This lodger. How long is she going to stay with us?" I expect him to gloat. I expect him to say there's isn't a lodger. That it's me who's made questionable life choices and now they're coming back to bite me.

"She'll stay for as long as it takes."

"What do you mean?"

He's quiet for a second, collecting his thoughts, choosing his words. "The way I see it— and correct me if I'm wrong— is that you and Tom had a good relationship—"

"We had a *great* relationship."

He nods. "You had a great relationship for over two and a half decades. You raised a family, you had your hardships, but you came through. And now, facing a new chapter in life, your relationship has crumbled. It needs to evolve and adapt to your new status. It takes time."

"How much time?" I yell. "I've been giving him nothing *but* time!"

"Which was very clever of you, Emily. Most women don't have as much patience as you do."

I sigh. "I guess that's the fixer in me. I've been called frugal, cheap, because I don't throw away broken stuff. I reuse, I re-purpose. I fix."

"Perhaps you can re-purpose your marriage."

"Into what? A decorative vase?" I shoot back.

He tilts his head back and laughs full-heartedly. "I was thinking more in the direction of friendship. Maybe in time, you can become friends with benefits."

I expect a smile, even half a smile. But he's deadly serious. He looks at me with eyes half-closed. I'm uneasy, trying to stealthily look at my phone and check when this session is going to end.

Leaning forward he asks, "Can I ask you something personal?"

"Because up until this moment it was just casual small talk?"

He chuckles. "You're a sharp one, aren't you? I can see why Tom loves you so much."

I forget to breathe. I can't believe he just said that. Did Tom tell him that he loves me still? Despite everything I did?

"Have you ever been in a relationship with a woman?" He asks it so casually, as if he's enquiring whether I remembered to get milk at the market.

"What?" I stutter. My face gets warm again. I lift my hand to my cheek, where my bruise was. "So, he knows." I get up and start pacing the room. "You should tell him it was a mistake. I shouldn't have gone to see her."

The look on his face. It's a total surprise.

"Tom never said anything," the therapist says. "I just got that vibe from you. As I mentioned earlier, most women would not have put up with their partner leaving the marital bed. They would have felt guilty. They would have felt unattractive. But not you."

"Of course I feel unattractive! How could I not?"

He gives me that scrutinizing look again. "Be honest, Emily, if not with me, at least be honest with yourself."

"I am."

He waits for an explanation.

I dive back into the chair and rest my forehand on the tip of my fingers, massaging my temples. I've made a mess. "I was in a relationship with a woman before I met Tom. But I've been loyal to him ever since we got together. I'm not gay."

"It's okay to like both men and women sexually. Nothing wrong with that."

"I know." I nod.

"Does Tom know about her?"

"Of course." I take a deep breath. "Recently, she resurfaced, and I went to see her."

"I see." He's quiet for a long time.

"I think we're done here," I finally say.

He nods. "Thank you for your time, Emily, I'm sorry if you found this meeting unpleasant. That was not my intention."

"Fine." I grab my purse and turn toward the door. My eyes are filled with a new set of tears. "Please don't tell Tom what I've said," I plead quietly when I'm at the door. "I'm waiting for the right moment to tell him."

"Are you going to leave him for this woman?" he asks.

I turn to face him. "It's the other way around. I left her to be with him, and I would do it all over again." And with that, I walk out, holding my head high.

Marni calls when I'm halfway home. There's been a crash on North street. The stationary row of cars finally starts moving like a lazy snail.

"Marni? Is everything alright?" She's usually too busy to call during the day.

"Mom, what's going on?" My heart misses a beat.

"What do you mean?" I stall.

"Why is Dad doing taxes for randos?"

For the first time on this miserable drive, I speed up to the limit. Then a yellow Chevrolet cuts me off. "Damn it!"

"Mom?"

I take a deep breath. "Sorry, dear. Road rage."

She's quiet. I can hear keyboard clacks. Poor girl. She's too busy to take a proper lunch break. My heart goes out to her.

"You're working too hard, Marni."

"Mom!" she snaps.

"Oh, yeah. Sorry. You were saying?"

"Remember my friend Willow? She sent me a snippet from Craiglist. Praised math teacher available for help with taxes. $50."

"What?"

"That's Dad. There's a photo. Why is he doing that? Why is he charging so low?"

I sigh. At least now I know what he's been up to. Tom and I agreed not to tell the kids more than they needed to know. But I can't keep any more secrets; I'm about to burst. "We have some money issues. Dad made a bad business move, and he's trying to make up for it."

She's so quiet. Even the tapping has stopped.

"I'm so sorry, Mom."

"We're going to keep our promise, though. We'll continue paying for your rent but—" I hesitate for a second. "Do you think there's a chance one of you will get a raise? The two of you are working so hard and all."

She chuckles bitterly. "Mom, you don't know what's it's like in the city. There are fifty people standing in line to replace either of us at any point. There's no raise in the foreseeable future for us. We're just lucky to have a job."

That makes me sad. And frustrated. It shouldn't be like that.

"Oh yeah," she adds after a short pause. "Dad texted me about a lodger? What the eff is that?"

I slow down as I pass the accident scene. A squashed Subaru is lying upside down in the ditch. It's terrifying, yet mesmerizing. A police officer diverts the traffic onto a side road. I don't know this area and just drive after the yellow Chevrolet in front of me, hoping it will lead me out of this mess to a recognizable street.

"Mom?" Marni whispers angrily into the phone.

"Yeah. Sorry. The lodger is part of Dad's treatment. He's going to a therapist."

"Dad's going to a *therapist*? Are you for real?" She laughs, certain it's nothing but a joke. Everyone knows how Tom feels about therapists.

"I'm afraid so. He's not well since grandpa passed." It's such a relief to share it with her.

The yellow Chevrolet stops by the curb, and I park right behind it without really thinking. The driver, a petite woman wearing a coral coat, steps outside, opens a hot-red umbrella over her head and runs to a bodega across the street. There's a fabric store right next to it. My breath is taken away. She *did* lead me to where I need to be.

When I started my business, I mapped out all the Joann's and Michael's and independent quilt shops within a 30-mile radius. This one must have slipped under my radar. Well, there's no better time than right now. I decide to check it out. I pull my hood over my head to protect myself from the rain. It's wide enough for me to hold the phone underneath.

Marni is whining about not having enough time to see Marcus, who needs to work on Saturdays as well and is so exhausted on Sundays he just sleeps in. I've heard it all before. She whines every time she calls, and it always ends with me telling her that they're working too hard and her getting angry, saying I don't know how it is in the city. So I listen only with half an ear as I go into the quilt shop.

"We just rented this place like a month ago so we could commute less, and now Dad is saying we need to find someplace cheaper. That means extra money on transportation and we can't afford that either," Marni whines.

"I'm sorry, honey," I say absentmindedly while checking the discount bins. They have a good size piece of Brussels lace laying there. I take it out and spread it against the light, immediately thinking about the stuff I could make with it.

"And I miss you all so much," Marni complains. "And we never have time to visit."

"We can Skype more often," I suggest as I step into the quilting cotton section. The shelves are stocked by color. A bold print in bumblebee yellow catches my eye, and I move closer. For me, a fabric shop is like a candy store for a child. I want to feel the fabric, and I need both hands for that.

"Talk to you later, Marni." I hang up, which is a first. Normally, she's the one who's in a hurry.

Then there's a familiar face near the blues.

"Eileen! What a pleasure." We hug firmly. She's a retired English teacher. We used to be friends but lost touch after she retired.

"Emily Swanson. Fancy seeing you here. And what on earth are you wearing?" Suddenly I'm aware of my outfit. Embarrassed, I take the hood off. I start to stutter. "It's...oh...funny story...it was supposed to..."

Eileen examines my tigress from top to bottom and back up again. "May I?" she asks and doesn't wait for an answer before she feels the fabric, crushing it between her fingers.

Other ladies in the store look at me. I smile a wary, self-conscious smile. One of the ladies—who is holding an interesting-looking jellyroll—interprets my smile as an invitation to move closer. She stands next to Eileen.

"This is just fabulous, Emily," Eileen says.

Overwhelmed, I can't tell if she's serious. So far, my jumpsuits have been the laughingstock of my family. Well, The men. Marni was thrilled. She put a photo of herself wearing one on her Instagram and got a lot of nice feedback.

"I love the way it flows," Eileen says. "There's so much life in it, yet it's not sleazy."

The lady with the jellyroll nods vigorously.

"Where did you get the pattern?" Eileen asks. There's a whole group of ladies around us now. They're from Eileen's quilt circle, so she says, and they all wait for my answer.

"I designed it myself," I say humbly. My cheeks are getting warm. Now everyone in the store is staring at me. I flush.

"Really?" Eileen asks. I take off my coat and they start circling me so they can take in all the fine details.

"Well, I got inspired by those onesie pajamas you see everywhere, but this one is styled so you can be comfortable wearing it outdoors as well."

The lady with the jellyroll looks at me with her eyes wide open. "Can you make one for me?"

Two hours later, I leave the store with five new orders. Three tigers, a cat, and a unicorn. I already took measurements in the back room, where the workshops are held. The ladies paid advances for my work and purchased the fabrics right there in the store. The fabric shop owner was thrilled with the unexpected extra business. She loved my jumpsuit so much, she offered to carry my patterns at her store. *And* we scheduled a workshop where I'll teach my method of using zippers as multipurpose elements.

And just like that, I've turned into a fashion designer.

∼

Riding the wave of my unexpected success, I drive to

Jefferson High. The teacher's parking lot is full, so I park in the student's zone.

Brenda lifts her head from the monitor when I burst into the office. She looks surprised and confused.

"Emily? What are you doing here?"

"She in?" I tilt my head toward Patrice's office.

"Well, yeah. She's in a conference call with— Emily!" The wheels of her chair squeak as she gets up and tries to stop me. Too late. I'm already in Patrice's office. She's also surprised to see me. Unlike Brenda, she recovers quickly, lifting one finger, asking me to wait quietly.

There's a man voice coming out of the speaker, talking about school dropout rates.

"Yeah, Zach. As I said, I'll get to the bottom of it. Give me a few days to check the numbers."

Ignoring her, Zach continues to talk.

"Zach. Zach. *Zach!*" It isn't until Patrice raises her voice that he stops talking. She can be quite intimidating when she wants to be. I lose my spirit. What was I thinking, bursting in here like that?

"I'll have to call you back. Something just came up." Patrice hangs up, then addresses Brenda and me at the same time. "Please, Emily. Sit," she says. "It's okay, Brenda, close the door behind you." Now I have her full attention, I'm discouraged.

"Yes, Emily. What can I do for you?" Patrice's eyebrows are knitted together. She's leaning back in her chair, her hands folded over her chest.

"It's...hmmm...it's about Tom," I stutter.

"What about him?" She picks a pen from the desk and starts twisting it in her hands.

"It's not right what you did to him, Patrice. Dumping him at his lowest? It's not like you to do that." On my way to the school, practicing what I wanted to say to her, that sentence sounded a lot stronger.

She slouches in her chair. Her face crumples. "I know. You're right. Believe me when I say I'm so sorry about that. It's just the school board—"

I find my voice again. "Fuck the school board, Patrice." Surprised she raises her eyes to look at my face. "Since when do you bend to their whims, huh?" I put my hands on her desk and lean forward. "You're the strongest person I know. The strongest *woman* I know. I used to look up to you, Patrice. You were this beacon of fairness and honesty." I shake my head a bit. "And now? Your politics disgust me." I spit those last words. "You should have been fighting for him, and instead, you're killing him, Patrice. You're killing a good man who gave his life to this school. To these kids. Whatever happens to Tom, it's on you!" I breathe heavily when I'm done. I feel like a tigress.

Patrice rearranges the stuff on her desk. Aligns the papers. Moves the stapler from right to left. I wait.

"First of all, Emily, you have no right to barge in here like this. And excuse me for saying this, but Tom is a grown man. He could have come in here by himself if he needed to. My door is always open for him. Secondly, I *did* reason with the board, and they agreed to revisit their decision at the next meeting since Tom is seeing a therapist now." She sounds hesitant when she says the last bit and looks at me as if she needs confirmation. I nod an acknowledgement

"And I was able to get him on a sick leave instead of suspension, so he'll get a paycheck. I think I'm doing every-thing within my power, Emily."

"Yes. Thank you," I utter. Tears fill my eyes. I hide my face in my palms.

"Now, I *am* sorry I didn't get to the bottom of it earlier," Patrice says. I don't see her get up, but then she's sitting in the visitor's chair right next to me. She touches my back comfortingly. "Tom was always so...stable. So trustworthy," she reminisces.

I sniffle. "Yeah," I agree.

Sitting on this side of her desk, she sounds informal, friendlier. "I should have offered my support way back. So, you are right, Emily. I do feel guilty for his breakdown. I was responsible, and I blew it. Please tell Tom that as well. He's refusing my calls, and I don't want to write it in a text."

I'm overwhelmed with gratitude.

"Please tell him he's an asset to this school, you *both* are. And you both have our full support." She grabs my hand and squeezes it. "You're not alone, Emily. You're not alone."

I nod. Tears are falling down my cheeks. She smiles empathetically. Still holding my hand, she taps the back of it.

"And now we've got that out of the way, tell me about this gorgeous outfit you're wearing."

Tom and I settle into our new routine, which isn't much different than our old one. He leaves every morning, and I hurry to my studio to get on with my orders. I'm going to need to hire some help soon, or I'll be drowning.

When he comes home, I rush downstairs. Now that I know he's been doing taxes and whatnot, I try my best to be supportive.

"Hi honey, how was your day?" I ask carefully. He's already sitting on the couch, hunched over his phone. He's humming. Well, that's new.

"Fine," he says. For a fraction of a second, he makes eye contact. He smiles at me, and my heart misses a beat. My hands ache with the need to hold him, to comfort him. For him to comfort me. But I don't. I wait for him to make the first move, and meanwhile, I'm dying a little every day, consumed by my secrets. I haven't shared my business success with Tom because, a) why rub it in his face when he's down? And b) the money I make is peanuts compared to the amount we need. And most importantly, c) because he doesn't ask. And that breaks my heart.

I bring drinks, then I order a pizza. We eat quietly by the coffee table. His eyes are on his phone. He doesn't seem to notice when I slip back to my room. There's so much work to be done with all the orders, and I'm not yet organized to sew multiple items at the same time.

When I come down again, creeping slowly down the stairs just to check if he noticed my absence, he's still in the same position.

"Oh, Em, there you are," he says. *Busted*, I think as I close my eyes. "Would you be a doll and make a fresh pot of coffee? I could really use some."

I grit my teeth. "Sure thing," I say.

"Thanks, hon. It's great, you having my back. I'm happy we get to do this together."

Are you kidding me? While the pot is boiling, I bang my head against the cabinet. This is not working. This is not working at all.

Every day that passes makes it harder to confess because now I need to explain why I didn't come forward sooner. And every day he doesn't say what he's really doing drives the wedge further between us.

Slowly, but surely, we're drifting apart. And I don't know what to do. I don't know how to fix it. We're ripping at the seams, and no thread in the world could sew us back together. I try to cling to the words the therapist said— "I get why he loves you so much," but then I ask myself, really? Does he?

As I fetch his coffee, I think about the deadline I set on our anniversary. "Hey Tom, you have a big birthday coming up. Want to do something special?" Like get a divorce? I don't say the last part.

He grits his teeth. "Thanks for reminding me how old I am. And no thanks. I want to have a quiet night at home. No parties, please." Lifting his eyes from his phone, he smiles at me, "No ballroom dancing either."

"And how about trekking the Appalachian Trail?"

"Sure. We can do that."

"Really?" I'm so excited. But then he gives me a look, and I know he was just teasing.

"How about a divorce?" I whisper. He doesn't react. Maybe he didn't hear.

"Talk to him already!" Katie yells when I call to complain. "It'll be like ripping off a Band-Aid. Excruciating pain for a brief of a second, and after that, you'll be fine."

But I can't do it. I can't.

When we go to bed together, I'm excited and full of hope. Although there's no sign of a lodger just yet, he stays with me. Then he kisses me goodnight, just a peck on the cheek, before turning his back toward me. He's right next to me, but I'm lonelier than ever.

2/21/17

Today I went to Mom's to say happy birthday. I took Scotty with me. I'm quite fond of the little creature. I think we humans can learn a lot from dogs, especially about grief and forgiveness and how to move on with your life. Scotty seems happy and content despite what he's been through. I know he's just a dog, but he has feelings too, I've seen them. And he must have been hurt when Charlie left and when they changed his name. Yet, he wiggles his tail happily whenever he sees Audrey. Always giving her another chance.

On our way to Mom's, we stopped at Sunjay's. There's a new girl working the counter now. Actually, there're a few of them, doing shifts. I can never tell who's who. I call all of them Doris. The Doris who was working said dogs were not allowed in the store. I don't know what possessed me at that moment, but I said Scotty was a service dog. And maybe he is.

Mom wasn't there. She's never there anymore. Taking an

example from Scotty, I gave her another chance. I said happy birthday to that stupid cold stone, and I was updating her with the latest when Scotty began growling. It was that man again, the one who took me to dinner on my birthday a week ago.

"Hello," he said.

"Are you stalking me?" I asked. It looked like he was eavesdropping on my private conversation with Mom.

"Oh no. I just came to visit my friend." Scotty sniffed his shoes, his pants, and gave him the tail wiggle of approval.

"Do you mean my Mom? Did you know my Mom?"

He examined me. "Do we really *know* someone?" He was being smart with me.

"Well, I sincerely hope so. I do know myself."

"Huh," he said and sat by me. He took out his flask and offered me a drink.

"My father was a no-good drunk," I said, refusing his offer. He took a long sip. "He left my mother when she was about to give birth to me."

"Do you think the dead can forgive?" he asked. "I wronged my friend many years ago."

"What did you do?"

He took another sip and smacked his lips. "Are you sure you don't want some?" He placed the flask close to me. It was lemon tea.

"The other day it was booze," I said.

He shrugged. "So how are you doing regarding your living situation?" he asked.

I didn't answer for a while. Scotty fell asleep. I wondered if Mom sent this man. Meeting him once could have been coincidental, but twice? It must mean something. Was it a sign and I was reading it wrong? "Why do you care about my living situation? What's in it for you?"

He looked at Mom's stone. Then he got up and moved his

finger over her engraved name. "Martha," he said. "That's a pretty name. Was your mother pretty?"

I gave him the photo from her wedding. He examined it for a long time before he handed it back.

"I help people. That's what I do. And I'd like to help you."

I hugged my knees. "What makes you think that I need help?"

He shrugged. "You seem lost."

"I lost my mother," I whispered. Scratching Scotty's chin, I found myself saying, "She used to talk to me. After she died, I mean. And now she's gone."

"Maybe she moved on," he said as he joined me in petting the dog. "Maybe you need to move on too. Let her rest in peace."

"Maybe," I whispered. I knew he was right. I needed to move on. But where should I go without a sign to guide me?

For a long time, we were quiet.

"So, about your living situation…" he said again.

"I get by." I didn't want to mention I spent last night in the storage unit. It was illegal.

"Would you be willing to move in with a married couple? They've been married for twenty-seven years and are looking for a lodger."

Would I!

CHAPTER 31

*E*mily

I'm sitting in my studio working on my jumpsuit orders when there's a knock on the door. I now have seven orders under my belt, including Patrice and Brenda's, who insist on paying full price despite the generous family and friends discount I offer.

I'm working hard to complete the first order, which should be delivered on Wednesday afternoon. I have less than forty-eight hours, and I'm already behind when the knocking disturbs me. It's a series of quick knocks that repeats itself twice. Surprised, I raise my head from the sewing machine. Glancing at my phone, I see it's 7:20 p.m. I've been so consumed with my work that I haven't felt the time passing.

Who could it be now? It's too late in the day for a delivery. Could it be Tom? He left for the therapist's only thirty minutes ago, and he wouldn't knock on the front door, he would probably just come through the garage. So, I decide to ignore it. Whoever is knocking will probably move on. But the knocking continues. It's a weird pattern of knocks. They come in bursts followed by a short period of silence.

I look at my phone again. There are no new messages. Nothing is scheduled. Yet, someone is out there, disturbing my peace. Angrily, I go downstairs in order to give the culprit a piece of mind.

A woman stands outside. She's looks in her early forties, but she's dressed like a much younger person, wearing a jean miniskirt and a tank top with the number twenty-seven printed on it. An outfit that certainly doesn't fit the weather either. Her lips are trembling from the cold.

"Oh, finally," she says with a big smile. Her teeth are very white. She holds a pink carry-on trolley bag with both hands, moving it to her left as she stretches the right one forward. "Seven Twenty."

I'm puzzled. Did she just ask for the time? "I believe it is," I say.

She chuckles. "You must be Emily."

I don't know how to wrap my head around that.

"I'm your lodger?" she says, her voices rising at the end, as though her announcement is actually a question.

"Oh, right," I say. She jumps up and down and crosses her arms over her chest. I can tell she's freezing, but she's not asking to come in. "Come on in, you poor thing," I say. "Sorry I didn't answer sooner, I figured it was a salesperson or something." I reach for her luggage.

"Oh, thank you so much! You don't have to do that." She won't let me take her suitcase. "The last place I lived, they thought I was a Jehovah's Witness when I came knocking," she says as she follows me into the house.

Inside, she looks at me as she exhales over her bare hands, trying to warm them up. Her nose and the tips of her ears are red. I guide her through the hall into the living room. I drag the wing chair closer to the fireplace.

"Why don't you sit here, and I'll bring you a hot drink to warm you up?"

"Thank you!" Her eyes fill with grateful tears.

"Tea? Coffee? Hot cocoa?"

She smiles a beautiful, innocent smile. "Whatever you're having. I don't want to impose."

When I return with two steaming mugs of herbal green tea, she's standing by the mantle and checking out the collage of family photos commemorating happy moments. She looks joyous, like a little kid who just got to open an unexpected present.

"Oh, Emily, you have such a pretty family!" She points at the family photo from Marni's wedding. She sounds so genuine, and I melt a little on the inside.

"The bride is my daughter, Marni." I point to the photo. Marni looks gorgeous in her white gown. "Her husband is Marcus." He looks handsome in a navy-striped suit that brings out his eyes. "My son Tommy, he's studying at MIT," I say proudly. "And that's my husband, Tom." Wearing a tux, Tom is eye candy.

"Ooh, He's hot," she says. "You're one lucky woman." She elbows me in the ribs as if we're two old friends getting together after a long-time-no-see.

"I knew I had to come here when I heard you've been married for twenty-seven years," she says. "You see, twenty-seven is my lucky number. It's my guide in this world. Whenever I see it, I know that's my next calling." Her eyes sparkle. She's crazy all right. Maybe she's harmless. Definitely sweet, but no question about it—a complete nut job.

"So, you changed your name to reflect your lucky number?" I ask casually. I need to stop the laughter straining to burst out of my chest, but this is just too funny.

"Well, Emily, thanks for asking." Oh no, she has a whole speech prepared. I get nervous goosebumps. "My mother named me Seven after the Seven Wonders of the World. She thought that I was all of them combined." She smiles and stares at an invisible object behind my head. I know it's invisible because I turn to look at what she's seeing, and there's nothing but thin air.

"She was a Twentyfive, my mom. It's a real surname. You can Google it if you don't believe me." I believe her. I think I've read about it somewhere, in an article listing strange surnames. "Well, she married a Smith, so officially, I'm Seven Smith. But he left before I was born, and my mom returned to her maiden name. I picked it up as well."

It's genetic. Crazy runs in her family.

"Anyways, I've changed it slightly. Reduced it to Twenty." She laughs. "So, I'm actually Seven Twenty, but you get the gist." She grins.

I nod, exhaustedly. She talks way too much. I need a drink.

"Anyways, since I was young, I've noticed that the digits two and seven are kind of magical. Have you ever experienced that?" She continues without waiting for my reply, which would have been a definite *no*. "Starting at birth. February 14th. That's two twos and one seven." She chuckles and stretches her hands out. "Is that a sign or what? Time of birth, twenty-seven minutes after midnight, which is the first twenty-seven occurrence of the day, right?"

She looks at me and I nod. This woman, she's in love with her own voice.

"The best years of my childhood were when we lived at 7227 on 7th street, can you imagine that? My mom and I lived in a small apartment just over a Chinese restaurant. It was smelly and loud, but we had great food… That can't be a coincidence, right? I mean—"

"Would you like to see your room?" I interrupt her mid-sentence. I can't listen to her ramblings anymore.

"Of course! I want to see all the rooms. Will you give me a tour?"

There's not much to see. It's not a mansion. We start in the living room, go past the kitchen and the guest bathroom. Upstairs, Marni's old room is the first one on the left. I point at it casually, which she interprets as an invitation to go in.

She shrieks. "Oh, Emily, I just love, love, love, your unicorn!"

Of course she does.

"I've always wanted to sew. Will you teach me, please?"

As much as I try, I simply can't refuse this Pollyanna. Her positivity is catching. It's like she came with fairy dust and is sprinkling it all around.

The next room on our tour in the master bedroom. The bed is all made up with a nice quilted spread on top. She's enchanted. "Did you make it? Wow! It's amazing. You're so talented!" Her reaction warms my heart, but I'm thinking about a saying I can't remember exactly, something about nobody ever getting slapped in the face for too much flattery. I need to be vigilant, though, not get caught in the wide net she's casting.

I show her the bathroom then we finalize our tour in Tommy's room.

"It's a beautiful space," she says with appreciation as she takes it all in, the slanted ceiling covered with Tommy's notes, graphs, and diagrams, the bookcase with his vast computer literature.

"It's kind of ironic, huh? My computer whiz likes reading from paper." I chuckle. She looks at me with those big puppy eyes, waiting for an explanation. "Because now you can get books digitally."

"Yeah, right," she says and giggles. I'm not sure she got my joke.

I open the closet. Its emptiness intensifies my longing for Tommy. My baby. I sigh.

"You can put your stuff in here."

She sniffs the wood, then taps it with her knuckles. "That's a great closet," she says. "Very sturdy."

"Thank you."

"No, Emily, thank you. For taking me in. I really need this." Her eyes sparkle.

"We have a humble home, but we're happy to help someone in need." Oh dear, now she's crying.

She grabs my arm for a moment. "Dear Emily, I'm not poor!" Then, going through her purse she starts jabbering again. "I have money. Funny thing, well, not so funny considering—" She giggles as she throws stuff out of her purse—dry lipstick, a few hygiene products, some gum—until she gets to a checkbook. "There it is." She waves it in front of my face. "I won the lottery a few years back. It was another one of my twenty-seven miracles." She smiles widely.

"Were all your numbers twenty-seven?" I ask and regret it immediately because she's clearly offended.

"Emily," she whispers, her lips shivering. She plunks down on Tommy's bed. *Her* bed.

"I'm sorry. That was rude. I didn't mean it like that."

She nods. Her head's down. I wait for her to say something, but she doesn't. Finally, I say, "Okay, I have work to do, so…" I retreat slowly. I'm almost out the door when she lifts her head.

Her eyes are still full of tears. She looks straight at me, and I see a new determination on her face. "Do you believe in God?"

I look at her, puzzled.

She lifts her voice and asks again. "Emily, do you believe in God?"

"Yes. I believe in God."

"And do you think God works in mysterious ways?"

I hesitate, not getting where she's going with this. "Yes," I say, "he is known to work in mysterious ways."

"Would you mock someone who told you she talks to God?"

"No. I would certainly wouldn't do that."

"Yet you mock me. What if it's my way to connect with God? What if the Holy Spirit is guiding me through numbers? Specifically, through the number twenty-seven?"

I swallow hard. "I'm sorry, Seven. You're right. I won't do that ever again." I close the door behind my back and take a deep breath. This isn't going to be easy.

TOM

I'm going to turn fifty in two weeks, and for the first time, I'm excited about it. It's the therapist I should be thanking. He compiled me a list of men who peaked way after their fifties. Charles Darwin, for instance. He published his evolution book when he was fifty years old. That's like seventy nowadays. Frank McCourt was a teacher just like me for thirty years before he wrote his award-winning books. I mean, the possibilities are endless.

"By the way," I say after I browse the list, "it seems I'm going to earn back what I lost just in time for my birthday." My nightly trades are paying off. I'm being careful, so very careful, with every transaction. I check everything thrice now.

"Have you shared this good news with your wife?" the therapist asks.

"I'm keeping it as a surprise." I'm smiling.

"Is it because you're afraid it's still premature, and you don't want to build up her hopes?" His face is sealed.

"Hmmm... I'm pretty confident. I've got a few things rolling, and I'm certain that more than one will be as fruitful as I expect. Also, I've got at least a dozen people lining up for me to do their taxes, so that's more money I can leverage."

He rests his chin on his hands. He looks tired. Worn out. He closes his eyes for a brief second. "Do you think it's wise to let your wife keep worrying about your finances while you know they're all right?"

"Yeah," I say with full certainty, but looking at his face, I hesitate. "I mean," I stutter, "I never really thought about it." Leaning back, I contemplate his question. It's our third meeting, and I already get his flow. I know he has a reason for everything he asks.

"Why do you keep parts of your life hidden from Emily?"

Do I? Thinking deeper I realize I haven't told her about the latest at school and where I go when I leave the house each morning. Why hadn't I thought of sharing it with her? Sighing, I shake my head. "I think it's because I want to protect her. I mean, isn't it my job to keep her safe from the burdens of life?"

He raises one eyebrow. "Seems to me she's not that fragile. You said she encouraged you to get back on that digital coin train after your mishap. So maybe it's the other way around? Maybe she's the one who shields you?"

I chuckle a little. This seems so absurd, Emily protecting me. But then I shift uneasily in my seat as I come to believe there's something true in what he says.

"When did it start?" he asks. "When did you start protecting her?"

The answer is very clear. "Right from the beginning. Emily was in an abusive relationship when we started dating. I rescued her from this wom—person." I don't want to go into details. Besides, it doesn't matter that Yolanda is a woman.

With a little nod, he encourages me to continue speaking.

I take a deep breath. "Over the years, this person has tried to contact Emily numerous times and I had to shield her." The image of Emily and Yolanda comes to mind, and I shiver. I look at it only when I'm certain I'm alone. Like in the bathroom. Every time I see Emily's carefree smile, it's like an arrow shot into my heart.

"I guess I didn't do a very good job because recently, this person was able to reach out to her," my voice cracks. "Emily went to see them." I bolt my face in my hands. I can't face him. The pain is too much.

"And how did she do without your protection?" he asks softly.

Behind the shelter of my hands I say, "I don't know."

"I'm guessing she didn't tell you about it," he says with that same soft tone.

"She never said a word!" I raise my head. My nostrils flare. "She lied about being at her sister's the whole time!"

Rage overcome me. His eyes follow me as I get up and pace the room. I depress the urge to kick something. To yell at the top of my lungs. "And I've asked her sister about it. Emily came back injured. I've asked Katie if Yolanda did it. All she said was to talk to Emily. Talk to Emily." It takes a moment to realize I'd said more than I intended.

His expression doesn't change. He waits for me to settle down again. "So. Do you think it's possible that Emily is trying to shield you as well?"

"Emily? No! She's—" but then his words sink in. Does she? Is that why she didn't tell me?

"Is it possible you're both caught up in a web of secrets created out of love and kindness, meant to protect each other?"

I exhale loudly.

"It's like that story, *The Gift of the Magi*," he continues. "A woman sells her hair to buy her husband a chain for his watch, while the husband sells his watch to buy a decorative hairpin for his wife."

My eyes wander to the ceiling. The cobweb is still there. Still gray. Still deserted. I wonder why it hadn't been cleaned. It's just a simple matter of climbing the ladder or even using a brush with a long handle. Looking at it I realize it's the perfect metaphor for my life. Here I am, old and gray, deserted by my offspring who'd moved on with their lives. Across the street, a window is lit, and with the bright light, I see it. A new, sparkling, white cobweb hanging onto the old one by a thread.

"Isn't it too late for us to change our ways?"

There's a hint of a smile on his face.

"I mean, we've been together for so long. We have our little habits, you now, patterns."

"What's the alternative?" he asks, and his voice is coarse.

I don't know how to answer that.

We sit quietly for a few moments. I become aware of the noises from the street. The humming of the elevator. Cars speeding.

"In nature," he finally says, "things that don't evolve become extinct. We humans change constantly. You don't see it daily, but you're probably not the same Tom you were when you met Emily."

I nod. He's stating the obvious.

"And Emily isn't the same person either. Why should your relationship stay the same?"

I get the point. Looking down at my dress pants, I clean away a tiny piece of dust. "I think my wife might be bi," I whisper. I can't look him in the eye. "That ex she went to meet is a woman. And now she has ladies coming over. She says it's for fittings. They go upstairs to her sewing room and lock the door after them. I hear giggling. I hear her ask them to take off their clothes." I inhale deeply. It feels good to say it out loud.

"Have you talked to her about it?"

I press my lips together. He knows the answer.

"You know that you should, right?"

I nod. Yeah. I Know.

"Maybe you'll find out it's innocent and they *do* come for fittings, or maybe what you dread is true. But knowing what you're facing would help you move on. Maybe you'll realize it's not a big deal as you think. Right now, you're stuck in a limbo state. Not here, not there."

He gets up, walks me to the door.

"Call to schedule our next meeting only *after* you've talked to her, otherwise we'll be just treading water."

I ponder about it in the elevator on my way down, and by the time I sit in the driver's seat, my mind is already made up. I'm going to have an honest and open talk with Emily. I'm going to do it tonight. Driving back home, I find myself singing along with the radio. As corny as it is, I'm singing with Louis Armstrong about this wonderful world, although the sky is gray, and the trees are still leafless and bare in their winter state. But still. It *is* a wonderful world. I laugh at being such a cliché. And then it occurs to me— I'm happy. How did that happen? I roll down the window and let the freezing wind caress my face. It's so invigorating.

CHAPTER 32

2/27/2017

New place requires a new journal, right?

So here I am, lying on my stomach, in yet another teenaged bedroom. At least this one isn't dead. Huh. What an improvement. Tommy. That's his name. He's away at college. I like his room. There's a big window that probably gets lots of daylight. And there's a lovely, heavy curtain I can draw if I want to keep the sunshine away.

I'm meant to be here. That man I met near Mom's grave knew that. I guess Mom guided him. She keeps taking care of me, even though she doesn't speak to me anymore. And that's fine. I get that she needs to rest in peace like he said.

I haven't met Tom yet, but I've seen pictures. He's such a handsome guy. Looks like one of those men who don't realize they look so fine. Emily is lucky; I've told her so. I do hope we can be friends, although we started off on the wrong foot when she mocked my beliefs. It reminded me of Audrey. I don't appreciate people who try to manipulate me like that. But I stood up to Emily, gave her a piece of my mind. I will not be ridiculed about my beliefs. And when I explained that to Emily, she apologized. I could see she really was sorry. She meant it from her heart. It was so rewarding. I will definitely use the explaining technique in my future twenty-seven voyages.

After we sorted things out, we became friends. She's so cool and talented. She's a fashion designer. I've never really cared about clothes and such, but when I saw her studio, I got an urge to create and guess what? She's going to teach me how to sew.

Now I'm going to go check on her. See what she's up too. Maybe offer my hand in making dinner. I don't know how things work in this household, and I'm anxious to find out.

Also, I'm starving.

Tom is so hot! I thought he would look older and wrinkly in real life, but he surprised me. Well, it was mutual. Emily said she's not much of a cook and gave me a free hand in the kitchen. I was about to start making a nice meal when he entered.

He rushed into the kitchen holding paper bags and with a happy grin. "Em! I brought us Beirut for dinner!"

Then he noticed me and froze in place. I was startled too and even let out a little scream, but then I recognized him from the family photos.

"You must be Tom," I said and reached my hand out. "I'm Seven. Your lodger." He seemed confused, and my cheeriness deteriorated with each word. The last one was nothing but a whisper.

He twitched his face. "Oh, yeah. The lodger. I completely forgot about that." He put the paper bag—which smelled divine, by the way—on the morning table and shook my hand. "Tom," he said with a little smile, but his eyes were still clouded.

"Yeah, I know. I've seen the photos," I said and pointed in the general direction of the living room.

"Right. Sure. The photos," he repeated after me like an echo. "Where's Emily?" he asked nervously. He seems upset, and that upsets me as well.

"She's working. And I was hungry, so—"

"Of course," he said, then went to the foot of the staircase where he yelled her name.

"What?" she yelled back from the landing. "What's going on?"

They turned quiet for about two minutes, and I knew they were signaling each other. Couples have this way of communicating without words. I've seen it with Audrey and Elijah. They picked up the habit in no time, and mainly, they signaled about me. I got it. I was a nuisance, and they didn't want to hurt my feelings by saying something, only they hurt me even more by doing it behind my back. Did Bill and I have a secret signaling language? Michelle and I did. Right from the start.

Oh dear, my thoughts are spreading all over the place.

Finally, I hear Tom say, "I brought dinner from Beirut." His voice is shaky.

"No thanks, I'm not hungry. And I have a lot of work to do," Emily says from upstairs. She sounds rigid and distant.

There's clearly some tension between these two, which is such a shame, because they're such a pretty couple, and I've seen how tender they feel toward each other. I heard it in the way they say each other's names.

So, we ate. The food was great. It reminded me of the place I had my birthday dinner.

❧

3/1/17

I have high hopes for this adventure. It's my second since Mom died, and my seventh all together.

I've been here for only two days, and already I feel like it's home.

Emily is so much fun. She's teaching me how to make her world-famous jumpsuits. She promised to make one for me once she's gotten over her current rush. How cool is that? Even though she's really busy, she made me a pillow with the number twenty-seven quilted on it. Or maybe it's embroidered? I'm still not familiar with the sewing world terms. She said it's her way of apologizing to me. Tom looked at me funny when I gave her a hug.

He's teaching me about cryptocurrencies. I didn't know anything about blockchain. Well, I'd heard about it, of course, but I thought it was only good for illegal money transactions, like drugs. So I never gave a thought to the math behind it. It's so interesting And I showed him the power of twenty-seven. We scrolled through the list of coins and picked the twenty-seventh. It's a new coin, just issued few days ago. How cool is that? He showed me how to get a digital purse, and how to purchase some coins. And then we waited and waited for the right moment to sell.

I made $2.70, which is a definite sign. Tom taught me about the algorithm Tommy came up with. It predicts the market trends up to the millisecond.

When I asked him to explain the algorithm, he dismissed me, saying, "It's very difficult to explain. It includes derivatives and other calculus terms."

"I happen to be a graduate of applied mathematics," I said.

He gave me a surprised look.

"Did my thesis about epidemiological models. I worked in a biology lab for several years," I added.

"You don't look it," he said with a new respect added to his tone.

I shrugged. I didn't know a math professional had to have a certain look. "You don't look it either," I said.

We both laughed so hard that Emily came downstairs to check on us.

~

3/8/17

Emily and I spend our mornings and afternoons together. I help her with her business, doing small tasks like ironing and adding zipper pulls on zipper tapes. She showed me how her sewing machine works and let me practice on scraps. Today, a lady came for a fitting. She was surprised to see me open the door.

"Who are you?" she asked, and I said I was the lodger. She put on an empathetic face when she spoke to Emily. "Poor you. I didn't know things were that tough that you needed to rent out one of your rooms."

"Well, Brenda, that's how it is," Emily said. "You threw us to the curb like we were garbage."

When she left, Emily asked me not to tell Tom about her visit.

"Why?" I wondered.

She hesitated before she explained he hates that Brenda woman, and she doesn't want to hurt his feelings.

Tom and I spend the evenings together, and I'm learning a lot. These guys, they can't pay me like Audrey did, but I'm still making money each day so I can keep paying the medical bills.

Tom earned a huge amount tonight. I was so excited, I whooped.

"Shh," Tom hushed me, "I don't want Emily to hear you."

"Why not?"

He shrugged and didn't explain. I didn't press the matter because Audrey called to check on me. She said she misses me, and that I'll always be welcome in her house. I said thanks. When she hung up, a sudden thought came to mind. Maybe it's the distance that gives me a new perspective. Up until that moment, I believed Mom had guided me there in order to help me, but maybe it was really meant to save Audrey. What if I was her rescuer after all, and I didn't know it?

And that got me thinking about Emily and Tom. Was I brought here for my sake or for theirs? The thought gave me shivers.

I wish I could help them. I'm in love with them both.

CHAPTER 33

mily

It's a minute past midnight when Tom wakes me.

"Emily," he whispers, "are you awake?"

"I am now," I say angrily. His eyes are like two bright stars in the dark.

"Marni?" he says. A lightning bolt flashes in the distance, and I notice the phone in his hand.

I sit up, alert. What happened? Why is she calling in the middle of the night?

"She called to wish me a happy birthday," Tom explains. "And she wanted you in on this too. Sorry." He shrugs.

"Hi Mom," Marni exclaims. She sounds delighted.

"Hi Mom," Marcus says. The thunder roars while he speaks and swallows his words.

Marni giggles. Since when does he call me Mom? Tom grabs my forearm. His eyes are sparkling. A huge grin spreads on his face. What?

"So, Mom, we wanted you to hear this too. We just found out. It's a boy!" She shrieks with joy.

"Oh Marni, Marcus! That's such wonderful news." Tom literally glows. He's been glowing like that ever since Seven arrived. She sits with him every night, flirting and giggling with his numbers and formulas.

"Marni is having a baby," Tom whispers. He realizes I'm miles away.

Marni is having a baby? I sit up straight. "What wonderful news! I'm so happy for you guys!" I say. And I *am* happy. Tom and I look at each other We're both overwhelmed with joy. It's is so unexpected.

"We're counting on you two to help us take care of Dylan."

"Dylan is a beautiful name!" I cry.

And at the same time, Tom says, "We'd love to!" His eyes are like two reflectors. More lightning strikes, far away.

"I can come and stay with you for a few weeks after he's born," Tom offers.

"No need," Marni's voice is high-pitched. "We're leaving the city and coming back to town. We're going to live at Nana's house until we get our own place."

"Nana recently moved to a retirement home," Marcus explains.

"That's great!" Tom is exhilarated. "That's the best birthday present ever!"

"But what about your work?" Am I the only one who's worried?

"Marcus is being relocated to Detroit, and I'm going to quit. I'm done with being treated like shit. They don't pay me enough."

"But you worked so hard!" I say. Tom touches my shoulder. He shakes his head.

"That's great news, honey. You're very talented. You'll land on your feet," he says.

Tom lies next to me. He's still grinning. I can see it whenever lightning flashes.

"A baby. Can you imagine that? Having little feet in the house again!" Tom is elated.

"It'll be wonderful!" he says. "I'm so looking forward to it," he says.

I remain quiet. I'm struggling to digest all this new information.

"It seems like she was a baby only a blip ago, and now she's going to be a mother." His fingers feel for mine. "We're going to be grandparents, Em. Can you believe it?"

I hear myself say, "I met with Yolanda." Boom. It just slipped out. My face is turned toward the ceiling. I don't dare meet his eyes. He was so happy, and I've ruined it.

The room turns quiet. Even the thunder seems subdued by my announcement.

"I know," Tom finally says.

"You know?" I turn on my side to look at him. He turns toward me as well.

"Yolanda posted a picture of the both on you on Facebook."

"Oh," I say. And after a short silence I add, "Why didn't you say something?"

He shrugs, I guess. There's a slight movement in his shoulder line.

Still facing me, he says, "I was fired from the school."

"You were only *suspended,* and Patrice is going to revisit that decision next week at the school board meeting," I say without really thinking about it.

"You knew?" he asks, surprised.

And we both laugh. We crawl closer to each other. He puts his hand on my waist. I put mine on his face. His scruff scratches my palm as I caress his cheek.

"Why didn't you tell me?" I ask softly.

"I didn't want to bother you with my stuff," he whispers. His mouth is so close to mine, I can feel the air coming out as he speaks. "You?"

"I wanted to tell you so badly. I was going to talk to you when I came back, but then you were having a crisis, and I was waiting for the right time, and—"

"That's all right," he says. He's so close now, our noses are touching. He moves his hand up and down my waist, from my chest to my hip and back up again. I hold my breath.

"She assaulted me," I say. My throat gets choked. "Sexually." His hand freezes in place. Then he sits up.

"I'm going to kill her," he says after a short silence. "Literally. I'm going to kill her."

"Tom." I sit next to him, trying to hold his face again. "I'm fine, Tom. I'm fine. It made me see things clearer."

He relaxes a bit and lies back, inhaling deeply. "That woman. She never let you be."

"She will now. I've ended it. I stood up to her, Tom. I did it."

He turns over and kisses my temple. "I'm so sorry you had to deal with that."

"She gave us faulty condoms, Tom. Back then. Marni—" My voice breaks.

"I suspected so." He nods.

And then we kiss. It's sweet and delicate, a reward for a job well done. The storm is close now, thunder roaring and lightning flashing, but we're in a bubble, looking deep into each other eyes. There's no need for words anymore. Yet, we say them.

"I have another bit of good news for you." Tom's eyes

sparkle in the dark. They're like two flashlights guiding me home. "As of today, we're debt-free," he says proudly.

"That's great, honey!"

"You made it happen." His voice is shaky with excitement as he embraces me.

"Hmmm... thanks? But all I did was make coffee." I chuckle. He's really exaggerating my part in all of it.

"What are you talking about? You encouraged me when I was down. You said to keep at it." As he talks, his breath catches in my hair. On my neck. It's cold and tingly and it makes me feel hot inside.

"I have something to tell you too," I whisper into his ear. He slides a little so he can look me in the eye. I see worry drawn over his face. What is he afraid of?

"My business has grown significantly this past month. Order are literally piling up."

"That's amazing." There so much love in his voice. "I'm so proud of you."

We kiss again. His lips are soft but demanding. Oh, I've missed it. We roll over and he's on top of me. Kissing my collarbone. My eyes. Undressing me as he gropes his way down.

"You know," he says, his voice heavy. "I didn't like those things you're—"

I see something in the corner of my eye. There's someone in our bedroom. I shriek with horror.

TOM

At first, I think it's a bear. I don't know how it got into the house. Upstairs. Into our bedroom. But that's the first thing that crosses my mind. It's big and scary and I hold on to Emily, certain we're going to die. Right here and now.

And then I realize it's Seven. The poor thing is covered in Tommy's comforter and is shivering. The TV set behind her flickers—it's exactly twenty-seven minutes after midnight. Seeing that time reassures me that it's her.

"You guys?" she whispers. Her voice is shaky, as if she's been crying. "I'm so scared of the storm. Can I climb into bed with you two? Just for a while? I could really use a boost from the twenty-seventh power, which is three to the power of three, as you must know."

She's babbling, and it's surreal. The whole situation is bizarre, yet it somehow feels right, especially after I glance at Emily, who's eating Seven with her eyes. I can't deny the little pinch of jealousy. She looks like that at me all the time, and it makes me feel nervous, pressured. But seeing her look like that at someone else is almost unbearable. Yet, at the same time, I realize this is something I could give her. A great peace falls upon me as I move to the edge of the bed and tap the gap between Emily and me.

Seven loses the comforter. She's naked underneath.

"I hope you don't mind. I can't stand the touch of clothes on my body when I sleep."

Now I'm interested too.

She slides in between us. Her body is warm, yet the poor thing is shivering. Every time lightning illuminates the room, I can see her face for a brief second. She looks terrified, like a rabbit; her breathing is shallow and quick. And when the thunder strikes, she becomes covered in sweat. I recognize the symptoms. Panic attacks seem so obvious when somebody else experiences it.

She grabs my hand and squeezes hard. By Emily's exclamation, I know she's grabbed hers as well.

And that's how it starts. One minute Emily is trying to

soothe Seven. "Don't worry sweetie, it'll be over soon. You're safe here with us."

"Oh, Emily, you're so pretty. I love you so much," Seven says. She turns to Emily and kisses her passionately. At first, I feel awkward. But then I realize Emily likes it. She kisses Seven back. Her eyes are closed.

Then Seven turns to me. "Oh, dear Tom. I love you too." Her lips tremble as she tries to kiss me. I don't cooperate. I just can't. It's too weird and different. I turn her back to Emily.

Leaning on top of Seven, Emily comes closer. "I love you," she says before her lips meet mine. Now *that* feels right. I pull her close and forget everything and everyone but the sweetness of her breath, the softness of her body. It's like we're young again, two eager, clumsy twenty-something trying to make love for the first time. Only this time we're not alone. When Seven butts between us, demanding her share, Emily just looks at me. I know that look; I've seen it a hundred times before.

"Hey, Tom," she whispers into my ear, "maybe *this* can be our activity? Something we to do together?"

I nod, although I'm not sure.

Emily welcomes Seven gladly into our intimate bond. Quite embarrassed, I join. We're a bunch of body parts slapping against each other and making funny noises. There's a lot of giggling and apologies, mainly on my part. Emily is completely into it, and I embrace the moment, readjust my position, and let the two ladies guide me into heavenly bliss.

It's the darkest moment before sunrise when the storm finally calms down. Emily and Seven sleeping soundly. The three of us are tangled together, just a bunch of limbs and torsos. Slowly, I pull back, unraveling myself. I walk downstairs to get a glass of water. This is not how I imagined the first day of the sixth decade of my life, and I can't help but snicker as I go outside.

The sun hasn't risen yet, but there's just enough light for me to see the contour of the trees in our backyard. I enjoy looking at them, flickering, dancing with the easy breeze. It gets brighter by the minute. Details start to emerge. The cherry tree is full of little buds. In a few days, they'll bloom in white and pink, creating a grand, astonishing sight.

I can't wait to experience the spring. I inhale deeply. The air is clear and sweet. For the first time in a long time, I feel complete.

The End

Thanks

I would like to express my deepest gratitude to the wonderful group of first readers especially Debbie Hart, Suzanne White, Erin Graham and David Turner. Thank you for reading numerous drafts of this story and taking the time to grant me with your wise advice.

Thank you, lovely ladies of Sew Fine sewing group, for your help with everything from fabric to needles to garments design. And thank you Gerry Gomez for patiently answering all my questions regarding Blockchain and digital coins. I took the liberty of changing some of the events regarding BitCoin values. It did dip 40% during one day on 2017, but that wasn't on February. And of course, thank you to my meticulous editor for encouraging me to delete the excess and refine the story. All textual mistakes remaining in this story are mine.

And last but not least, my family. I would be nothing without your constant support. Thank you for enduring with my quirks, and allowing me to frequently withdraw into my imagination.

To join the First Readers group email: beth@bethloure.com

Beth Loure is a 19th century soul living inside a millennial body. She longs for the simpler times and is still looking for a Mrs. Darcy. Beth Lives by the coast with a companion gray parrot named Johnny, who keeps reminding her to sit down and write. With these exact words. When she's not writing or reading you can find her attending the roses in her garden.

You can find her here:
bethloure.com
info@bethloure.com

www.ingramcontent.com/pod-product-compliance
Lightning Source LLC
Chambersburg PA
CBHW030901060726
47591CB00005B/1367